D0271827

208

BALTIC MISSION

BALTIC MISSION

Richard Woodman

JOHN MURRAY · LONDON

3470

© Richard Woodman 1986
First published 1986
by John Murray (Publishers) Ltd
50 Albemarle Street, London W1X 4BD

Typeset by Inforum Ltd, Portsmouth
Printed and bound in Great Britain
by The Bath Press, Avon

British Library CIP Data
Woodman, Richard
  Baltic mission
  I. Title
  823'.914[F]   PR6073.0617
  ISBN 0–7195–4340–1

Contents

For Regine and Neil

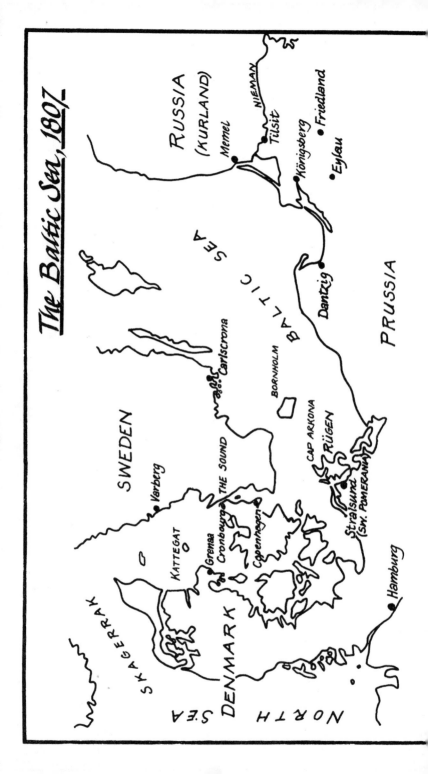

The Baltic Sea, 1807

PART ONE

The Ship

'I was born on a battlefield – what are the lives of
a million men to me?'
Napoleon, Emperor of the French

Eylau

The horses of the two squadrons of Cossacks were labouring as they breasted the low ridge dominating the shallow valley and the frozen river behind them. They were almost blown by the speed of their recent charge and the violence of their clash with the enemy along the line of the river. As the officer at their head caught sight of the red roofs of the village of Schlöditten, he threw up his blood-stained sabre, stood in his stirrups and ordered the fur-swathed cavalry to wheel their shaggy mounts. They reined in, faced about and halted as their officers trotted back to their posts.

'Well done, my children!' the Russian officer called with patriarchal familiarity, smiling and nodding his clean-shaven face to the swarthy and bearded troopers who grinned back at him. The Cossack horses tossed their heads in a jingle of harness, edging their tails round into the biting northerly wind. Breath erupted in clouds from their distending nostrils and the snowflakes that were again beginning to fall melted on contact with their steaming flanks. Lowering their lances across their saddle-bows, the Cossacks exchanged ribaldries and remarks, incongruously crossing themselves as they called the unanswered names of men they had left behind them in the valley. A few bound each other's wounds, or ran their filthy hands gently down the shuddering legs of horses galled by the enemy. Most remained in their saddles, reaching under their sheepskins for flasks of vodka, or for carcasses of chickens that hung in festoons from their belts.

Reaching his post at their head, the clean-shaven officer abandoned the dialect of the Don. 'Hey, my friend! Come!' he called in French to another officer. Sheathing his sabre he fumbled in a pistol holster for a flask which he beckoned the other to share.

'What does the esteemed representative of the staff think of today's work?' He held out the flask, his blue eyes intently observing him. 'We made short work of those French bastards, didn't we, eh?'

3

The staff-officer grinned, but his eyes kept returning to the valley below them, into which they had charged twenty minutes earlier.

'They were Lasalle's bastards, you know, Count. The best light cavalry in the Grand Army.'

'And we beat them, by Almighty God.' The count crossed himself piously and his companion raised a sardonic eyebrow at the practice.

'We haven't finished the business yet,' he said, pointing to the southward, where the little town of Preussisch-Eylau lay engulfed in smoke. Only its church belfry showed above the pall as, house by house, it crumbled beneath the storm of shot from two massive Russian batteries close to its eastern outskirts. Beyond the town and spreading out over the gently rolling snow-covered countryside of East Prussia, the dark masses of the Grand Army of France and her allies attempted to roll up the Russian left wing.

Four miles away to the north, just beyond the frozen river at the other extreme of the contending armies and immediately in front of the Cossacks, Lasalle's repulsed hussars were reforming. Between them the bloody corpses of two dozen men were already stiffening like the trampled and frozen reeds of the river margin. To the south of the French cavalry, the dark swirl of Marshal Soult's Fourth Army Corps had been thrown back from their own assault upon the Russians. The Cossack commander slapped his thigh and laughed with satisfaction.

'Ha! You see, my friend, they *are* beaten! And was it not us, the squadrons of Count Piotr Petrovich Kalitkin, that took the very orders of the great Napoleon himself from the hands of his courier? Eh? Well, wasn't it?'

'Indeed, your Excellency,' said his companion with exaggerated courtesy, 'I think we may take a measure of credit for today.' He returned the vodka flask amid an outburst of indignation.

'Measure of credit! Measure of credit!' spluttered Kalitkin. 'As a result of *us*, Marshal Bernadotte never received his orders, and . . .' he waved his gloved hand over the battlefield, 'is not here to support his Emperor.'

The staff-officer nodded, his expression of amused irony altering to one of concern. It was quite true that Napoleon's courier had fallen into the Cossacks' hands at Lautenberg, but the staff-officer had a wider appreciation of events than Count Kalitkin.

'You are quite right, Count, but Ney is not here either, and that worries me.'

'Bah! You know too much and it makes you worry too much.'

'That', said the staff-officer, levelling a small telescope to the north

4

where snow was falling thickly from a leaden sky, 'is my business, Count, and the reason for my attachment to your brilliant command.'

'Ah, you and your damned reports. I know you are a spy; though whether you spy for Bennigsen on me, or for St Petersburg on Bennigsen, I have not yet determined.'

The staff-officer lowered his telescope and grinned at the Count. 'You are too suspicious, Count, and too good a light-cavalryman to need a nursemaid.'

'Bah!' repeated Kalitkin good naturedly, apparently unconcerned at the purpose of the staff-officer's attachment to his squadrons. 'You are an impudent rascal and I should have you whipped, but you would report me and I should be reduced to a troop again, damn you.'

'If I were you, my dear Count,' said the staff-officer, staring again through his glass, 'I should forget about whipping me and send a patrol to find out who is approaching from the northward; if it's Ney we shall be outflanked.' He passed the glass to Kalitkin whose manner was immediately transformed.

'I'll go myself.' He turned in his saddle. 'Hey! Khudoznik, stop doing that and mount up with your men!' A score of Cossacks fastened their saddle-bags and slung their lances, detaching themselves from the main body and forming a loose column. Kalitkin turned to the staff-officer. 'I shall leave the fate of Holy Russia in your hands and save Bennigsen's reputation again.' Kalitkin threw the vodka flask to his friend and kicked his horse to a trot. In a few moments he was no more than a blur in the swirling snow.

The staff-officer edged his horse forward to catch a glimpse of the battlefield before more snow flurries obscured it. To his left a battery of 60 cannon kept up a ruthless fire into the re-forming battalions of Soult. Beyond, the orange flashes of a further 120 guns pounded Eylau; but in the far distance heavy columns of French infantry could be seen advancing to attack. For a while the snow curtained everything, even deadening the concussion of the guns, but when it cleared again the French attack seemed to have failed.

Nearer at hand a greater drama was unfolding. About a mile away from the ridge a huge column of Russian infantry, grey-coated and with feet muffled in sacking, hurled themselves forward against the houses of Eylau. Six thousand peasant soldiers followed their officers with the obedience of small children and fought their way into the town like furies. Unseen by the distant Cossacks, Napoleon was driven from his post in the church belfry and only escaped by the self-sacrifice of his bodyguard. But the Cossacks observed his angry response to this insolent bravery; they shook up their horses' heads and grasped their lances, in case they were called upon to react to the great counter-attack that burst out of the French position.

The snow cleared completely, torn aside by the biting wind as swiftly as it had come, and this lull was accompanied by a sudden brightening of the sky as Napoleon's brother-in-law, Marshal Murat, led forward more than ten thousand horsemen to burst through the Russian line. Wheeling in its rear and repeatedly breaking the centre, they sabred the indomitable gunners and cut up the devoted Russian infantry that had so recently threatened their Emperor. Behind Murat's cuirassiers and dragoons, Marshal Bessières followed with the Horse Grenadiers of the Imperial Guard, big men on huge black horses who trampled the remains of Bennigsen's frontal assault beneath their hooves. But the tide of cavalry had reached its limit. It was unsupported and ebbed inexorably back towards Eylau. The guns of the Russian centre were remanned and began to pour shot into the enemy as they retreated. Then another curtain of snow closed over the mass of dying and mutilated men, so that their cries and groans were unheard.

The staff-officer finished the flask of vodka and tucked it into the breast of his coat. He nodded companionably to a subaltern who rode up from the Cossack flank.

'Well, young Repin, this is a bloody business, but a sweet revenge for Austerlitz, eh?'

'Indeed, sir, it is.'

'Count Kalitkin should rejoin us soon . . . ah, here he comes, if I'm not mistaken . . .' Kalitkin rode up and reined in, his eyes gleaming with triumph, his horse steaming.

'Well, my friend, I have done it again! I have found your Ney for you. *Voilà!*' Kalitkin pointed behind him where some of Lasalle's hussars were moving out to form a screen behind which the head of a marching column could just be made out through the snow. 'And also I have found our valiant ally, or, at least, what remains of him . . .'

'General Lestocq's Prussians?' asked the staff-officer sharply.

'Exactly, my dear wiseacre. Lestocq and his Prussians, and we must move to the right and cover their march across our rear.' Kalitkin suddenly drew his sabre with a rasp and pointed it across the shallow valley. 'There! See, those French pigs are ahead of us! They will try and harry the Prussian flank . . .'

'I told you they were the best light cavalry in the Grand Army.'

6

'You go and tell Bennigsen that the squadrons of Piotr Kalitkin have saved Mother Russia again . . . and if he gives me a division I will win the whole damned war . . .' He stood in his stirrups and bawled an order. This time the whole mass of the Cossacks moved forward and the staff-officer wheeled his horse aside to let them pass. For a moment he remained alone on the ridge to watch. The trot changed to a canter and then to a gallop; the lance points were lowered, the pennons flickering like fire as the dark wave of horsemen swept over the frozen marshes bordering the river, and crashed into the ranks of the French hussars. The enemy swung to meet them, their breath steaming below their fierce moustaches and their hair braided into dreadlocks beneath their rakish shakoes. The staff-officer pulled his horse round and spurred it towards the headquarters of the Russian army at Anklappen.

Night fell early, the short winter afternoon expiring under heavy clouds and the smoke of battle. The French attack failed, largely due to the timely arrival of General Lestocq's Prussians and the late appearance of Ney: Napoleon had received the worst drubbing of his career, but Lasalle's hussars had had their revenge, and Kalitkin's Cossacks had been pushed back beyond the village of Schlöditten, to bivouac and lick their wounds. It was past midnight when Kalitkin had posted his vedettes, rolled himself in his cloak and lain down in the snow. A few moments later he was roused as one of his men brought in a strange officer, wearing an unfamiliar uniform and raging furiously in a barbarous French at the Cossack trooper whose sabre point gleamed just below the prisoner's chin.

Kalitkin sprang to his feet. 'Mother of God! What have you there, Khudoznik? A Frenchman?' Kalitkin addressed the prisoner in French: 'Are you a French officer?'

'God damn it, no, sir!' the man exclaimed. 'Tell this ruffian to let me go! I am Colonel Wilson, a British Commissioner attached to General Bennigsen's headquarters. I was reconnoitring when this stinking louse picked me up. Who the devil are you?'

Kalitkin ordered the Cossack Khudoznik to return to his post and introduced himself. 'I am Count Piotr Kalitkin commanding two squadrons of the Hetman's Don Cossacks. So, you are a spy of the British are you?' Kalitkin grinned and made room round the fire.

'You Russians are a damnably suspicious lot,' said the mollified Wilson, rubbing his hands and extending them to the warmth of the fire.

'But you have come to see we don't waste your precious English gold, eh?'

'To liaise with the headquarters of the army, Count, not to spy.'

'It is the same thing. Where are your English soldiers, Colonel, eh? Your gold is useful but it would have been better if some English soldiers could have helped us today, would it not? There would be fewer widows in Russia tomorrow.'

'My dear Count,' replied Wilson with a note of tired exasperation creeping into his voice, 'I am plagued night and day with pleas for which I can offer no satisfaction until the ice in the Baltic thaws and His Majesty's ships can enter that sea. Until then we shall have to rely upon Russian valour.'

'So, Colonel,' said Kalitkin, still grinning in the firelight, 'you are a courtier *and* a spy. I congratulate you!'

'I hope', said Wilson with a heavy sarcasm, 'that I am merely a diplomat.'

A stir on the outskirts of the firelit circle among the half-sleeping, half-freezing men caused both Kalitkin and the Englishman to turn.

'And', exclaimed Kalitkin triumphantly, 'here is another spy. Welcome back, my friend. I expected you to spend the night in a whore's bed at headquarters. Are there no women with General Bennigsen?'

'Only pretty boys dressed as aides,' said the staff-officer emerging from the night, 'in accordance with the German fashion. Besides, I came back to bring you . . . *this!*' The staff-officer produced a bottle from the breast of his cloak with a magician's flourish.

'Ah! Vodka! Next to a woman, the best consolation.'

'One can share it with more facility, certainly . . . I see you have company.'

As Kalitkin laughed, snatching the bottle and wrenching the cork from its neck, the staff-officer's expression of cynical levity vanished at the sight of the British uniform.

'Yes, my friend,' explained Kalitkin after wiping his mouth, 'a spy like you. He is an English officer; a *commissioner* no less.'

In the firelight the staff-officer's mouth set rigid, his eyes suddenly watchful. 'I am Colonel Wilson,' said the Englishman again, waving aside the vodka that Kalitkin companionably offered him after liberally helping himself, 'His Britannic Majesty's representative at the headquarters of His Imperial Majesty's army.'

'Colonel Wilson . . .' the staff-officer muttered under his breath, his eyes probing the face of the English officer.

'Count Kalitkin has introduced himself,' said Wilson, referring obliquely to Kalitkin's failure to introduce the staff-officer. 'Whom have I the honour of addressing?'

The staff-officer hesitated, looked down and with a muddy boot kicked back a piece of wood that had been ejected from the heart of the fire by a small explosion of resin deep in its core.

'Tell him, my friend,' said Kalitkin, swigging again at the vodka. 'Tell him who you are.'

The staff-officer's obvious reticence combined with the scrutiny to which he had been subject to awaken suspicions in Wilson's mind. Kalitkin's flippant allusions to espionage had been initially attributed to the subconscious reaction to excessive centralisation that Wilson had encountered in his dealings with the Russians. Watching the staff-officer's face he was aware of a quickening interest in this man.

'Come, sir,' he prompted, 'you have the advantage of me.'

'I am Captain Ostroff, Colonel Wilson, aide-de-camp to Prince Vorontzoff and presently attached to Count Kalitkin's squadrons of the Hetman's Don Cossacks.'

But Wilson paid little attention to the details of the staff-officer's status. What interested him far more was the way in which this Ostroff had pronounced Wilson's own name. For the first time since his secondment to the Russian army Wilson had heard his surname without the heavy, misplaced accent upon its second syllable. In a flash of intuition he realised he was talking to a fellow Englishman.

'Your servant, Captain Ostroff,' he said, bowing a little from the waist and holding the other's eyes in a steady gaze. But Ostroff's expression did not alter, not even when a sharp crack at their feet ejected another sliver of wood from the bivouac fire.

'How interesting,' went on Wilson with the smooth urbanity of the perfect diplomat, 'I have not had much opportunity to study the Russian tongue of your *muzhiks*, but if I am not mistaken, your name is the Russian word for . . .'

'*Island*,' snapped Ostroff suddenly and it was not the abruptness of the interruption that surprised Wilson but the fact that where he had been about to employ the French noun, Ostroff had chosen to head him off with a sideways glance at Kalitkin and the use of a definition in plain English.

As the two men strolled with an affected nonchalance away from the recumbent Kalitkin and his bivouac, the Count lounged back on his sheepskin. 'Spies,' he muttered to himself, 'spies, the pair of them . . .' and he stared up at the stars shining through the rents in the clouds, aware that their motion had become suddenly irregular.

The Kattegat

His Britannic Majesty's 36-gun, 18-pounder frigate *Antigone*, commanded by Captain Nathaniel Drinkwater, lay at anchor off the Swedish fortress of Varberg wrapped in a dense and clammy fog. Her decks were dark with the moisture of it; damp had condensed on the dull black barrels of her cannon, giving them an unnatural sheen, and her rigging was festooned with millions upon millions of tiny droplets like the autumn dew upon spiders' webs. Wraiths of fog streamed slowly across her deck, robbing the scarlet coats of her marine sentries of their brilliance and dulling all sounds.

The duty midshipman leant against the quarterdeck rail with one foot upon the slide of a carronade and contemplated the dark oily water and the ice-floes that bumped and scraped alongside. Fifty yards out from the ship's side he could see nothing and the view from the deck was too familiar to engage his slightest interest.

Not that the slowly swirling ice-floes were worthy of study in themselves, for they were fast melting and puny by comparison with those he had seen in the Greenland Sea, but they were hypnotic and drew all active thought from the brain of the idle young man. They set him to dreaming aimlessly and endeavouring to pass the time as pleasantly as possible without the tiresome need to exert himself. For the past forty minutes Midshipman Lord Walmsley had been the senior officer upon the upper deck and in that capacity he saw no reason to exert himself. The sentries were at their posts, the duty watch fussing about routine tasks, and he was perfectly content to leave them to the supervision of the petty officers and their mates. Besides, Walmsley had been cheated of the prospect of an early repast and the trivial sense of grievance only reinforced his inertia. In the absence of the captain ashore, the first lieutenant, Mr Samuel Rogers, had repaired to the gunroom for a meal he felt he was more entitled to than the midshipman.

Lord Walmsley did not seriously dispute the justice of the

contention, for to do so would have involved far more effort than he was capable of. So he let the silly sense of grievance paralyse him and dreamed of a distant milkmaid whose willing concupiscence had long since initiated him to the irresponsible joys of a privileged manhood.

Inertia was endemic aboard the *Antigone* that morning. Captain Drinkwater had zealously pushed his frigate from the Nore through a succession of gales and into the breaking ice of the Baltic to reach Varberg as soon as he could. The whole of *Antigone*'s company was exhausted, and they had lost a man overboard off the Naze of Norway: a sacrifice to the elements which seemed determined to punish them for every league they stole to windward in a searing succession of freezing easterly gales. It was, therefore, scarcely surprising that once the anchor had bitten into the sea-bed off the coast of Sweden and the captain departed in his barge, the mood on board *Antigone* should have been one of euphoria. As if confirming the frigate's company in their own merit, the elements had softened, the wind dropped, and within an hour of Captain Drinkwater's departure the fog had closed down on them, wrapping them in a chill, damp cocoon.

'Well now, d'you intend to spend the entire day in that supine way, laddie?'

Walmsley straightened up and turned. Mr Fraser, the frigate's second lieutenant, crossed the deck to stand beside him.

'I was merely ascertaining whether I could hear the captain's barge returning, Mr Fraser, by removing my ears from the sounds of the deck and leaning over the side.'

Fraser raised a sandy eyebrow. 'Your lordship is a plausible liar and should have his ears removed from the sounds of the deck to the masthead. A spell of sky-parlour would cure your impudence . . . but cut along and have something to eat . . . and send young Frey up in your place,' he added calling after the retreating midshipman.

The Scotsman began a leisurely pacing of the deck, noting the other duty-men and sentries at their places. A few minutes later Midshipman Frey joined him.

'Ah, Mr Frey,' remarked Fraser in his distinctive burr, 'you well know how my flinty Calvinist soul abhors idleness. Be so kind as to pipe the red cutter away and row a guard around the ship.'

'Aye, aye, sir.'

Fraser regarded the activity that this order initiated with a certain amount of satisfaction. His mild enjoyment was marred by the unnecessary appearance of Rogers, the first lieutenant. Fraser had just left Rogers at table, his big fist clamped proprietorially around the neck of the gunroom decanter as though it was his personal property. Rogers's face was flushed with the quantity of alcohol he had consumed.

'What the devil's all this fuss and palaver, Fraser?'

' 'Tis nothing, Mr Rogers. I'm merely hoisting out a boat to row guard about the ship while this fog persists . . .'

'You take a deal too much upon yourself . . .'

'I think the captain would have . . .'

'Damn you, Fraser. D'you threaten me?'

Fraser suppressed mounting anger with difficulty. 'Reflect, sir,' he said with frigid formality, 'we have a considerable sum in specie under guard below and I think the captain would object to its loss in his absence . . .'

'Oh, you do, do you? And who the hell's going to take it? The Swedes are friendly and the Danes are neutral. There isn't an enemy within a hundred leagues of us.'

'We don't know there isn't an enemy a hundred *yards* away, damn it; and as long as I'm officer o' the deck there'll be a guard pulled round the ship!' Fraser had lost his restraint now and both officers stood face to face in full view of the men at the davit falls. Fraser turned away, flushed and angry. 'Lower away there, God damn you, and lively with it!'

Rogers stood stock still. His befuddled mind recognised the sense in Fraser's argument. He was aware that he should have sent off a boat as soon as the fog settled that forenoon. Knowledge of his own failure only fuelled his wrath, already at a high pitch due to the amount of wine he had drunk. And his mind was clear enough to realise that Fraser had committed the unforgiveable in losing his temper and answering a senior insolently. 'Come here, Fraser!' Rogers roared.

Fraser, supervising the lowering of the cutter, turned. 'D'you address me, sir?' he asked coldly.

'You know damn well I do! Come here!'

Fraser crossed the deck again slowly, grasping the significance of Rogers's new attack. Once again the two officers were face to face.

'Gentlemen, gentlemen, this is no time for such discordant tom-foolery . . .'

Rogers's colour mounted still further as he spun round on the newcomer who, called by the sudden interest stirring between decks, now arrived on the quarterdeck.

'You keep out of this, Hill,' snarled Rogers at the sailing master.

'No, sir, I will not.' He lowered his voice. 'And you are making damnable fools of yourselves. For God's sake stop at once!' Hill's warning ended on an urgent hiss.

'And I suppose, Hill, you'll feel obliged to inform the captain of this matter?' Rogers snarled.

'I'll hold my tongue if you'll hold your temper,' Hill snapped back sharply, fixing the first lieutenant with a stare. Rogers exhaled slowly, his breath strong with the odour of liquor. He turned abruptly and went below. Hill walked forward.

'Coil down those slack falls! Bosun's mate, chivvy those men and put some ginger into it! By God you're as slack as the draw-strings of a Ratcliffe doxy!'

Normality settled itself upon the ship again.

'Thank you, Mr Hill,' said Fraser somewhat sheepishly. 'The old devil had me provoked there for a moment . . . it would never have happened if the captain had not been out of the ship.'

'Forget it. Fortunately that is a rare occurrence. I must confess to a certain uneasiness, considering the contents of the hold, the fog and the absence of the captain.'

'Mr Frey is at least a diligent young man . . .'

'Boat 'hoy!' The midship's sentry's call stopped the conversation dead and the two officers rushed to the rail while the suspicious marine cocked his musket. The bow of a boat emerged from the fog.

'*Antigone!*' came the coxswain's Cornish accent.

'By God, it's the captain returning!' Fraser flew to the entry, aware that fog and anger had caused him to fail in his duty and that Captain Drinkwater would reboard his ship with less than half a side-party because of his own inattentiveness. To his chagrin the captain's barge had not even been challenged by Frey's guard-boat which was still on the other side of the ship.

As Captain Drinkwater's head came level with the deck, Fraser set his right hand to the fore-cock of his own hat. He was relieved to hear the squeal of a pipe in his right ear. The marine sentry presented arms and the side-party, though not complete, was at least presentable.

Drinkwater swung his weight from the baize-covered man-ropes and stood on the deck, his eye taking in the details of *Antigone*'s waist even as his own right hand acknowledged the salutes.

'Mr Fraser,' he said, and Fraser braced himself for a rebuke.

'Sir?' The captain's sharp grey eyes made him apprehensive.

'My compliments to the first lieutenant and the master, and will they attend me in the cabin . . .'

'Aye, aye, sir.'

'And Mr Fraser . . .'

'Sir?'

'Mr Mount is to come too.'

'Very well, sir.'

'Damn this fog.'

'Aye, sir. We were not expecting you so soon.'

'So I perceived,' Drinkwater said drily, 'but the t'gallant masts are clear above the fog from the ramparts of Varberg castle.' He reached beneath his boat-cloak and fished in the tail pocket of his coat. 'I took the precaution of taking this.'

Fraser looked down at the folded vanes of Drinkwater's pocket compass.

'I see, sir.'

With a dull knock of oar looms on thole pins the guard-boat swung clear of the bow and pulled down *Antigone*'s starboard side.

Drinkwater nodded his satisfaction. 'A wise precaution, Mr Fraser,' he said and made for the ladder below, leaving the second lieutenant expelling a long breath of relief. Fraser turned to the boatswain standing beside him, the silver call still in his hand.

'I'm indebted to ye, Mr Comley, for your prompt arrival,' Fraser muttered in a low voice.

'Wouldn't like to see 'ee caught atween two fires, Mr Fraser, sir,' said Comley, staring after the young Scotsman as he went off on the captain's errand. Then he turned and put the call back to his lips. Its shrill note brought silent expectation to the upper deck again.

'Man the yard and stay tackles there! Prepare to 'oist in the barge!'

Captain Nathaniel Drinkwater took off the boat-cloak and unwound the muffler from his neck. He handed them, with his hat, to his steward, Mullender.

'A glass of something, Mullender, if you please.'

'Blackstrap, sir?'

'Capital.' Drinkwater's tone was abstracted as he stared astern through the windows at the pearly vapour that seemed oddly substantial as it swathed the ship. He rubbed his hands and eased his damaged shoulder as the chill dampness penetrated the cabin.

'Damn this fog,' he muttered again.

Mullender brought the glass of cheap blackstrap and Drinkwater took it gratefully. He relaxed as the warmth of the wine uncoiled in his belly. He could hear the creaks of the tackles taking the weight of the barge, felt the heel of the ship as she leaned to it, then felt the list ease as, with half-heard commands, the heavy boat swung inboard. A dull series of thuds told when it settled itself in its chocks amidships. The guard-boat swam across his field of vision, rounded the quarter and vanished again.

He was recalled from his abstraction as a knock at the door announced the summoned officers. Turning from the stern windows he surveyed them. Hill, the sailing master, he had known for many years. Fifty years of age, Hill was as dependable as the mahogany he appeared to be carved from. Balding now, his practical skill and wisdom seemed undiminished by the passing of time. Like Drinkwater himself, Hill bore an old wound with fortitude, an arm mangled at Camperdown ten years earlier. Drinkwater smiled at Hill and addressed Rogers, the first lieutenant.

'All well in my absence, Mr Rogers?' he asked formally.

'Perfectly correct, sir. No untoward cir . . . circumstances.' Roger's reply was thick. Like Hill, Rogers was an old shipmate, but he was showing an increasing dependence upon drink. Disappointed of advancement and temperamentally intolerant, his fine abilities as a seaman were threatened by this weakness and Drinkwater made a mental note to be on his guard. For the moment he affected not to notice that Rogers had over-indulged at the dinner table. It was not a rare occurrence among the long-serving officers of the Royal Navy.

'Very well.' Drinkwater diverted his attention to the third officer. Mr Mount was resplendent in the scarlet, blue and white undress uniform of the Royal Marines. His inclusion in the little group was pertinent to *Antigone*'s purpose here, off Varberg. It was Mount who, in addition to his customary duties of policing the frigate, had had in his especial charge eighty thousand pounds sterling, and whom Drinkwater was anxious to keep abreast of the latest news.

'Well, gentlemen, I wished that you should be informed of some news I have just gleaned from the Swedish authorities at Varberg. About five weeks ago, it seems, the Russians administered a severe check to the French army under Napoleon. No,' he held up his hand as Mount began to ask questions, 'I can give you little more information, but that which I can tell you would be the more convivially passed over dinner. Please pass my invitation to the other officers and a few of the midshipmen. Except Fraser, that is. It'll teach him to keep a better lookout in future.'

An expression of satisfaction crossed Rogers's face at this remark and Drinkwater was reminded of the burgeoning dislike between the two men.

'That will be all, gentlemen, except to say that there is, as yet, no news of our convoy. They have not yet come in after the gale but that is not entirely unexpected. Neither Captain Young's nor Captain Baker's brigs are as weatherly as *Antigone*, but we shall make for the rendezvous at Vinga Bay as soon as the wind serves and disperses this fog.'

They left him to his glass, Mount chattering excitedly about the news of the battle, and Drinkwater dismissed the preoccupations of the ship in favour of more important considerations. The bad weather had separated him from the two brigs whose protection he had been charged with. He had every confidence in locating Young and Baker at Vinga Bay. The Swedes had told him the ice was breaking up fast and the Sound was clear, except for the diminutive fragments of pancake ice that spun slowly past them towards the warmer waters of the Skagerrak and the grey North Sea. Carlscrona was already navigable and he might have landed his diplomatic dispatches there, closer to Stockholm than the Scanian fortress of Varberg. However, the Swedish governor had assured him that was unimportant. He had personally guaranteed their swift delivery to King Gustavus who eagerly awaited news of support from London.

Drinkwater drained the glass. Exactly how accurate the news was of a check to the French he did not know, but he was acutely aware that the events of the coming summer were likely to be vital in the Baltic.

As the cabin door opened to admit the officers the noise of a fiddle came from forward where the hands had been piped to dance and skylark. Drinkwater stood and welcomed his guests as Mullender moved among them with a dozen glasses of blackstrap to whet their appetites.

'You ordered the purser to issue double grog to all hands, Mr Rogers, I trust?'

'Aye, sir, I did.' Rogers had made some effort to sober up from his injudicious imbibing earlier that day.

'That is as well. I am conscious of having made all hands work hard on our passage. Despite the disappearance of the convoy, which I don't doubt we shall soon remedy, it was necessary that we deliver the Government's dispatches without delay.' Drinkwater turned to a tall, thin lieutenant who wore a hook in place of his left hand and from whose pink nose depended a large dewdrop. 'I see you have come from the deck, Mr Q. Is the fog still as dense?'

17

Lieutenant Quilhampton shook his head, sending the dewdrop flying. 'Doing its damnedest to lift, sir, though I cannot depend on half cannon-shot at the moment. But a dead calm still and no sign of any merchantmen.'

'And unlikely to be, Mr Q. They'll have snugged down and ridden out that gale like sensible fellows, if I don't mistake their temper.'

'Rather an unusual convoy for a frigate of our force, sir, wouldn't you say?' put in Midshipman Lord Walmsley. 'I mean two North-country brigs don't amount to much.'

'I don't know, Mr Walmsley,' replied Drinkwater who from their earliest acquaintance had avoided the use of the young man's title on board, 'their lading is almost as valuable as our own.'

'May one ask what it is?'

'One hundred and sixty thousand stand of arms, Mr Walmsley, together with powder and shot for sixty rounds a man.'

Drinkwater smiled at the whistles this intelligence provoked. 'Come gentlemen, please be seated . . .'

They sat down noisily and Drinkwater regarded them with a certain amount of satisfaction. In addition to the three officers he had summoned earlier, James Quilhampton the third lieutenant, Mr Lallo the surgeon, and four of *Antigone*'s midshipmen were present. Mr Fraser was absent on deck, pacing his atonement for failing to sight the captain's barge that forenoon, an atonement that was spiced by Rogers's passing of the instruction, leaving Fraser in no doubt of the first lieutenant's malicious triumph.

In the cabin Drinkwater paid closest attention to the midshipmen. Mr Quilhampton was an old friend and shipmate, Mr Lallo a surgeon of average ability. But the midshipmen were Drinkwater's own responsibility. It was his reputation they would carry with them when they were commissioned and served under other commanders. Their professional maturation was, therefore, of more than a mere passing interest. This was the more acutely so since most were protégés of another captain, inherited by Drinkwater upon his hurried appointment to the corvette *Melusine* during her eventful Greenland voyage. By now he had come to regard them as his own, and one in particular came under scrutiny, for he had both dismissed and reinstated Lord Walmsley.

Midshipmen Dutfield and Wickham were rated master's mates now and little Mr Frey was as active and intelligent as any eager youngster, but Lord Walmsley still engaged Drinkwater's speculation as, laughing and jesting with the others, he addressed himself to the broth Mullender placed before them. A dominating, wilful and dissolute youth, Drinkwater had discerned some finer qualities in him during the sojourn in the Arctic. But the boy had abused his powers and Drinkwater had turned him out of the ship for a period, only taking him back when Walmsley had gone to considerable lengths to impress the captain of his remorse. There were still streaks of the old indolence, and touches of arrogance; but they were tempered by a growing ability and Drinkwater had every confidence in his passing for lieutenant at the next available Board.

Drinkwater pushed his soup plate away and hid a smile behind his napkin as he watched Walmsley, at the opposite end of the table, talking with a certain condescension to Mr Dutfield, some three years his junior.

'A glass of wine with you, sir?' Sam Rogers leaned forward with exaggerated cordiality and Drinkwater nodded politely, raising his glass. The conversation swelled to a hubbub as Mullender brought from the little pantry the roast capons and placed them before the captain. The homely smell of the meat emphasised the luxury of this fog-enforced idleness and combined with the wine to induce a comfortable mellowness in Drinkwater. He felt for once positively justified in putting off until tomorrow the problems of duty. But Mr Mount was not of so relaxed a frame of mind.

'Excuse me, sir,' put in the marine lieutenant, leaning forward, his scarlet coat a bright spot amidst the sober blue of the sea-officers, 'but might I press you to elaborate on the news you gave us earlier?'

'I did promise, did I not, Mr Mount?' said Drinkwater with a sigh.

'You did, sir.'

Drinkwater accepted the carving irons from his coxswain Tregembo, assisting Mullender at the table. He sliced into the white meat of the fowl's breast.

'It seems that a pitched battle was fought between considerable forces of French and Russians at a place near Königsberg called . . . Eylau, or some such . . . is that sufficient, Mr Rogers? Doubtless,' he continued, turning again to Mount, 'it is noted upon your atlas.'

A chuckle ran round the table and Mount flushed to rival his coat. He had been greatly teased about his acquisition of a large Military Atlas, purporting to cover the whole of Europe, India, North America and the Cape of Good Hope to a standard 'compatible with the contemplation, comprehension, verification and execution of military campaigns engaged in by the forces of His Majesty'. Armed with this *vade mecum*, Mount had bored the occupants of the gunroom rigid with

19

interminable explanations of the brilliance of Napoleon's campaign in Prussia the previous year. The double victory of Jena-Auerstadt, which in a single day had destroyed the Prussian military machine, had failed to impress anyone except James Quilhampton who had pored over the appropriate pages of the atlas out of pity for Mount and was rewarded by a conviction that the likelihood of a French defeat was remote. The completeness of the cavalry pursuit after Jena seemed to make little difference to the naval officers, though it had brought the French to the very shores of the Baltic Sea and reduced the Prussian army to a few impotent garrisons in beleaguered fortresses, and a small field force under a General Lestocq. Mount's admiration for the genius behind the campaign had led him to suffer a great deal of leg-pulling for his treasonable opinions.

'And the outcome, sir?' persisted Mount. 'You spoke of a check.'

'Well, one does not like to grasp too eagerly at good news, since it has, in the past, so often proved false. But the Russians gave a good account of themselves, particularly as the French were reported to have been commanded by Napoleon himself.'

Drinkwater looked round their faces. There was not a man at the table whose imagination was not fired by the prospect of real defeat having been inflicted on the hitherto triumphant Grand Army and its legendary leader.

'And the Russkies, sir. Who was in command of them?'

Drinkwater frowned. 'To tell the truth, Mr Mount, I cannot recollect . . .'

'Kamenskoi?'

'No . . . no that was not it . . .'

'Bennigsen?'

'You have it, Mr Mount. General Bennigsen. What can you tell us of him?'

'He is one of the German faction in the Russian service, sir, a Hanoverian by birth, something of a soldier of fortune.'

'So your hero's taken a damned good drubbing at last, eh Mount?' said Lallo the surgeon. ' 'Tis about time his luck ran a little thin, I'm thinking.' Lallo turned to Drinkwater, manifesting a natural anxiety common to them all. 'It *was* a victory, sir? For the Russians, I mean.'

'The Swedes seemed positive that it was not a French one, Mr Lallo. It seems they were left exhausted upon the field, but the Russians only withdrew to prepare positions of defence . . .'

'But if they had beat Boney, why should they want to prepare defences?'

'I don't know, but the report seemed positive that Napoleon received a bloody nose.'

'Let us hope it *is* true,' said Quilhampton fervently.

'And not just wishful thinking,' slurred Rogers with the wisdom of the disenchanted.

'Napoleon's the devil of a long way from home,' said Hill, laying down his knife and fork. 'If he receives a second serious blow from the Russkies he might overreach himself.'

Drinkwater finished his own meat. The uncertainty of speculation had destroyed his euphoria. It was time he turned the intelligence to real account.

'I believe he already has,' he said. 'Those decrees he issued from Berlin last year establishing his Continental System will have little effect on us. Preventing the European mainland from trading with Great Britain will starve the European markets, while leaving us free to trade with the Indies or wherever else we wish. Providing the Royal Navy does its part in maintaining a close blockade of the coast, which is what the King's Orders in Council are designed to achieve. I daresay we shall make ourselves unpopular with the Americans, but that cannot be helped. Napoleon will get most of the blame and, the larger his empire becomes, the more people his policies will inconvenience.' He hoped he carried his point, aware that a note of pomposity had unwittingly crept into his voice.

'So, gentlemen,' Drinkwater continued, after refilling his glass, 'if the Royal Navy in general, and you in particular, do your duty, and the Russians stand firm, we may yet see the threat to our homes diminish. Let us hope this battle of Eylau is the high-water mark of Napoleon's ambition . . .'

'Bravo, sir!'

'Death to the French!'

'I'll drink to that!' They were all eagerly holding their glasses aloft.

'No, gentlemen,' Drinkwater said smiling, relieved that his lecturing tone had been overlooked, 'I do not like xenophobic toasts, they tempt providence. Let us drink to our gallant allies the Russians.'

'To the Russians!'

Drinkwater sat alone after the officers had gone. Smoke from Lallo's pipe still hung over the table from which the cloth had been drawn and replaced by Mount's atlas an hour before. He found the lingering aroma of the tobacco pleasant, and Tregembo had produced a remaining half-bottle of port for him.

He had watched the departure of his old coxswain with affection. They had been together for so long that the demarcations between master and servant had long since been eroded and they were capable of anticipating each other's wishes in the manner of man and wife. This uncomfortable thought made Drinkwater raise his eyes to the portraits of his wife and children on the forward bulkhead. The pale images of their faces were lit by the wasting candles on the table. He pledged them a silent toast and diverted his thoughts. It did not do to dwell on such things for he did not want a visitation of the blue devils, that misanthropic preoccupation of seamen. It was far better to consider the task in hand, though there was precious little comfort in that. Locked away beneath him lay one of the subsidies bound for the coffers of the Tsar with which the British Government propped up the war against Napoleon's French Empire. Eighty thousand pounds sterling was a prodigious sum for which to be held accountable.

He drew little comfort from the thought that the carriage of the specie would earn him a handsome sum, for he nursed private misgivings as to the inequity of the privilege. The worries over the elaborate precautions in which he was ordered to liaise with officials of the diplomatic corps, and the missing shipment of arms in the storm-separated brigs, only compounded his anxiety over the accuracy of the news from Varberg. There seemed no end to the war, and time was wearing away zeal. Many of his own people had been at sea for four years; his original draft of volunteers had been reduced by disease, injury and action, and augmented by those sweepings of the press, the quota-men, Lord Mayor's men and any unfortunate misfit the magistrates had decided would benefit from a spell in His Majesty's service.

Drinkwater emptied the bottle and swore to himself. He had lost six men by desertion at Sheerness and he knew his crew were unsettled. In all justice he could not blame them, but he could do little else beyond propitiating providence and praying the battle of Eylau would soon be followed by news of a greater victory for the armies of Tsar Alexander of Russia.

Occasional talks with Lord Dungarth, Director of the Admiralty's Secret Department, had kept Drinkwater better informed than most cruiser captains had a right to expect. Their long-standing friendship had given Drinkwater a unique insight into the complexities of British foreign policy in the long war against the victorious French. All the British were really capable of doing effectively was sealing the continent in a naval blockade. To encompass the destruction of the

Grand Army required a supply of men as great as that of France. 'It is to Russia we must look, Nathaniel,' Dungarth had once said, 'with her endless manpower supported by our subsidies, and the character of Tsar Alexander to spur her on.'

He had one of those subsidies beneath him at that moment; as for the character of Tsar Alexander, Drinkwater hoped he could be relied on. It was rumoured that he had connived at the assassination of his own sadistically insane father. Did such acquiescence demonstrate a conviction of moral superiority? Or was it evidence of a weakness in succumbing to the pressure of others?

Wondering thus, Captain Drinkwater rose, loosened his stock and began to undress.

An Armed Neutrality

'Here's your hot water, zur,' Tregembo stropped the razor vigorously, 'and Mr Quilhampton sends his compliments to you and to say that we'll be entering The Sound in an hour.' Tregembo sniffed, indicating disapproval, and added, 'And I'm to tell 'ee that Mr Hill's on deck . . .'

Drinkwater lathered his chin and jaw. 'And my presence ain't necessary, is that it?'

Tregembo sniffed again. 'That's the message, zur, as I told it.'

Drinkwater took the razor and began to scrape his lathered face, his legs braced as *Antigone* leaned to the alteration of course. 'Huh! We're off Cronbourg, Tregembo, and the Danes are damned touchy about who goes through The Sound. Where are the two brigs?' he asked after a brief pause, pleased that he had located his charges at Vinga Bay as predicted.

'Safely tucked under our larboard beam, zur.'

'Good. We'll keep 'em on the Swedish side.' He concentrated on his shave.

'You'll pardon me for saying, zur,' Tregembo pressed on with the familiarity of long service, 'but you've been under the weather these past two days . . .'

'You talk too much, too early in the day, damn you . . . God's bones!' Drinkwater winced at the nick the razor had given him.

'You'd do better to take more care of yourself,' Tregembo persisted, and for a second Drinkwater thought he was being insolent, referring to his own bloodily obvious need to keep his mouth shut. But a single glance at the old Cornishman's face told him otherwise. Tregembo's concern was touching.

'You cluck like an old hen,' Drinkwater said, his tone and mood mellowing. He had to admit the justice of Tregembo's allegation, although 'under the weather' was an inadequate description of Drinkwater's evil humour. He wiped off the lather and looked at

Tregembo. It was impossible for him to apologise but his expression was contrite.

' 'Tis time we went ashore, zur. Swallowed the anchor, in a manner of speaking.'

'Ashore?' Drinkwater tied his stock, peering at himself in the mirror. 'Ashore? No, I think not, Tregembo, not yet. I don't think I could abide tea and gossip at the same hour every day and having to be polite to the train or gentlewomen who infest my house like weevils in a biscuit.'

Tregembo was not so easily diverted, knowing full well Drinkwater's exaggeration only emphasised his irritability. ' 'Tis time you purchased a bit of land, zur. You could go shooting . . .'

Drinkwater turned from the mirror. 'When we swallow the anchor, as you quaintly put it, Tregembo,' he said with a sudden vehemence, holding his arms backwards for his coat, 'I pray God I have done with shooting!'

Tregembo held out the cocked hat, his face wearing an injured look.

'Damn it, Tregembo, I've a touch of the blue devils lately.'

'You know my Susan would run a house fit for 'ee and Mistress Elizabeth, zur.'

'It's not that, my old friend,' said Drinkwater, suddenly dropping the pretence at formality between them. 'Susan and Mistress Elizabeth would both be full of joy if we went home. But d'you think they'd tolerate our interfering indefinitely?' He made an attempt at flippancy. 'D'you think you'd be content to weed the onion patch, eh?' He took the proffered hat and smiled at the old Cornishman.

'Happen you are right, zur. There's many as would miss 'ee if 'ee took it in mind to go.'

Drinkwater hesitated, his hat half raised to his head, sensing one of Tregembo's oblique warnings.

'I know the people are disaffected . . .'

'It ain't the people, zur. Leastways not as cause, like. They be more in the nature of effect.'

'Meaning, Tregembo?' asked Drinkwater.

'Mr Rogers, zur, is shipping a deal of the gunroom *vino*. 'Tis a fact 'ee cannot hide from the people, zur. They hold 'ee for a fair man, zur. 'Twould be a pity to see Mr Rogers become a millstone, zur, if 'ee takes my meaning.'

Drinkwater jammed the hat on his head. He should be grateful for Tregembo's warning, yet the old man had only revealed the cause of his own recent ill-humour. Carrying eight thousand pounds around in an explosive corner of the world with one hundred and sixty thousand muskets tucked under his lee for good measure was bad enough, but to have to contend with a pot-tossing first lieutenant to boot was well-nigh intolerable.

'Belay that infernal prattle,' he snapped and threw open the cabin door. Ducking through with a nod to the marine sentry he sprang for the ladder to the quarterdeck.

Behind him Tregembo shook his head and muttered. 'Jumpy as a galled horse . . .' He rinsed the razor, dried and closed it, nodding at the portrait of Elizabeth on the adjacent bulkhead. 'I did my best, ma'am.'

Lifting the bowl of soapy water he threw it down the privy in the quarter-gallery where it drained into *Antigone*'s hissing wake as she sped past the fortress of Cronbourg at the narrow entrance of The Sound.

On deck, Drinkwater's sudden arrival scattered the idle knot of officers who stared curiously ahead at the red-brick ramparts and the green copper cupolas of the famous castle, above which floated a great red and white swallow-tailed flag, the national colours of neutral Denmark. Drinkwater took Hill's report and left the master in charge of the con. He stopped briefly to stare at the two trim brigs with their cargoes of arms that they had found two days earlier in Vinga Bay, just as predicted; then he fell to pacing the starboard rail, watching the coast of Denmark. The shreds of conversation that drifted across to Drinkwater from the displaced officers were inevitably about the great expedition, six years earlier, which had culminated in Lord Nelson's victory at Copenhagen. Although he had distinguished himself both before and during the famous action, Drinkwater's already morbid humour recalled only a dark and private episode in his life.

It was here, among the low hills and blue spires already slipping astern, at the village of Gilleleje, that Drinkwater had secretly landed his own brother Edward on the run from the law. Edward had had a talent with horses and drifted into the life of a gambler centred on the racing world of Newmarket and the French emigrés who had settled there. His entanglement with a young Frenchwoman had resulted in him murdering his rival. Drinkwater had always felt his honour had been impugned by the obligation Edward's ties of blood had held him to. Even at this distance in time, even after Drinkwater had discovered that in murdering his rival, Edward had inadvertantly killed a French agent, Drinkwater was still unable to shrug off the shadows that had so isolated him then. Nor did it seem to mitigate Drinkwater's personal guilt that Edward had found employment as an agent himself. For after landing at Gilleleje and going to Hamburg, Lord Dungarth had sent him eastwards, relying on his ability to speak the French he had learned from his faithless mistress. Drinkwater knew that Edward had been at the battle of Austerlitz and was the origin of accurate intelligence about the true state of affairs in the Russian army after that bitter and shattering defeat. The news, it was said, had killed Billy Pitt; and this too seemed full of a dark accumulation of presentiment. With an effort, Drinkwater cast aside his gloom. Sunshine danced upon the water and they were rapidly approaching the narrowest point of The Sound commanded by the Danish guns in their embrasures at Cronbourg. It was, he thought with sudden resolution, time to make a show, a flourish. He spun on his heel.

'Mr Rogers!'

The first lieutenant's florid features turned towards him. 'Sir?'

'Call all hands! Stuns'ls aloft and alow! Then you may clear for action!'

'Stuns'ls and clear for action, sir!' The order was taken up and the pipes twittered at the hatchways. Drinkwater stood at the starboard hance and watched the temper of the hands as the watches below tumbled up. Topmen scrambled into the rigging and Comley's mates chastised the slower waisters into place as they prepared to send up or haul out the studdingsails. Drinkwater's gaze rose upwards. Already the agile topmen were spreading out along the upper yards on the fore- and main-masts. Out went the upper booms, thrust through their irons at the extremities of the topsail and topgallant yardarms. At the rails by the fore-chains, the lower booms were being swung out on their goosenecks. Festoons of guys straightened into their ordered places. He watched with satisfaction as the midshipmen, nimble as monkeys in their respective stations, waved their readiness to the deck. The upper studdingsails, secured to short battens, were stowed in the tops. At the signal first the weather and then the lee studding-sails were run up to the booms next above. They fluttered momentarily as the halliards secured them, then their lower edges were spread to the booms below. On the fo'c's'le two large bundles had been dragged out of their stowage in the boats. They were similarly bent onto halliards and outhauls stretched their clews to the guyed ends of the lowest booms which were winged out on either side of the frigate's fore-chains. In a minute or so *Antigone* had almost doubled the width of her forward sail plan.

Rogers, satisfied with the evolutions of the ship's company, gave the men permission to lay in. Watching, Drinkwater knew that there had been a few seconds' hesitation before the nod to Comley had brought the bosun's pipe to his mouth and the topmen had come sliding down the backstays. Rogers crossed the deck and knuckled the fore-cock of his hat.

'Very well, Mr Rogers, you may beat to quarters.'

As Rogers turned away, Drinkwater caught again that slightly malicious grin that he had noticed when he had ordered Fraser to keep the deck off Varberg. Whipping a silver hunter from his fob, Rogers flicked it open as he roared the order. Again, and with a mounting disquiet that he could not quite place, Drinkwater watched the motions of the men. To a casual glance they appeared perfectly disciplined, tuned to the finest pitch any crack cruiser captain could demand but . . . that element of perplexity remained with him.

The marine drummer doubled aft, unhitched his drum and lifted his sticks to his chin in a perfunctory acknowledgement of the prescribed drill; then he brought them down on the snare drum and beat out the urgent ruffle. The frigate, alive with men still belaying ropes and laying in from aloft, suddenly took on a new and more sinister air. Along the length of her gundeck the ports were raised and round each of the twenty-six 18-pounder cannon and the ten long 9-pounder chase guns the men congregated in kneeling and expectant groups. Others mustered elsewhere, the marines at the hammock nettings and in the tops, the firemen unreeled their hoses and worked the yoke of their machine to dampen the decks. Boys scattered sand or stood ready with their cartridge boxes. The activity died to an expectant hush. Each gun-captain's hand was raised. Rogers lifted his speaking trumpet.

'Run out the guns!'

The deck beneath Drinkwater's feet trembled as the gunners manned their tackles and hauled the heavy cannon out through the gun-ports.

With every man at his station, her yards braced to catch the quartering breeze and her charges safely tucked under her lee, *Antigone* entered The Sound. Drinkwater indulged Rogers in a final look round the upper deck while he studied the ramparts of Cron-bourg less than a mile away. Through his glass he could see the tiny dots of heads beneath the gigantic swallow-tailed standard which rippled gallantly in the breeze. At this distance those men could not fail to remark the belligerent preparedness of the British cruiser. Denmark was a neutral state, but not therefore without influence upon international affairs. Her trade, particularly in the matter of naval stores, if directed towards the beleaguered fleets of France, could be damaging to the war-efforts of Great Britain. And since Napoleon had decreed that no European country, whether under the control of his legions or attempting to maintain a precarious neutrality, might trade with Britain, the British must treat her with suspicion.

'Ship cleared for action, sir.' The snap of Rogers's hunter made Drinkwater lower his glass.

'Very well. An improvement?'

'About the same, sir,' replied Rogers non-commitally, and in a flash Drinkwater knew what he had been witness to, what had been going on under his very nose. He fixed his keen glance on the first lieutenant.

'I thought they were a trifle faster that time.'

He saw a hint of uncertainty in Rogers's eyes. 'Well, perhaps a trifle faster,' said Rogers grudgingly, and Drinkwater was certain his instinct was right. Between first lieutenant and the hands there existed a state of affairs exactly analogous to that between Britain and Denmark: a neutrality in which each warily sought out the weakness and the intentions of the other. Rogers, the first lieutenant, the all-powerful executive officer, was always ready to punish any gun-crew, yardarm party, or individual, whose standard was not in his opinion of the highest. Against him were pitted the people, hydra-headed but weak, vulnerable to one simple, silly slip, yet knowing that they had only to wait and the bottle would destroy the first lieutenant. The certainty of this knowledge came as a shock to Drinkwater and the colour drained from his face, leaving his eyes piercing in the intensity of their anger.

'By God, Sam,' he said softly through clenched teeth, 'I will not have you judge, lest you be judged yourself.' Rogers's glance fell as they were interrupted.

'I think we have not bared our fangs in vain, sir,' said Hill, stumping across the deck to draw Drinkwater's attention to the events unfolding on the starboard bow. Hill paused, sensing an open breach between captain and first lieutenant where he had anticipated only an exchange of remarks concerning the ship's internal routines. He coughed awkwardly. 'Beg pardon, sir, but I . . .'

'Yes, yes, I see them,' snapped Drinkwater and raising his glass once more, affected to ignore Rogers.

Standing out from Elsinore Road to the south of Cronbourg was a two-decked line-of-battleship, and astern of her a small frigate. They too were cramming on sail, coming in at an angle to *Antigone*'s bow as though to intercept her.

'Their bearing's opening, sir,' offered Hill, coolly professional again, 'only slowly, but they'll not catch us.'

'Very well, Mr Hill, but we ought not to outrun our charges.' Drinkwater nodded at the brigs, now some distance astern of them. The Danish warships would pass between *Antigone* and the two British merchantmen.

'Notified of our approach from the castle, I'll warrant,' remarked Hill.

'Yes.' Drinkwater subjected the two ships to a further scrutiny through his glass. The Danes had proved tough opponents in 1801, reluctant to surrender and forcing from Lord Nelson the remark that they played the hottest fire he had ever been under. The two Danish ships broke out their own studdingsails. He watched critically. It was well done.

'I thought we had buggered their damned fleet for them,' said Rogers with characteristic coarseness in an attempt to defuse the atmosphere between himself and Drinkwater.

'Apparently not,' Drinkwater replied as if nothing untoward had occurred, watching the ships as their respective courses converged. But Hill was right, the bearings of the Danes were drawing aft, showing that the *Antigone* was the faster ship. 'They've had six years to right the damage,' he said, turning to look again at the lumbering brigs on the larboard quarter. 'I don't like exposing our charges like this and I'm rather disposed to test their mettle . . . Secure the guns where they are, Mr Rogers,' he said with a sudden sharpness, 'and get the stuns'ls off her!'

Rogers began bellowing orders. Again *Antigone* seethed with activity. Whatever discontents might be running through her people, the chance of demonstrating their superiority as seamen before a mob of tow-haired Danes animated the ship. In a few minutes her studdingsails fluttered inboard.

'Clew up the courses!' Drinkwater ordered sharply, for he had not wanted anything to go wrong, or the Danes to put a shot across his bow, turning a voluntary act into a submissive one.

'Lower the t'gallants on the caps!' *Antigone*'s speed slowed, yet she held her course and the hands were sent back to their battle-stations as the Danish warships came up, the frigate ranging out to larboard so that they overtook on either quarter.

Hill was looking at him anxiously.

'My God,' said Rogers to no one in particular, 'if they open fire now they will . . .' His voice trailed off as he wiped the back of his hand across his mouth. It was, Drinkwater noted, the gesture of a thirsty man.

'They are neutrals, gentlemen,' he said. 'They dare not fire upon us without provoking an act of war. They simply wish to demonstrate their readiness not to be intimidated on their own doorstep . . . Just keep the men at their stations in silence if you please, Mr Rogers, and perhaps we may yet surprise 'em,' Drinkwater added as an outbreak of chatter started up in the waist.

Drinkwater strode forward as the line-of-battleship ranged up on their starboard beam, her two tiers of guns also run out so that they dominated the much lower deck of the British frigate.

'Mr Mount!' Drinkwater called to the marine officer.

'Sir?'

'Form your men in two divisions, facing outboard on either side, then bring 'em to attention.'

'Very good, sir.'

As the quarterdecks of the three ships drew level the marines stood rigid. Drinkwater casually mounted the starboard rail in the mizen rigging. He turned back inboard. 'Have the hands piped aloft to man the yards, Mr Rogers.' He ignored the puzzled apprehension in Rogers's eyes and turned to the Danish ship, not two hundred feet away and stealing their wind. He doffed his hat in a wide sweep.

'Good day, sir!' he shouted.

A line of Danish officers regarded him and there was obviously some conferring going on on her quarterdeck. After a pause a junior officer was pushed up onto her rail.

'Gut morning, Capten. Vat ship is that, please?'

'His Britannic Majesty's frigate *Antigone*, upon a cruise with merchantmen in company, sir,' Drinkwater bawled back cheerfully.

'Ve hope you do not vish to stop Dansk ships, no?'

'My orders are to stop all ships carrying cargoes of war material to His Majesty's enemies. This policy is clearly stated in His Majesty's Orders in Council, sir, copies of which have been delivered to your Government's representatives in London.'

The Danish officer bent down, obviously in consultation with a senior, for he stood again. 'You are varned against stopping Dansk ships, Capten.'

'I shall carry out my orders, sir, as I expect you to maintain your neutrality!' He turned to Rogers: 'I want three hearty cheers when I call for 'em.'

He heard Rogers mutter 'Good God!' and turned again to the Dane. The big battleship was drawing ahead now and he could read her name across her stern: *Princesse Sophia Frederica.*

'Three cheers for His Majesty the King of Denmark! Hip! Hip! Hip!'

'Hooray . . .' The three cheers ripped from over his head and Drinkwater jumped down from the rail.

'Now, Sam, let fall those courses, hoist the t'gallants and reset the stuns'ls!' He turned to the sailing master, standing by the wheel. 'Hold your course, Mr Hill . . . Bye the bye, did you get the name of the frigate?' Drinkwater nodded to larboard.

'Aye, sir, *Triton*, twenty-eight guns.'

'Very well.' Drinkwater clasped his hands behind his back and offered up a silent prayer that his pride was not to be humbled in front of such witnesses. But he need not have worried. It was not merely his own pride that was at stake; some of the defiance in his tone had communicated itself to the hands. This was no longer a petty internal matter, no empty evolution at the behest of the first lieutenant, but a matter of national pride. Now the captain was handling the ship and they behaved as though they were in action and their very lives depended upon their smartness.

Antigone gathered speed as she again spread her wings. Her long jib-boom swung across the great square stern of the two-decker as she pointed closer to the wind. She began to overhaul the Danish ship to windward and with an amiable insouciance Drinkwater again waved his hat at the knot of officers who stared stolidly back at him.

The cheering provoked no response from the Danes.

'Miserable bastards,' remarked Rogers sullenly, coming aft as the studdingsail halliards were coiled down. In their wake the Danish battleship hauled her wind and put about, turning back towards her anchorage off Elsinore.

Triton kept them company as far as the island of Hven, then she too put about and the incident was over. To larboard the Scanian coast of Sweden lay in the distance, while closer to starboard the coast of Zealand fell away to a low-lying, pastoral countryside dotted with church towers and white farms. Astern of *Antigone* the two brigs followed in their wake, while ten miles ahead, faintly blue in the distance, the spires of Copenhagen broke the skyline.

The British frigate and her small convoy entered the Baltic Sea.

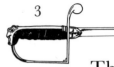

3   April 1807

The Shipment of Arms

Mr James Quilhampton peered over the ship's side and watched the little bobbing black jolly-boat, from the nearer of the two brigs, hook neatly onto the frigate's main chains. The man in her stern relinquished the tiller, stepped lightly upon a thwart and, skilfully judging the boat's motion, leapt for the man-ropes and the wooden battens that formed a ladder up the frigate's tumblehome. He was met by Midshipman Lord Walmsley and Quilhampton straightened up as the man, hatless despite the cold and in plain civilian dress, strode aft.

'Good morning, Lieutenant,' he said in the rolling accent of Northumbria.

'Good morning, Captain Young,' responded Quilhampton civilly. 'I have informed Captain Drinkwater of your approach and here he comes now.'

Drinkwater mounted the quarterdeck ladder and cast a swift and instinctive glance round the horizon. *Antigone* and the two brigs lay hove-to on a smooth grey sea which was terminated to the north and east by an ice-field that seemed at first to stretch to the horizon itself. But beyond it to the east lay the faint blue line of land, a low country of unrelieved flatness, almost part of the sea itself.

'Captain Young,' said Drinkwater cordially, taking the strong hand and wincing with the power of its grip. His right arm already ached from the cold seeping into the mangled muscles of his wounded shoulder and Young's rough treatment did nothing to ease it. 'I give you good day. I take it that you and Captain Baker and your ships' companies are well?'

'Why aye, man. As fit as when we left London River.'

'What d'you make of this ice?' Drinkwater disengaged his arm from Young's eager, pump-handle grasp and gestured eastward.

'The Pregel Bar is not more than two leagues distant, Captain Drinkwater. It is unlikely that the ice will last more than another sennight.' He smiled. 'Why, man, Baker and I'll be drinking schnapps in Königsberg by mid-month.'

'You think the ice in the Frisches Haff will have cleared by then?'

'Aye, man. Once thaw sets in 'twill soon clear.'

'In view of the presence of ice I think it better that I should remain with you. You might have need of my protection yet.'

'As you wish, Captain.'

'You have your instructions as to the formalities necessary to the discharging of your arms and ammunition?'

'Aye, Captain.' Young smiled again. 'You may allay your fears on that score. They will not fall into the wrong hands.'

'Very well. But I could wish for more positive assurances. News from the shore that Königsberg is not in danger from the French . . .'

'No, Captain, I doubt there's any fear o' that. At Vinga we heard that Boney's had both his eyes blacked proper by them Russians. You've no need to fear that Königsberg's a French port.'

'Let's hope you are right,' said Drinkwater.

'What about your own cargo, Captain Drinkwater?' Young asked.

'Eh? Oh. You know about that do you?'

'Of course,' Young chuckled, 'have you ever known a secret kept along a waterfront?'

Drinkwater shook his head. 'I have to deliver it to Revel but, as you can see, the ice prevents me for the time being.' He attempted to divert the conversation. He had no business discussing such matters with Young. 'What will you do once you have discharged your lading at Königsberg?'

'Coast up to Memel and see what Munro has for us.'

'Munro?' asked Drinkwater absently.

'A Scottish merchant who acts as my agent at Memel. He and I have been associates in the way of business for as many years as I've owned and commanded the *Jenny Marsden*. The rogue married a pretty Kurlander at whom I once set my own cap.' Young grinned and Drinkwater reflected that here was a world as intimately connected with the sea as his own, but about which he knew next to nothing.

'The trade and its disappointments seem to keep you in good humour, Captain Young.'

'Aye, and in tolerable good pocket,' Young added familiarly.

'We had better anchor then . . .'

'Aye, Baker and I will work our way inshore a little, if you've a mind to close in our wake.'

'It won't be the first time I've worked a ship through ice, Captain,' said Drinkwater returning Young's ready smile. 'Mr Q! Have the kindness to see Captain Young to his boat.' He could not avoid having his wrist wrenched again by the genial Northumbrian and felt compelled to dispel his anxiety by more of the man's good-natured company. It would do him no harm to learn more of the Baltic for he might yet have the convoy of the whole homeward trade at the close of the season. 'Perhaps you and Baker would do me the honour of dining with me this afternoon, Captain. 'Tis a plain table, but . . .'

'None the worse for that, I'm sure. That's damned civil of ye, Captain Drinkwater. And I'll be happy to accept.'

'Very well. Ah, Mr Q . . .'

As the little jolly-boat pulled away, Drinkwater raised his hat to Young and then, his curiosity aroused after the conversation, he fished in his tail-pocket for the Dollond glass and levelled it at the distant smudge of land. The sand-spit that separated the open sea from the great lagoon of the Frisches Haff was pierced at its northern end, allowing the River Pregel to flow into the Baltic. Twenty miles inland lay the great fortress and cathedral city of Königsberg, once the home of the Teutonic knights and later a powerful trading partner in the Hanseatic League. Now it was the most eastern possession of the King of Prussia and the only one, it seemed, that contained a Prussian garrison of any force to maintain King Frederick William's tenuous independence from Napoleon. As such it formed an important post on the lines of communication between Russia and the Tsar's armies in Poland, a depot for Bennigsen's commissariat and the obvious destination for one hundred and sixty thousand muskets, with bayonets, cartridge and ball to match.

'Beg pardon, sir, but the brigs are hauling their main-yards.'

Mr Quilhampton recalled Drinkwater from his abstraction. He shut the glass with a snap, aware that he had seen nothing through it apart from grey sea, ice and the blue line of a featureless country. It seemed odd that history was being made there, among what looked no more substantial than a streak or two of cobalt tint from Mr Frey's watercolour box.

'Filling their sails, eh, Mr Q? Very well. Do you do likewise. And you may pass word to rouse up a cable and bend it onto the best bower. We shall fetch an anchor when those two fellows show us some good holding.'

Captain's Young's forecast proved accurate. Within a few days the ice began to melt and disperse with dramatic rapidity. A soft wind blew from the south-east, bringing off the land exotic fragrances and stray birds that chirruped as they fluttered, exhausted in the rigging. From here the boys were sent aloft to chase them off and prevent them fouling the white planking of *Antigone*'s decks. The relative idleness of the enforced anchorage served to rest the men, settling those new-pressed into a more regular routine than the demands of passage-making allowed, and Drinkwater detected a lessening of tension about the ship. His warning to Rogers seemed to have been heeded and he felt able to relax, to consider that their earlier problems had been part of the inevitable shaking-down necessary to the beginning of every cruise.

As the ice broke up, the three ships moved closer to the estuary, and ten days after their first anchoring, Drinkwater began to send boat expeditions away to determine the effect of the thaw upon the fresher waters of the Frisches Haff. A few days later local fishing boats appeared and then there were signs of coastal craft beyond the sand-spit that was in sight of them now. And then, quite suddenly and with unexpected drama, proof came that confirmed that navigation was open up the Pregel to the quays of Königsberg itself. While Drinkwater was breakfasting one morning an excited Midshipman Wickham burst into his cabin with the news that a large and 'important-looking barge' was coming off from the shore. Hurriedly swallowing his coffee, Drinkwater donned hat and cloak and went on deck.

Lieutenant Fraser had already caught sight of the unmistakable flash of scarlet under a flung-back grey cape and the ostentatiously upright figure of a military officer standing in the big boat's stern. He had had the presence of mind to man the side, Drinkwater noted, as he joined Fraser at the entry.

'My congratulations, Mr Fraser,' he said drily. 'Your vigilance has improved remarkably.'

'Thank ye, sir,' replied the Scotsman sensing the captain's good humour, 'but to be truthful I think yon gentleman was of a mind to draw attention to himself.'

'Yes.' Drinkwater nodded and stared curiously at the approaching stranger. 'He seems to be British, and in full regimentals,' he remarked as the boat came alongside below their line of vision.

A twitching of the baize-covered man-ropes, and then the cockerel plumes, bicorne hat and figure of a British colonel rose above the rail to a twittering of pipes, stamp of marines' boots and the wicked twinkle of sunshine upon Mount's flourished hanger. The officer saluted and Drinkwater tipped his own hat in response.

'Good morning, sir. This is an unlooked-for pleasure. Permit me to introduce myself, Captain Nathaniel Drinkwater of His Britannic Majesty's thirty-eight-gun frigate *Antigone*.'

The newcomer managed a small, sharp bow. 'Your servant, sir. Robert Wilson, Colonel in His Britannic Majesty's Service, attached to the headquarters of His Imperial Majesty's armies in Poland and East Prussia.' He held out a paper of accreditment taken from his cuff and stared about him with an intelligent and professional interest.

Drinkwater gave the pass a cursory glance and said, 'Perhaps we should adjourn to my cabin, Colonel Wilson . . .'

'Delighted, Captain . . .'

The two men went below leaving an air of unsatisfied curiosity among the men on deck.

In the cabin, as Mullender poured two glasses of wine, Drinkwater checked Wilson's pass with more thoroughness. 'Please be seated, Colonel Wilson,' he said and then handed back the document with a nod. 'Thank you. How may I be of service?'

'You have two brigs with you, sir. The *Nancy* and the . . . *Jenny Marsden*. They are filled with a consignment of arms and ammunition for the Russian army, are they not?'

'They are indeed, Colonel,' said Drinkwater, relieved that Wilson had come off to assume responsibility for them. 'Are you intending to see them to their destination at Königsberg?'

'I shall do what I can, though Russian methods can be damnably dilatory.'

'Then I am doubly glad to see you.' Drinkwater smiled, 'And I'd welcome reliable news of the action we heard had been fought in February. I have been concerned as to the accuracy of the reports I had from the Swedes and the safety of such a shipment if left at Königsberg.'

Wilson stretched his long legs and relaxed in his chair. 'You need have no fear, Captain. The Russian outposts confront the French all along the line of the Passarge. They have not moved since Eylau . . .'

'So they *were* held . . .'

'The French? Oh, good God, yes! Had they been under Suvoroff, well . . .' Wilson sipped his wine and shrugged.

'Were you there?'

'At Eylau, yes. The Russians fought with great stubbornness and although Bennigsen left the field the French had been fought to a standstill; Boney himself had had the fright of his life and the Grand

Army were dying in heaps *pour la gloire*. Their cavalry were magnificent of course, but even Murat was powerless to break the Russkies.'

'Will Bennigsen complete the matter when you come out of winter quarters?'

'Bennigsen? Perhaps. He's a German and unpopular with many of the Russian-born officers who will want some of the credit if a victory's to be had; but they're only too happy to blame a scapegoat if they're defeated. Bennigsen's competent enough, and he's close to the Tsar.'

'How so?' asked Drinkwater, fascinated by Wilson, whose close contacts with the Russians were interesting to him on both a professional and a personal level.

'Bennigsen was one of the officers present when Alexander's father, Tsar Paul, met his end in the Mikhailovsky Palace. It is said that Bennigsen was the first man to lay his hands on the Tsar. Outside the room was the Tsarevich Alexander, who happened to be Colonel-in-Chief of the Semenovsky Regiment which stood guard that night. Not an attractive story, but Alexander's complicity is well known. Paul was a highly dangerous man. Apart from his secret accord with Bonaparte, he *was* a vicious and cruel monster. Alexander, on the other hand, nurtures ideal views on kingship.' Wilson tossed off his glass and Drinkwater refilled it.

'Your post is a curious and fascinating one, Colonel. Tell me, what is your candid opinion of the likelihood of the Russians finally trouncing Bonaparte?'

Wilson raised his eyebrows in speculative arches. 'I know that's what your friend Lord Dungarth wants, hence the arms and the specie you have below . . .'

Drinkwater coughed into his wine and looked up sharply. 'You know a great deal, Colonel Wilson. What the devil makes you say Lord Dungarth is my friend?'

'Well he is, ain't he?' replied Wilson. 'That's why *you* are here, Captain Drinkwater, as I understand it.'

Drinkwater assumed an air of sudden caution. Stories of murder and intrigue from St Petersburg were all very well, but Colonel Robert Wilson figured nowhere in his instructions from the Admiralty. 'I have my orders, Colonel Wilson, respecting the specie about which you seem to know everything. I am directed to hand it over at Revel to Lord Leveson-Gower in his *diplomatic* capacity as Ambassador to St Petersburg and not to yourself.'

'My dear sir,' said Wilson smoothly, crossing his legs, 'that ain't what I mean at all, damn me. I assumed that it was you as had been given this assignment in view of your unusual personal connections hereabouts.'

Drinkwater felt the colour leave his face. Surely Wilson could not know about his brother? The feeling that, in some way, providence would make him expiate his guilt for Edward's escape from justice suddenly overwhelmed him. It was an irrational fear that had haunted his subconscious for six years. 'What the devil do you mean?'

Drinkwater's extraordinary reaction had not escaped Wilson, but he had not thought it caused by guilt.

'Come, Captain Drinkwater, I think you need not alarm yourself. I have myself been, if not directly employed by Lord Dungarth's Secret Department like yourself, connected with it in view of my duties here. I am frankly amazed that my presence surprises you. Were you not told? Is it not part of your orders to liaise with any British agents in the field?'

'In so far as I am permitted to discuss my orders, Colonel, I can only shake my head to that question,' Drinkwater said cautiously.

'Some damnable back-sliding between the Horse-Guards and the Admiralty I don't doubt. A confounded clerk that's forgotten to copy a memorandum, or lost a note he was supposed to deliver.' Wilson smote his thigh with a relatively good-natured and contemptuous acceptance. 'Still, that's as may be. Then your orders, after you've turned your convoy and your specie over, are those usual to a cruiser, eh?'

Drinkwater nodded. 'Watch and prey is the formula off Brest, but here 'tis tread the decks of neutrals without upsetting anyone. A difficult task at the best of times.'

'Then you had better know more, Captain, in case we want you . . .'

'*We?*'

'Yes. Doubtless Lord Leveson-Gower will have something to say to you, but there are men in the field whom I will advise of your presence on the coast. Should they want swift communication with London they will be looking out for you. Often a frigate is the best and safest way. Chief among them is Colin Mackenzie. Whatever names he uses in his work he is not ashamed to own Rosshire ancestry on his father's side, though what his mother was only his father knows. I would advise you offer him whatever assistance he might require. There is also another man, a Captain Ostroff, in the Russian service. Both these fellows use a cryptogramic code for their dispatches – I am sure you are familiar with the type of thing – and all are sent to Joseph Devlieghere, Merchant of Antwerpen . . .'

'The clearing house . . .'

'Yes. And for all I know, where Bonaparte's people open 'em up before popping them into a Harwich shrimp-tub together with a keg or two of Hollands gin. The way Paris seems to know what's going on is astounding. That man Fouché is diabolical . . . You smile, Captain . . .'

'Only because he outwits us, Colonel,' said Drinkwater drily. 'If he was one of our fellows he would be considered brilliant.'

'True,' said Wilson smiling.

'I understand. I shall, of course, do what I can, but I assure you I have had no direct orders from Lord Dungarth, nor have I executed any commission for him since April last year.' Drinkwater refilled the glasses, then went on, 'But tell me, if you are confident about Russian prospects, why all this anxiety about agents? Indeed you did not fully answer my question about the military situation.'

'No more I did.' Wilson sipped his wine, considered a moment, then said, 'It is not entirely true to say the situation is static. With Napoleon in the field any thoughts of immobility can be discounted. Colberg and Dantzig have been invested and may fall to the French any day; that much we must expect. Marshall Mortier is occupying our supposed allies, the Swedes, before Stralsund, in Pomerania . . .' Wilson shrugged, 'Who knows what might happen. As to the main theatre here, well . . . I will give Boney one last throw. He is a damned long way from Paris. He's been absent for a year and when the cat's away we all know what the mice get up to. Bennigsen gave him a drubbing. He can't afford to retreat, either politically or militarily. But then he can't risk a defeat which the Russkies are quite capable of giving him. My guess is a battle of his own choosing and a big stake on a single hand.'

Drinkwater digested this. 'I should not care to bear such a responsibility,' he said slowly.

'No more would I,' said Wilson tossing off his glass and making to stand. 'The Russians are a rum lot, to be sure. Touchy, secretive and suspicious, but brave as lions when it comes to a fight.' He rose and looked pensively round the cabin. 'You seem to have a little piece of England here, Captain.'

Drinkwater smiled and drained his own glass. 'The other man's grass always appears a little greener.'

Wilson rose. 'The sooner you deliver your specie to Revel, Captain, the better. My stock at Imperial headquarters may rise a little and I may be less importuned and accused of British lassitude. The Russians are constantly asking why we do not send troops to their assistance. Money and arms seem to disappear without effect.'

'God knows it costs enough without our having to fight their battles for them!' Drinkwater said indignantly.

'Ah, the pernicious income tax!'

'I was not thinking merely of the money, Colonel.' Drinkwater gestured vaguely around him.' It is not merely ships that make up the navy. It takes many men. Do the Russians not appreciate that?'

Wilson raised his eyebrows, his expression one of amused cynicism, and, pulling himself upright, caught his head on the deck beam above. Wincing, he said, 'They are a land-power, Captain. We cannot expect them to understand.' He extended his hand.

'Let us hope', said Drinkwater, shaking hands, 'that you and Bennigsen finish the business. Then we can enjoy our next glass together in London.'

'A cheering and worthy sentiment, Captain Drinkwater, and one that I endorse with all my heart.'

Drinkwater accompanied Wilson on deck and saw him over the side. He watched as the barge was pulled across to Young's brig, the *Jenny Marsden*. Wilson looked back once and waved. Drinkwater acknowledged the valediction then turned to the officer of the watch. 'Well, Mr Fraser . . .'

'Sir?'

'Not all the lobsters strut about St James's. Now do you prepare to get the ship under weigh.'

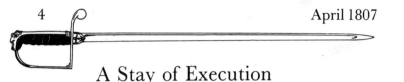

A Stay of Execution

'It comes on to blow, Mr Q!' Drinkwater clamped his hat more securely on his head. 'You were quite right to call me.' He staggered as *Antigone*'s deck heeled to the thump of a heavy sea. The wave surged past them as the stern lifted and the bow dropped again, its breaking crest hissing with wind-driven fury as it was torn into spume.

'We must put about upon the instant! Call all hands!'

'Aye, aye, sir!' Quilhampton shouted forward and the bosun's mate of the watch began to pipe at the hatchways, then he turned back to the captain who had crossed the heeling deck to glance at the compass in the binnacle. 'I've had Walmsley aloft this past hour and there's no passage as yet . . .'

Drinkwater moved to the rail, grasped a stay and stared to leeward as *Antigone* lay down under the sudden furious onslaught of a squall. Through his hand he could feel the vibration of the wind in the frigate's rigging, feel the slackness in the rope as it bowed to leeward. He wiped his eyes and stared across the white-streaked water that heaved and boiled in the short, savage seas that were the result of comparatively shallow water and a quickly risen gale. The rim of the sea terminated, not at the skyline, but in a line of ice.

'Damned unseasonable,' Drinkwater muttered – unconsciously rubbing his shoulder which ached from damp and the chill proximity of the ice – while he considered the effect of the gale on the sea. It occurred to him that it might bring warmer air to melt the ice, and the thought cheered him a little, for it was clear that until the ice re-treated further northwards any hope of reaching Revel was out of the question.

Drinkwater left Quilhampton to tack the ship. The frigate came round like a jibbed horse, her backed fore-yards spinning her high-stabbing bowsprit against the last shreds of daylight in the west.

'Mains'l haul!' The blocks clicked and rattled and the men hauled furiously, running the lee braces aft as the main- and mizen-yards spun round on their parrels.

'Pull together there, damn you!' Comley roared, his rattan active on the hapless backs of a gaggle of men who stumbled along the larboard gangway.

'That's well with the main-braces! Belay! Belay there!'

'Fore-braces! Leggo and haul!' The fore-yards swung and *Antigone* gathered headway on the starboard tack.

'A trifle more on that weather foretack there! That's well! Belay!'

Hill stepped up to the binnacle then looked at the shivering edge of the main-topsail. 'Full and bye now, lads,' he said quietly to the four men at the frigate's double wheel, and the overseeing quartermaster acknowledged the order.

'She's full an' bye now, so she is.'

'Very well.' He turned to Drinkwater. 'She's holding sou' by east a quarter east, sir.'

'Very well. Mr Q! Do you shorten down for the night. We'll keep her under easy sail until daylight.'

'Aye, aye, sir!'

Drinkwater watched patiently from his place by the weather hance, one foot on the little brass carronade slide that he had brought from the *Melusine*. The big fore-course, already reefed down, was now hauled up in its buntlines and secured, forty men laying out along the great yard to secure the heavy, resistant canvas. When they came down it was almost dark. They were waiting for the order to pipe down.

'Mr Quilhampton!'

'Sir?'

'Pass word for Mr Comley to lay aft.'

'Aye, aye, sir.' The lieutenant turned to Walmsley. 'Mr Walmsley, cut along and pass word for the bosun to lay aft and report to the Captain.'

'Aye, aye, sir.'

Lord Walmsley made his way along the lee gangway to the fo'c's'le where Mr Comley stood, the senior and most respected seaman in the ship, at his post of honour on the knightheads.

'Mr Comley!'

'Mr Walmsley, what can I do for you?'

'The Captain desires that you attend him on the quarterdeck.'

'Eh?' Comley looked aft at the figure of Drinkwater, shadowy in the gathering gloom. 'What the devil does he want me on the King's

44

parade for?' he muttered, then nodding to Walmsley he walked aft.

'You sent for me, sir?'

Drinkwater stared at Comley. Hitherto he had never had the slightest doubt that Comley's devotion to duty was absolute. 'Have you anything to report, Mr Comley?'

'To report, sir? Why . . . no, sir.'

'The four men at the lee main-brace, Mr Comley – Kissel, Hacking, Benson and Myers, if I ain't mistaken – are they drunk?'

'Er . . .'

'Damn it, man, you'd do well not to try and hide it from me.'

Comley looked at the captain, his expression anxious. 'I, er, I wouldn't say they was drunk, sir. Happen they slipped . . .'

'Mr Comley, I can have them here in an instant. They are all prime seamen. They didn't slip, sir. Now, I will ask you again, are they drunk?'

Comley sighed and nodded. 'It's possible, sir. I . . . I didn't know until . . . well when they slipped and I got close to 'em. I could smell they might be in liquor, sir.'

'Very well, Mr Comley.' Drinkwater changed his tone of voice. 'Would you answer two questions without fear. Why are they drunk and why did you not report it?'

Even in the twilight Drinkwater could see the dismay on Comley's face. 'Come, sir,' he said, 'you may answer without fear. And be quick about it, the watch below are waiting for you to pipe 'em down.'

'Well, sir, beggin' your pardon, sir, but the men ain't too happy, sir . . . It's nothing much, sir, we ain't asking no favours, but we . . . that is the old Melusines, we was volunteers, sir, back in the year three. Now we're all shipped with pressed men an' quota-men, men that ain't prime seamen, no, nor don't take no shame from that fact, sir; and the length of the commission and there bein' no pay last time at the Nore, sir, and the men beginning to run . . .' His voice faded miserably.

'Personal discontent is not a crime, Mr Comley. I too should like to go home, but we have not yet destroyed our enemies . . . Be that as it may, you have not answered my question. Why did you not report it?'

Drinkwater could see a gathering of pale and expectant faces staring aft, waiting to be dismissed from the tasks they had been called on deck to carry out. All hands were witness to Mr Comley's talk with the captain.

'I don't want no trouble, sir . . . that's all . . .'

'I understand that, Mr Comley . . .' Drinkwater saw Comley's eyes slide across to the figure of the first lieutenant whom, he realised with a sharp feeling of guilt, he had not noticed on deck until that moment. Comley's predicament was obvious. He was supposed to report all misdemeanours direct to Rogers, but Rogers had not been on deck. No doubt Comley, if he really had intended to report the four men, would have let the matter blow over, since the first lieutenant had failed to answer the call for all hands. Rogers's strictness was well known and in that game of each trying to catch out the other, first lieutenant and crew had developed a subtlety of play that Drinkwater was only just beginning to grasp. Even now Comley's stuttering excuses, although they might be understood as the genuine, if ill-expressed, discontent of the best and oldest hands on board, were evidence of a game that became increasingly deadly with every round.

Drinkwater thrust his own culpability out of his mind for a moment or two. Although Rogers's absence had compromised Comley in the strict line of his duty, it had given a round to the hands. That much was obvious to all of them as they stood there in the twilight watching. And now Rogers was compromising Drinkwater, for it was clear that the first lieutenant was the worse for drink. In a second Drinkwater would be compelled to take very public notice of Rogers's condition; and at the moment he wanted to avoid that. He affected not to have noticed Rogers.

'Mr Comley,' he said with every appearance of ferocity, 'I'll not have the ship go to the devil for any reason. D'you clearly understand me?'

His tone diverted Comley's eyes from the person of Rogers to himself.

'Aye, aye, sir.'

'I hold you personally responsible. It's your duty to report such things, and if you can't I'll turn you forrard and find someone who can!' He paused, just long enough to let the words sink in. 'Now have those four men confined in the bilboes overnight and pipe down the watches below.'

'Aye, aye, sir.'

Drinkwater left the deck as Comley put the silver call to his mouth. The captain was raging inwardly, furious with Rogers and himself, himself most of all for his self-delusion that all was well on board. The marine sentry held himself upright at what passed for attention on the heeling deck as Drinkwater stalked past him.

'Pass word for the first lieutenant and the marine officer!' he snapped, banging the door behind him.

Mullender was fussing about in the cabin. 'Why aren't you on deck, Mullender? Eh? Ain't the call at every hatchway enough for you? Don't you hear properly, damn it? The call was for *all* hands, Mullender!'

'But, sir, the first lieut . . .'

'Get out!' It was no good Drinkwater making Mullender the surrogate for his anger. The unfortunate steward fled, scuttling out through the pantry. Drinkwater flung off his cloak, massaged his shoulder and groaned aloud. The damp was searching out the old wound given him long ago by the French agent Santhonax in an alley at Sheerness and made worse by a shell-wound off Boulogne. It reminded him that his cross was already heavy enough, without the added burden of Rogers and the fomentation of an exhausted crew. The pain, resentment and momentary self-pity only fuelled his anger further and when Mount and Rogers came into the cabin they found him sitting in the darkness, staring out through the stern windows where the heaving grey sea hissed and bubbled up from the creaking rudder and as suddenly dropped away again.

'Gentlemen,' he said after a pause and without turning round, 'the men are in an evil mood. The grievances are the usual ones and most are justified. Mr Mount, your own men must be aware of the situation, but I want them to be on their guard. Any reports of meeting, combinations . . . the usual thing, Mr Mount. Make sure the sentinels are well checked by your sergeant, and change their postings. I know they've enough to do watching the specie but I'll not have a mutiny, by God I'll not!'

He turned on them, unwilling to let them see the extent of his anger. A light wavered in the pantry door and Mullender stood uncertainly with the cabin lamps he had obviously been preparing when Drinkwater threw him out. 'Yes, yes, bring them in and ship 'em in the sconces for God's sake, man!' He looked at Mount, 'You understand, don't you, Mr Mount?'

'Yessir!'

'Very good. Carry on!'

'Sir.'

Mullender and Mount both left the cabin and Drinkwater was alone with Rogers who remained standing, one arm round the stanchion that rose immediately forward of the table.

'Well, sir,' said Drinkwater, looking upwards at Rogers, 'it was

47

ever your dictum to flog a man for every misdemeanour. I have apprehended four men drunk at their stations tonight. Had you been on deck you might have attended to the matter yourself, as you are in duty bound. Had you brought those men to the gratings tomorrow I would have had to flog 'em. But now your conduct has ensured that if I am to flog them I must, in all justice, flog you, sir! Yes, you, sir! And hold your tongue! Not only are you in liquor but you prevented my steward from mustering on deck as he should have done. Why that was I'll forbear enquiring, but if it was to obtain the key to the spirit-room, by God I'll have you broke by a court martial!'

Drinkwater paused. There was a limit in the value of remonstrance with a drunken man. Either rage or self-pity would emerge and neither was conducive to constructive dialogue. Rogers showed sudden and pathetic signs, not of the former, as Drinkwater had expected, but of the latter. Drinkwater had had more than enough for one day and dismissed Rogers as swiftly as possible.

'Get to bed, Mr Rogers, and when you are sober in the morning, be pleased to take notice of what I have said.'

Rogers stepped forward as though to speak, but the ship's movement, exaggerated here at the stern, checked him and the lamps threw a cautionary glint into Drinkwater's grey eyes. In a sudden access of movement Rogers turned and fled.

Samuel Rogers woke in the night, his head thick and his mouth dry. He lay staring into the creaking darkness as the ship rose and fell, riding out the last of the gale under her reefed topsails and awaiting the morning.

The events of the previous evening came back to him slowly. The pounding of his headache served to remind him of his folly and, once again, he swore he would never touch another drop. He recalled the interview with Drinkwater and felt his resolve weaken, countered by his deep-seated resentment towards the captain. They were of an age; once a few days had differentiated them in their seniority as lieutenants. Now there was a world of difference between them! Drinkwater a post-captain, two steps ahead of Rogers and across the magic threshold that guaranteed him a flag if he lived long enough to survive his seniors on the captains' list.

It was convenient for Rogers, in the depths of his misery, to forget that it was Drinkwater himself who had rescued him from the gutter. Samuel Rogers was no different from hundreds of other officers in the navy. He had no influence, no fortune, no family. Fate had never put him into a position in which he could distinguish himself and he lacked that spark of originality by which a man might, by some instinctive alchemy of personality, ability and opportunity, make his own luck. To some extent Rogers's very sense of obligation fired his steady dissolution; his jealousy of Drinkwater's success robbed him of any of his own. In his more honest moments he knew he had only two choices. Either he went to the devil on the fastest horse, or he pulled himself together and hoped for a change of luck. In the meantime he should do his duty as Drinkwater had advised and the consideration that he was on a crack frigate under an able officer seemed to offer some consolation. But after that one drink that was all he needed to settle himself, the axis of his rationality tilted. After the inevitable second drink it lost its equilibrium, leaving him ugly with ill-temper, inconsiderate and tyrannical towards the gunroom, cockpit and lower deck.

As he lay in the darkness, while above him the bells rang the middle watch through the night, he knew that some form of turning-point had been reached. Up until that moment his drunkenness had not come to Drinkwater's attention. Until that had happened, Drinkwater was simply the captain, a man of influence and advantage, one of the lucky ones in life's eternal lottery seen from the perspective of one of its losers. Now, however, the captain assumed a new role. His power, absolute and unfettered, could confront Rogers and demolish his alcoholic arrogance with fear.

For although the service had disappointed him, Rogers had nothing beyond the navy. If he was broken by a court martial as remorse said he deserved to be, he would have only himself to blame. The penury of half-pay in some stinking kennel of lodgings alongside the whores and usurers of Portsmouth Point was all that disgrace and dismissal would leave him with.

He lay in his night-shirt, sweat sticking it to his body, staring into the darkness of his tiny cabin. Loneliness possessed him in its chill and unconsoling embrace as he knew that, come the morning, he would be unable to resist the drinks that even now he swore he would never touch again.

Drinkwater was on deck at dawn. He, too, had slept badly and woke ill-at-ease. He had not liked humiliating Rogers any more than discovering four men turned-up drunk from their watch below. It was manifestly unfair to expect men who had more than a liberal amount of alcohol poured into them by official decree to offset the deficiencies of their diet, to remain as sober as Quakers, particularly in their watch below. But, Drinkwater reasoned, four drunkards probably indicated that a hardened group had illicit access to liquor. In addition to these men, Rogers was obviously abusing his own powers to gain access to the spirit-room. The addictive qualities of naval rum were well known and many a man, officer and rating alike, had died raving from its effects upon the brain. Furthermore it was possible that whoever was aiding and abetting the first lieutenant was probably taking advantage of the opportunity to plunder an equal quantity for the hardened soaks among the crew.

The thought tormented Drinkwater as he lay awake, shivering slightly as a faint lightening of the sky began to illumine the cabin. He abandoned his efforts to sleep, swung his legs out of the cot and began to dress. Ten minutes later he was on deck. The wind had eased during the night and the approaching daylight showed it to be backing. They would have to tack again soon, and stand more to the west-north-westward. Hill had the morning watch and, having passed instructions to tack at the change of watch, Drinkwater fell to pacing the quarterdeck.

His mind was in a turmoil. He loathed using the cat o' nine tails except for serious crimes. For most minor punishments, public humiliations and loss of privilege served to make a man regret his folly. Besides, it was Drinkwater's firm belief that a strong discipline, strictly enforced, prevented most men from overstepping the mark. At home he tired of debates with Elizabeth upon the subject. She considered his rule illiberal, but failed to understand the cauldron of suppression that a man o' war on a long commission became: some ten score of men whose only reason for existence was to pull and haul, to hand, reef and steer, to load and ram and fetch and carry and fight when called upon to do so, in the name of a half-witted old king and a country that cared more about the nags and fillies of Newmarket than their seamen.

Drinkwater's anger grew as he paced up and down. It was Rogers's business to manage this motley mixture of seamen, this polyglot collection of the 'jolly-jack tars' of popular imagination, who were everywhere shunned once they got ashore among the gentry of the shires. It was a simple enough matter, if attended to sensibly. The might of the Articles of War stopped the poor devils from being men and turned them into pack-animals deserving of a little attention. God knew they asked little enough! Damn Rogers! He had no business behaving like this, no business prejudicing the whole commission because he could not leave the bottle alone!

Little Midshipman Frey skidded across the deck on some errand for the master.

'Mr Frey!' he called, and the lad turned expectantly. 'Mr Frey, give my compliments to the surgeon and ask him to step on deck as soon as he can.'

'Aye, aye, sir.'

Drinkwater stared grimly after the retreating figure. It was not yet time for Mr Lallo to be called. He was one of the ship's idlers, men whose work occupied them during daylight hours and absolved them from night duty except in dire emergencies. From his eventual appearance it was obvious Drinkwater's summons had called him from the deepest slumber. Drinkwater was suddenly touched by envy of the man, that he could so sleep without the intereference of troublesome thoughts.

'You sent for me, sir?' Lallo suppressed a yawn with difficulty. 'Is there something amiss? Are you unwell?'

Drinkwater turned outboard, inviting Lallo's confidence at the rail. 'The matter is not to become common gossip, Mr Lallo.'

Lallo frowned.

'The first lieutenant . . . I want you to have him confined quietly in his cabin for a day or two, starve him of liquor and convince him it is in his own best interests. Tell the gunroom he is sick. D'you understand?'

'Yes, I think so, sir. You want Mr Rogers weaned from the bottle . . . ?'

'And quickly, Mr Lallo, before he compels me to a less pleasant specific. I cannot hold my hand indefinitely. Once I am forced to recognise his true state then he is a ruined man. Quite ruined.'

'I cannot guarantee a cure, sir, I can only . . .'

'Do your best, yes, yes, I know. But I am persuaded that a few days reflection may bring him to his senses. Do what you can.'

'Very well, sir.' Lallo sighed. 'I fear it may be a violent business . . .'

'I am sure that you will see to it, Mr Lallo. And please remember that the matter is between the two of us.'

'The three of us, sir,' Lallo corrected.

'Yes, but it is *my* instructions that I want obeyed, damn it! Don't haze me with pettifoggin' quibbles and invocations of the Hippocratic oath. Rogers is half-way to the devil unless we save him,' Drinkwater said brusquely, turning away in dismissal.

'Very well, sir, but he is a big man . . .'

'Just do your duty, Mr Lallo, if you please.' Drinkwater's exasperation communicated itself to Lallo at last and he hurried off. Drinkwater watched him waddle away then stared again over the sea. The waves were no longer spume-streaked. Fluttering up into the wake a bevy of gulls hunted in the bubbling water where the tiny creatures of the deep were caught up in the turbulence of *Antigone*'s passing hull. The crests broke infrequently now and the vice had gone out of the wind. He watched the pattern of quartering gulls broken up by the predatory onslaught of a sudden swift skua. The dark bird selected its **quarry** and hawked it mercilessly, folding its neck beneath one wing until the gull, terrified into submission, evacuated its crop in one single eructation. The skua released its victim and rounded on the vomited and part-digested food, folded its long dark wings over its back and settled in the frigate's wake.

He was startled by someone at his elbow.

'Beg pardon, zur, but your shaving water's getting cold in the cabin.'

Drinkwater nodded bleakly to his coxswain. He thought that Tregembo already knew of the strong words that had been passed between captain and first lieutenant the previous evening. Doubtless Mullender had let the ship's company know too, but that was unavoidable. He led Tregembo below.

Taking off cloak, coat and hat, and unwinding the muffler from his neck, he began to shave. 'Well, Tregembo . . . what do they say?'

'The usual, zur.'

'Which is one law for the officers . . .'

'And one for the hands, zur.'

'And what do they expect me to do about it, eh?' He pulled his cheek tight and felt the razor rasp his skin. The water was already cold. He swirled the blade and scraped again.

'They are content that you are a gennelman, zur.'

Drinkwater smiled, despite his exasperation. It was a curious remark, designed to caution Drinkwater, to place upon him certain tacitly understood obligations. Only a man of Tregembo's unique relationship could convey such a subtlety so directly to the commander of a man o'war; while only an officer of Drinkwater's stamp would have taken notice of the genuine affection that lay beneath it. 'Then I am content to hear it, Tregembo.'

'There *are* four men in the bilboes, zur . . .'

'Quite so, Tregembo.' The eyes of the two men met and Drinkwater felt forced to smile again. 'Life is like a ship, Tregembo.' He saw a puzzled look cloud the old man's face. 'Nothing ever stays still for long.'

Picking up the napkin he wiped the remaining lather from his face and held his hands out for his coat.

Drinkwater looked down at the faces of the ship's company assembled in the waist. They were the usual mixed bag, some thirteen score of men from all four corners of the world, but most from Britain and Ireland. There were the prime seamen, neat in their appearance, fit and energetic in their duties, those men for whom, in the purely professional sense, he had the highest regard. Yet they were no angels. Long service had taught them all the tricks of the trade. They knew when to 'lay Tom Cox's traverse' and avoid work, how to curry favour with the petty officers and where to get extra rations, tobacco or spirits in the underworld that flourished aboard every King's ship. Neither were they exclusively British or Irish. There was at least one Yankee, on board a British ship for a reason he alone knew though many suspected. There was also a Swede, two Finns and a negro whose abilities aloft were, within the little world of the *Antigone*, already part of legend. But the bulk of the frigate's people were made up of 'ordinary' seamen, waisters and landsmen, in a strictly descending order of hierarchy as rigid as its continuation upwards among the officers. It was a social order imposed by the uncompromising nature of the sea-service and extended in its inflexible formality from Drinkwater to the stumbling, idiotic luetic whose only duty consisted of keeping the ship's lavatories clean. Each man had a clearly defined task at sea, at anchor, in action and during an emergency in which the strength of his arm and the stamina of his body were the reason for his existence.

They spread right across the beam of the ship, no further aft than the main-mast. Some ships bore a white line painted across their deck planking there, but not the *Antigone*. She had been acquired from the French and no such device had ever been added. They were perched in the boats on the booms, up on the rails and sitting on the hammock nettings. Men crowded into the lower ratlines of the main shrouds and all wore expressions of expectancy.

Between the untidy mob of 'the people', the midshipmen, master's mates and warrant officers occupied the neutral ground. Abaft them the files of marines made a hedge of fixed bayonets, cold steel ready for instant employment in defence of the commissioned officers.

The murmur of comment that noted the absence of Rogers subsided the instant Drinkwater's hat began to rise in the stairwell, but he heard it, as he was meant to. He strode to the binnacle and looked at the men and took his time, opening the punishment book with great deliberation, gauging the mood of the hands. He looked about him, checking that the helmsmen, quartermaster, sentinels and look-outs were at their stations.

'Bring up the prisoners!'

The ship's corporal guarding the four seamen with a drawn bayonet shoved them forward from the companionway. They stood miserably after a cramped night in the bilboes, their ankles sore from the chafing of the irons. They could expect, by common custom, three dozen lashes apiece. Drinkwater turned to Fraser and raised an eyebrow. 'Mr Fraser . . .' he reminded.

'Off hats!'

'Benson, Hacking, Kissel and Myers . . .' Drinkwater read their names and then fixed the four guilty men with a baleful grey eye. He was not in the mood for the lugubrious formalities of the Articles of War with their dolorous recital of the punishment of death for each and every offence, scarcely suggesting that 'such lesser punishment' was ever employed in mitigation. 'You four men were drunk last night at the call for all hands . . .' Drinkwater pitched the words forward so that they could all hear. 'If you had been topmen such conduct might have caused you to fall to your deaths. Indeed you might have killed others. Understand that I will not tolerate drunkenness . . .' he looked from the four wretches in front of him and raked the whole assembly, officers included, with his eyes, '. . . from anyone, irrespective of station. At the next occurrence I shall punish *to the very extremity* of the regulations.'

He turned to the four prisoners. 'You four men are stopped all grog until further notice. Mr Pater,' he turned to the purser, 'do you see to it: no grog.'

'Aye, aye, sir.'

A murmur broke out amidships, but this time Fraser needed no prompting. 'Silence there!'

'Very well. Dismiss the ship's company, Mr Fraser, and send Mr Comley aft.'

Drinkwater stalked away and, tucking the punishment book in his pocket, grasped the taffrail with both hands and stared astern. Behind him Fraser ordered the ship's company to disperse and they did so in noisy disorder, only the measured tramp of the marines' boots

54

conveying the impression of discipline. A few minutes later Comley appeared.

'You sent for me, sir?'

'Yes.' Drinkwater turned and faced the bosun. 'I *shall* flog on the next occasion, Mr Comley, be quite certain of that.'

'Yes, sir.'

'You must see to it that it ain't necessary.'

'Very well, sir. Them four men'll suffer more from loss o' grog . . .'

'A flogging still hurts 'em, Mr Comley, and I'd not have any of them thinking I've no stomach for it. You do understand, don't you?'

Comley looked at the captain. He was not used to being intimate with Drinkwater twice in two days, preferring his daily encounters with the first lieutenant. He had the measure of Mr Rogers who was no different from half-a-hundred first luffs in the navy. He had seen the captain in action and heard more of him from his old Cornish coxswain. For all that a shrewd cockney knew that a Kurnowic man could spin a lie like an Irishman and make it sound like the unvarnished truth, there was something in Drinkwater's eyes that bade Comley take care.

'I understand, sir,' he said hurriedly.

'Very well. And now, Mr Comley,' said Drinkwater more brightly, 'I want you to put it about the hands that there'll be a good-conduct payment at the end of this cruise, payable in cash . . . do close your mouth, there's a good fellow.'

Comley did as he was bid, but stared after the retreating figure of the captain as he was left standing thunderstruck by the taffrail.

'Did you hear that, soldier?' he asked the marine whose sentry post was across the frigate's stern, ready to hurl a lifebuoy at any man who went overboard.

'Does that include the sojers, Bose?'

'I dunno,' ruminated Comley.

'He's a rum bastard,' offered the marine.

'He is that,' said Comley, going forward with the extraordinary news.

Mr Lallo stared unhappily at the snoring figure in the cot. Inert, Lieutenant Rogers seemed even larger than the surgeon remembered him when standing. If he woke now, what the devil did one say to him?

'Please, Mr Rogers, the captain says you're a drunken oaf and would you be so kind as to keep quietly to your cabin for a day or so.

After you have rested and your body has acclimatised itself to no rum, you'll be fit as a fiddle to resume your duties.' It was impossible. For days Rogers would toss and rave and drive himself to the edge of sanity. Lallo shook his head. In his younger days the surgeon had eaten opium. It had only been a mild addiction, but the memories of those hallucinations still haunted him.

' 'Ere ye are, Mr Lallo . . .'

He turned, his finger to his lips, as his loblolly boy, Skeete, entered the first lieutenant's cabin. Skeete wore an expression of impish glee that revealed a mouth full of carious teeth. Lallo took and shook out the heavy canvas strait-jacket.

'Very well, work your way round the cot and if you wake him I'll have you at the gratings.'

Rogers stirred as Lallo moved forward and Skeete moved round the cot. 'What the . . . what the devil?'

'Hold him!'

'I *am* holding him!'

'Let me go, damn you! Help, murder!'

Lallo thrust a rag into Rogers's gaping mouth and knelt upon his struggling body, trying to avoid the halitosis of Skeete. They passed the lashings of the jacket, rolling Rogers over and avoiding his thrashing feet. In that position it was easy to secure the leather gag and, wiping the sweat from their eyes, roll him face upwards once again.

'There! It is done.' Skeete grinned, his face hideous. ' 'Tis like trussing a chicken . . .' His pleasure in so dealing with a person of Rogers's importance was obvious.

'Hold your tongue!' snapped Lallo as the man's stinking breath swept over him yet again. 'Help me settle him a little more comfortably.'

The fight had gone out of Rogers. The skin on his forehead was pallid and dewed with drops of heavy perspiration. His eyes were wide open, the pupils unnaturally dilated and expressive of a bursting sense of outrage.

'Get out . . . and Skeete, try and keep your damned mouth shut about this, will you?'

'Anything to oblige.'

Lallo stared disgustedly at his assistant. His manner had the sincerity of a Jew proclaiming a bargain. The surgeon sighed and turned to Rogers when they were alone. He and Skeete were guardians of the frigate's most arcane secrets. Mostly they consisted of who was receiving treatment for the clap or the lues, but now Rogers's infirmity was to be included, under disguise, since the whole ship knew he was 'indisposed'. Such an open secret had to be treated with due form, in accordance with the ritual that maintained the inviolability of the quarterdeck.

Rogers grunted and Lallo gave his patient his full attention. 'Now, Mr Rogers, please try and behave yourself. You have been drinking far too much. Your liver is swollen and enlarged, man. You are killing yourself! You know this, don't you?' Rogers's eyes closed. 'You have got to stop and the captain has ordered you be confined for a day or two, to see you over the reaction . . . now you try and relax and we'll see if we can't dry you out, eh? Until I'm sure you'll behave, I am compelled to restrain you in this way. Do you understand?'

Rogers grunted, but the malevolent glare from his eyes was full of a terrible comprehension.

News from Carlscrona

Drinkwater laid down the pencil and stared at the little column of figures with a sense of quiet satisfaction. With only a one per cent commission on the specie in the strong-room, to which as captain he was entitled, he would be able to pay a 'good conduct' bounty of three pounds per man and still have a few guineas left over for himself. Not only that, he had acquired another form of punishment: that of cancelling the bounty if an individual deserved it.

It was true that his own fortune would be the poorer, but he was not a greedy man. The days of being an indigent midshipman and making free with gold taken aboard a prize or two were behind him, thank God. A small bequest by an old and bachelor shipmate had rescued him from the poverty of reliance upon pay and his home was comfortable if modest. Although he had withered Tregembo's suggestion that he purchase a gentleman's estate, the idea occasionally occupied his thoughts, but in a sense he thought the money better spent this way. Commissions on specie were a perquisite of which his puritan soul did not whole-heartedly approve. Besides, he knew Elizabeth would have appreciated his action and that she, unlike so many post-captains' wives, did not measure her husband's success by the number of horses that drew her carriage.

Drinkwater's mood of self-esteem was ruptured by the sudden appearance of Midshipman Frey. 'Beg pardon, sir, but the look-out's reporting a sail . . .'

A few minutes later he stood beside the master, levelling his glass and focusing upon the newcomer. 'What d'you make of her, Mr Hill?'

'Swede, sir . . . naval dispatch vessel, from Carlscrona probably . . . ah, that's interesting.'

Drinkwater saw it at the same time. In addition to the yellow and blue of the Swedish national colours at her main peak, the schooner had broken out a flag at her fore-masthead as she altered course towards them. The flag was the British Union.

'She wants to speak to us. Heave to, Mr Hill, and a whip and a chair at the main-yard arm.'

Half an hour later a damp civilian gentleman in a caped sur-tout stood uncertainly upon *Antigone*'s deck and looked curiously about him. Drinkwater approached and extended his hand. 'May I present myself. I am Captain Nathaniel Drinkwater of His Britannic Majesty's . . .'

'I know, Captain,' the stranger cut him short, 'and damned glad I am to have found you.' He laughed at Drinkwater's surprise. 'Yes, I'm British. Straton, British Resident at Stockholm.' They shook hands. 'May we adjourn to your cabin? I have something of the utmost importance to communicate.'

'Of course, Mr Straton.'

'Would you be so good as to hoist in Johansson, the pilot?'

'Pilot? Why should I need a pilot? Where is he for?'

'Carlscrona, Captain. Come, let me explain in your cabin.'

'Very well. Mr Hill, you are to hoist in another person. It seems you are right about Carlscrona. Come, sir, this way.' He led Straton below.

In the cabin he indicated a seat and sent Mullender for a bottle of wine.

'Our present position is about twenty miles south-east of Gotland, I believe, Captain,' said Straton non-committally as Mullender fussed around.

As soon as the steward had gone Drinkwater said, 'Well, sir?' expectantly.

'Well, sir. To be brief, you are not to deliver your consignment of specie to the Russians.'

'The devil I'm not! And on whose instructions, may I ask?'

'Those', said Straton, drawing a slim leather wallet from a volumi-nous pocket in his greatcoat, 'of His Majesty's Government . . .' He handed a paper to Drinkwater who took it and examined it closely. As he did so Straton studied the captain.

Grey eyes were masked by his eyelids, one of which was freckled by blue powder burns, tattooed into the soft skin like random ink-spots, his tanned face was disfigured by a thin scar that ran down his left cheek and the mop of brown hair bowed over the paper was shot with grey and tied at his nape in an old-fashioned queue. The epaulettes, Straton noticed shrewdly, were not level, betraying an inequality in the height of the shoulders, the evidence of a serious wound. It was obvious to Straton that Captain Drinkwater had seen a deal of service, but to his courtier's eye the captain still seemed something of a tarpaulin officer, perhaps too set in his ways to appreciate the tangled diplomacy of the Baltic. He would have preferred a younger man, in his late twenties perhaps, and from his own class. The captain looked up and returned the papers.

'You must forgive me my suspicions, Mr Straton.'

'They are quite understandable.'

'The truth is I am astonished at the change in my orders, but they are dated recently.'

'Yes, they arrived by fast cutter at Helsingborg and were delivered overland by a courier. I received them less than a fortnight after your own dispatches from Varberg. All I can tell you is that there is some doubt as to the wisdom of forwarding further subsidies to the Tsar at the moment.'

Drinkwater frowned. 'Why is that? Not many days ago Colonel Wilson sat in that very chair and emphasised how important they are to the continued maintenance of the alliance. Besides, from what I hear, Sweden is scarcely a safe haven for such a sum.'

Straton dismissed his doubts about the political capacity of Captain Drinkwater.

'You are concerned about the reliability of the King, no doubt, Captain. Well, it is common knowledge that His Majesty King Gustavus Vasa is quite mad, but he isn't insane enough to lose sight of reality. This situation creates a state of uncertainty which keeps even his court guessing! Although he has foolishly quarrelled with Berlin and petulantly withdrawn troops from Stralsund as a consequence, he is unlikely to fall out with us. It is true that internally Sweden is in trouble, for Gustavus has no interest in the welfare of his people, hates the French and therefore hates the reforming faction of his own nobility who are Francophile in sentiment. The people of Sweden are opposed to the King's foreign policy, concerned about their ruined economy and apt to contrast their plight with their prosperously neutral neighbours in Denmark whom they used to regard as inferior.'

'On the face of it then, hardly a place for eighty thousand pounds . . .'

'Government instructions are explicit, Captain Drinkwater,' Straton said and Drinkwater shrugged. It was no concern of his, but he remained curious.

'But why deny Russia the money?'

'I believe it is only a temporary delay.'

'What on earth for?'

'As an inducement, I assume. You have heard of the action at Eylau?'

'Yes.'

'Well, there has been some agitation in St Petersburg to have General Bennigsen removed, a court intrigue you understand, probably related to the fact that certain people do not want a German to reap the credit for the death-blow to Napoleon.'

'Let them argue about that when they have secured the victory. At least the Russian rank and file have proved themselves the equals of the Grand Army . . .'

'Exactly, Captain, and the removal of Bennigsen would be a disaster. The campaigning season is already open. If the Tsar is swayed by the anti-German lobby then the damage to the Russian army may be incalculable. A large number of officers of German extraction occupy key posts; Bennigsen's dismissal would unsettle them and reduce the chances of success in the next, vital, clash with the French. A brief withholding of your subsidy is the British Government's caution to the Tsar to maintain the status quo. Bennigsen's army did well at Eylau and he has it in his power to deal the fatal blow to the over-extended divisions of France. Then . . .' Straton brought the edge of his hand down on the table like the blade of a guillotine, '*c'est fini, n'est-ce pas?*'

'It seems a devious and damned risky gamble to me,' replied Drinkwater uneasily, 'but then it doubtless would to a sailor.' He paused and drained his glass. 'So I am to accompany you to Carlscrona, eh?'

'Exactly, Captain.'

'Then perhaps I can offer you the hospitality of my cabin while I go and pass the requisite orders.'

As the south-westerly gale blew itself out, the warm air it had drawn into the southern Baltic cooled on the distant ice-edge and *Antigone* became shrouded in rolling banks of damp fog. To the north the ice began to melt rapidly but, in the open sea south of Gotland, the fog and the calm kept the British frigate and her smaller Swedish consort immobilised for almost two weeks. Then, quite suddenly, as if impetuously relenting, the long northern winter metamorphosed into summer and on a day of brilliant sunshine, on a sea as blue as the Mediterranean ruffled by a light easterly breeze, the *Antigone* closed the Swedish coast. Only the islands littering the approaches to

61

Carlscrona remained gloomy, hump-backed under their dense mantles of fir trees.

Johansson, the pilot, stood at the weather rail and guided their course as they wove between the islands. All hands were on deck, trimming the yards as the frigate followed the schooner towards the Swedish naval arsenal of Carlscrona. Drinkwater remarked the dark spikes of the fir trees and the scent of the resin they gave off, sharp in his nostrils. Under her three topsails and a jib, *Antigone* ghosted through the still water, the hiss and chuckle of her wake creaming out from under her round bows.

'You seem to have a most expertly drilled company, Captain, though I am no judge of such matters.'

'You are very kind, Mr Straton, but I daily wonder how long they can be kept at this ceaseless task. Many of these men have not seen home for four years.'

'Yours is not an enviable task.'

'Nor yours, sir.'

'We must both stand to our posts, Captain,' Straton said sententiously, 'and bring this damnable war to an advantageous conclusion.'

'I should rather you had said "victory", Mr Straton. "Advantageous conclusion" smacks too much of half-measures for my liking now.'

Straton laughed. 'You are right, Captain Drinkwater. I have been too long at the Swedish court!' He pointed ahead to where, beyond a rocky point, the citadel and anchorage of Carlscrona was coming into view. There were men-of-war anchored in the road. 'And here we are. The nearest vessel is the *Falken*. She flies the flag of a rear-admiral which you should salute as we arranged. It is into her that you are to turn the specie.'

Drinkwater nodded. 'Mr Fraser! Have the chasers manned and prepare to make the salute. Mr Hill, you may bring the ship to her anchor under the lee of yonder man o' war.'

A few minutes later the hands were away aloft to stow the topsails and the surrounding islands flung back the echoes of *Antigone*'s guns as she paid her respects to her Swedish allies.

Drinkwater leaned over his chart of the Baltic Sea. He was tired and the candlelight played on features that betrayed his anxiety. He had fondly imagined that, once the specie had been discharged and he had Straton's signature for it, he would be free. But one responsibility had exchanged itself for another and he was now faced with the unnerving problem of what to do next. Once free of his convoy and the Tsar's subsidy his orders were far from explicit. He was instructed to act 'with discretion, bearing in mind the paramount importance of His Majesty's Orders in Council'. Theoretically the duties of blockading were simple enough, but during his brief stay at Carlscrona he had learned that in the tangled diplomacy of the Baltic states, where the very crisis of the war seemed to be developing, the discretionary part of his orders might place far greater demands upon him. He recalled Wilson's surprise that he had no specific instructions from Lord Dungarth and now he studied the chart as if, like Mount's Military Atlas, it would provide him with all the answers.

Along the southern shore of the Baltic lay the coast of Germany, mostly the territory of Frederick William of Prussia, but now under the control of the French. The large island of Rügen was still in Swedish hands, as was the town of Stralsund, now under seige by Marshal Mortier's army corps. Drinkwater's gaze moved east, along the coast from Pomerania towards another port holding out against a French force: Dantzig. Beyond this allied outpost and its bight, the coast swept northwards, past the Frisches Haff and Königsberg to Russia beyond and the Kurland ports of Memel and Revel. Somewhere near Königsberg the main armies of France and Russia faced each other along the line of the River Passarge.

Straton had made it clear that the British Government was now meditating moves which not only could influence Drinkwater, but also be significantly affected by his own operations in this period of uncertainty. This was the nub of his own dilemma.

A knock at the door interrupted his deliberations. 'Enter. Ah, come in, Mr Hill.'

'She's under easy sail for the night, sir.' His eyes fell on the chart.

'Very well.' Drinkwater studied the face of the master. 'What the deuce d'you make of it, Mr Hill, eh? Do we sit here and stop neutrals or d'you fancy a spar with Johnny Crapaud?'

Hill grinned. 'I don't understand, sir.'

'Would to God that I did,' said Drinkwater, 'but Straton came off to see me again before we left Carlscrona. He told me his instructions from London, just arrived, are to urge King Gustavus to reinforce his troops in Rügen and Stralsund . . .' Drinkwater laid his finger on the chart. 'Gustavus insists our subsidies are too small and wants British troops to help him. The problem seems to be that if London sends troops, Gustavus insists on commanding them personally.'

'Good God,' Hill chuckled, 'then he's as mad as they say!'

'Yes. But that ain't all. There's a considerable faction at his court which is pro-French and wants reform. In short, the threat of a revolution is simmering in Sweden.'

'What a mess!'

'My head aches with the complexity of it all.' Drinkwater looked up and, catching Hill's eye, appeared to make up his mind. 'Damn it, we can't dither like this, Hill. We're like a couple of old women! The men are spoiling for a fight . . .' He bent over the chart and Hill leaned over with him. Drinkwater's finger traced a strait of water between the island of Rügen and the mainland where it ran past the engraved outline of the town of Stralsund.

'Let's see what is to be done against Marshal Mortier.'

'Beg pardon, sir . . .'

Fraser turned at the waft of malodorous breath. The obscenely grinning features of Skeete, Lallo's elderly loblolly boy, were thrust expectantly into his face.

'Skeete, what the de'il d'you want on the upper deck?'

'Mr Lallo's compliments, sir, and would you step down to the first lieutenant's cabin.'

'The first lieutenant?'

'Mr Rogers, sir.'

'I know fine well who the first lieutenant is, damn your insolence.'

'Aye, aye, sir.' Nothing seemed to wipe the grin from Skeete's face. He had been too long an intimate with death not to find most situations in life full of morbid amusement. He followed Lieutenant Fraser below.

The door to Rogers's cabin swung ajar with the roll of the ship and from inside Lallo beckoned him. The surgeon closed the door against Skeete. After the upper deck the cabin was dark, the air stale and for a second he did not see the trussed figure of Rogers lying in the cot. His dislike of Rogers had not encouraged him to enquire too eagerly into the nature of the first lieutenant's 'indisposition'.

As his eyes focused he saw a pale face, the hollow cheeks slashed by the cruel line of the gag, and was unable to master an over-riding feeling of revulsion at the harshness of the surgeon's treatment.

'Dear God, Lallo, take that thing off him!'

'I cannot, Mr Fraser . . . the captain . . .'

'The captain did not tell you to gag him. Take it off, I say.' Fraser leaned forward and began to fumble.

'No, sir! Don't, I beg you!' Lallo put out his hands to prevent Fraser's loosening of the gag. 'I asked for you to come down in the hope that you might help . . .'

'Sweet Jesu, Lallo, how much of all this does the captain know?' Unable to get the gag off, Fraser gestured round the tiny cabin.

'Look, Mr Fraser, I have no mind to confine him a moment longer than I have to . . .'

'Then let him out of that . . .'

'For God's sake, sir, do me the favour of listening,' hissed Lallo, suddenly very angry. 'I have twenty-eight men on the sick list and cannot molly-coddle one who's over-fond of the bottle. There are the usual bruises and ruptures, three consumptives, an outbreak of the flux, a man with gravel and one with a paraphimosis, plus the usual clutch with clap. Rogers can only be treated by Procrustean methods and I'm damned if I'm prepared to have *you* interfere like this!'

'Away with your blather, man! What the de'il d'ye want with me then?'

'I do want your assistance to enable me to get him out of that thing as fast as possible.'

Now that his active participation was required Fraser was suddenly cautious.

'In what way?' Fraser looked at the first lieutenant, whose eyes seemed unnaturally large and held his own in a glare of intensity.

'I am prepared to release him today, but if I do I need you to stand surety for me.'

'Why me?'

'Because', said Lallo, a note of weary contempt entering his voice, 'you are the next senior lieutenant and I am concerned that he may attempt to revenge himself.' Lallo spoke as though Rogers was not there, but his worry was clear enough to Fraser.

'Look, Mr Lallo, if the captain ordered you to confine the first lieutenant, why must you drag me into the imbroglio?'

'The captain didn't order me to truss him up.'

'He didn't? But you just claimed he did!'

'No, he ordered me to keep the first lieutenant quiet for a day or two . . . Mr Fraser, where the hell are you going?'

But Fraser had gone. Uncertain of the correct course of action, he thought it proper to inform Captain Drinkwater. Much though he disliked Lieutenant Rogers, the thought of a man of Lallo's stamp having the power to truss up a commissioned officer like a pullet appalled him.

Lallo shook his head over his patient. 'Another young pipsqueak with all the answers, Mr Rogers,' he said, putting the palm of his hand on the lieutenant's sweating forehead, 'and I thought we might have you quietly out of there today.'

Fraser found the captain poring over Mount's atlas and the charts spread out on the cabin table.

'Ah, Mr Fraser, and what brings you rushing in here?' Drinkwater asked, looking up.

'It's the first lieutenant, sir. The damned surgeon has him trussed like a lunatic!'

Drinkwater frowned. It was in his mind to enquire how Fraser had come by this knowledge, but he knew it had been a vain hope to expect the confinement of the first lieutenant to be kept a secret. He recollected he had given Lallo a free hand and had thought the surgeon would have used the powerfully sedative properties of laudanum, but, on reflection, that was Lallo's business.

'Mr Fraser, you are a young man. Your outrage does you credit but I am sure that Mr Lallo was only being cruel to be kind. What was your business in the matter?'

'The surgeon sent for me . . .'

'The devil he did!' Drinkwater snapped. So Lallo had deliberately involved Fraser in direct contravention of his own instructions: 'To what end?' he enquired coldly.

'To stand guarantee for Rogers's good behaviour.'

Drinkwater frowned and felt the sense of affront drain out of him. He had, he realised, been unreasonable in expecting Lallo to work a miracle in secret. Rogers presented them with a problem that only proved their woeful inadequacy to deal with such things. He sighed. 'Well, Mr Fraser,' he said wearily, his thoughts drifting back to the plan formulating in his mind, 'you are the next senior lieutenant. Hadn't you better heed the surgeon?'

'But sir, he's no' a man of much sensibility.'

Drinkwater looked up sharply. 'What the devil d'you mean by that? That he ain't got a commission like yourself? By God, Mr Fraser, you surprise me! Mr Lallo's a professional officer holding a warrant as surgeon, just as Hill holds one as master. Your own status as a gentleman of honour does not entitle you to make such social distinctions among persons of ability! You seem an able and active enough fellow but I'll have none of that damnable cant aboard here!

You may save that for the pump-room or Lord Keith's withdrawing room, but not here, sir, not here!'

The unexpected onslaught from the captain took Fraser aback. His face was white and his mouth hung open. Drinkwater cast another look at the papers spread out before him and then up again at the hapless young officer. 'Very well, Mr Fraser; I am aware there is a growing fashion among young men of breeding to consider these matters of some importance, and that may well be the case ashore. However I suggest you might see Lallo at his true worth were a ball to shatter your thigh. Now cut along and pass word to him to get Rogers up here at once.'

Only the direct summons to the captain's cabin prevented the outbreak of rage the surgeon feared from a freshly released Rogers. Pale from his confinement, Rogers entered the cabin and stood menacingly close to Drinkwater, his mouth a hard line, his eyes glittering.

Drinkwater, sensitive to Rogers's fury, ignored it and, after a brief look at the first lieutenant, stared down at the maps and charts.

'Mr Rogers,' he said levelly, 'you're better, I understand. Now I have it in mind to employ you . . .'

'Do you mean to pretend that nothing has happened?' Rogers's voice was strangled as he sought to control himself. 'I have been bound and gagged, you heartless . . .'

Drinkwater looked up, his own eyes blazing. 'What would you have me do? Eh? If I wished, Sam, you'd be going home for a court martial for that remark alone! What was done was done for your own good, and you know it. Lallo says you're over the worst. Hold off the drink for a month and your victory is complete. If I pretend that you've had the flux that's my own business. What would you have me write in the Sick Book?'

Rogers opened his mouth and then shut it again.

'Look,' persisted Drinkwater, 'I'm meditating an attack on the French here. You lead it. Take the post of honour. It's an opportunity. God knows it's one you can't afford to pass up.'

'Opportunity,' Rogers's voice became almost wistful, 'I haven't had an opportunity . . .'

'Well, enough's said then. Come, this will be a boat attack. We are crossing the Greifswalder Bight and will anchor somewhere here, work our way into the strait as far as we can. Then you take all the boats, the marines and a hundred-odd seamen and press an attack against the French lines around Stralsund; do what damage you can and come off again before Johnny Crapaud knows what's hit him. Just the very thing for you. Get you a mention in the Gazette.'

Drinkwater smiled encouragingly and met Rogers's eyes. The confusion of the man was plain to be seen. 'A perfect opportunity, Sam.'

A Perfect Opportunity

'Well, gentlemen,' said Drinkwater, glancing round at the assembled officers, 'when the sun gets high enough to burn off this mist I think we might find some amusement for the hands today.' He kept his tone buoyant. The awkwardness of the officers in Rogers's presence was obvious. The poor fellow was being treated like a leper. A single glance at his face told Drinkwater that Rogers's torments were not yet over. He could only guess at the remarks that had been passed at every mess in the ship: from the gunroom to the cockpit, from the marines' mess to the ratings messing on the berth deck, the scuttle-butt would have been exclusively about the first lieutenant and his mysterious illness. Drinkwater hoped the action today would give them all something else to talk about and, more important, make them act as a ship's company again.

Antigone lay on a sea as smooth as a grey mirror in the twilight of the dawn. In the distance, scarcely discernible, a reedy margin could be seen dividing sea and sky. From time to time the quack of ducks came from the misty water's edge.

'From what information we have gleaned,' Drinkwater resumed, 'Mr Hill and I estimate that the French siege lines are no more than about five miles from the ship. They are investing the Swedish town of Stralsund but at present a state of truce exists between Marshal Mortier, commanding the French, and the garrison of Stralsund. No such armistice exists between ourselves and the French, however, while anything we might do to provoke more activity on the part of the Swedes can only be of benefit to the Alliance. So we intend to annoy the French by mounting a boat attack on their lines wherever opportunity offers. The mist offers you good cover for your approach.' He smiled again and felt the mood changing. The officers' preoccupation with the restitution of Rogers was diminishing: fear and excitement were stirring them now. He had only one more thing to say to complete the shift in their thinking.

'Mr Rogers will command the expedition in the launch.' He paused, measuring the effect of his words. Disappointment was plain on Fraser's face, but he ignored it and went on. 'Now, gentlemen, I think you had better break your fasts.' They trooped below and Drinkwater added, 'Perhaps, Sam, you would join me in my cabin.'

In the gunroom, as the burgoo was cleared away and the toast and coffee spread its crumbs and ring-stains upon the less-than-clean tablecloth, the officers deliberated over the coming day.

'Don't look so damned *bereaved*, Wullie,' said Mount, impishly aping Fraser's accent. 'You couldn't expect the Old Man to have done anything else.'

'It's all right for you and your leathernecks,' grumbled Fraser, irritated by Mount's eagerness at the prospect of action, 'you're just itching to get at the enemy. At least you've something to do.'

'So have you.' Mount took up a piece of toast and regarded it with some interest. 'D'you know this looks quite palatable, damned if it don't.'

'Just a bloody boat-minder . . .'

'You might get an opportunity to distinguish yourself,' put in James Quilhampton, pouring himself more coffee. 'I can tell you that poor Rogers will be looking for an opportunity to cover himself with glory.'

'Rogers?'

Quilhampton looked at the second lieutenant. 'You haven't known him as long as I have, Willie. He might be an old soak, but he's no coward.'

'Ah,' said Mount, 'but if he leads, will the men follow?'

The question and the doubt associated with it hung over the table, stirring the cold and personal apprehensions that forgathered before action. Quilhampton shrugged the shadow off first. Like Rogers he too awaited his 'opportunity' and his youth was easily convinced it might be soon. He stood up, his chair scraping in the silence.

'Mount,' he said lightly, 'you rumble like a bad attack of borborygyms.'

'Thank you, my young and insolent friend. I suppose I could prescribe myself the carminative of being proved right.'

'I hope you're damn well not,' said Fraser, obviously getting over his pique, 'I haven't written my will this commission.'

'I didn't know you had anything to leave behind you,' laughed Mount.

Fraser made a face, wiped his mouth and looked up. Lord Walmsley stood in the gunroom door.

'What do you want?'

'Mr Hill's compliments, gentlemen,' said Walmsley in his easy manner, 'but the mist's beginning to clear, the first lieutenant is making the dispositions for the boats and the captain's going aloft. Mr Hill is also awaiting the opportunity to come below and have his breakfast.'

'Oh! Damn me, I forgot.' Quilhampton shoved his chair in and reached for his hat and sword. Fumbling with the belt as he made for the door he shouted over his shoulder to the negro messman, 'King! Be a good fellow and bring my pistols on deck!'

In the main-top Drinkwater trained his glass carefully, anxious not to miss the slightest detail emerging from the upper limit of the mist as it hung low over the marshy shore. From their landfall at Cape Arcona they had sailed round the east coast of the island of Rügen, across the mouth of Sassnitz Bay where the Swedish fleet lay at anchor, and round into the Greifswalder Bight. Yesterday they had worked patiently westwards, towards the narrow strait that separated Rügen from the Pomeranian mainland. With a man in the chains calling the soundings they had manoeuvred *Antigone* as far into the strait as wind and daylight permitted, and learned of the state of truce between the Swedes and French from a Swedish guard boat. As daylight finally faded, and with it the breeze, they had fetched their anchor.

Above the mist, the rising sun behind Drinkwater picked out tiny reflections ahead: the pale gold of a church spire, a sudden flash as a distant window was opened. It was curious how he could see these details twelve miles away, while closer-to there was nothing to see beyond the rounded shapes of tree-tops, elms he thought, and some willows lower down; but that was all that emerged from the nacreous vapour that hung over the water margin. An observer in one of those trees would be able to see *Antigone*'s masts and spars above the mist, while her hull, with its rows of cannon, was invisible. Not that he thought for a moment they had been observed, and the presence of the Swedish fleet in Sassnitz Bay had persuaded him that by flying Swedish colours he would be perfectly disguised.

He heard a distant trumpet and a drum beat, staccato and oddly clear as it rolled over the water, its rat-a-tat-tat mustering Mortier's corps to morning parade. Drinkwater pondered the wisdom of his proposed attack. It was to be made on slender intelligence and he knew his intention had far more to do with the state of his command than any real damage he would inflict upon the enemy. Somehow the unreality was emphasised by the mist and it seemed that the only real danger lay below him in that unhappy relationship between Lieutenant Rogers and the people.

Drinkwater had taken Rogers as his first lieutenant out of pity, knowing him for a dogged fighter and competent seaman. But drink and disappointment had soured the man, and although Drinkwater curbed Rogers's excesses, in his everyday behaviour he had given ample cause for offence and grievance among the hands. He received their daily petitions with an unpleasant contempt, used an unnecessary degree of foul language towards them and provoked a general grumbling. Drinkwater's reluctance to flog was a liberality Rogers disapproved of and which seemed to provoke him to greater unpleasantness towards men whom the iron rule of naval discipline held in a state of thrall.

It was clearly a situation that could not go on. A boat attack under Rogers, Drinkwater had reasoned, gave them all a chance to wipe the slate clean; or at least as good a chance as men in their circumstances were likely to get.

Drinkwater felt the mast jerk and looked down into the waist. Wraiths of mist trailed across the deck but he could clearly see the ordered lines of men straining at the tackles as they lifted the heavy launch off the booms and began to transfer its weight from the stay to the yard tackles. He watched the boat lifted outboard and then lowered into the water. Drinkwater pocketed compass and glass, swung himself over the edge of the top and felt for the futtocks with his feet.

As he jumped down onto the deck, Rogers, Fraser and Quilhampton were telling the men off into the waiting boats. Marines filed along the deck, their muskets slung over their shoulders. Together with the seamen being armed with cutlasses and tomahawks at the main-mast, they scrambled down the nets hung over the ship's side and into their allocated places in the boats.

Drinkwater crossed the deck to where Rogers was stuffing loaded pistols into his waistband. He smiled encouragingly. 'Good luck, Mr Rogers,' he said formally.

Rogers nodded his acknowledgement and paused, as though to say something. But he seemed to think better of it, murmured 'Aye, aye, sir,' and slung a leg over the rail.

'It's up to you, Sam,' persisted Drinkwater, 'you and those men down there.'

Their eyes met and both knew what the other thought.

Then Rogers had gone, and a few minutes later the boats had vanished in the mist.

Lieutenant Rogers, his hand on the tiller of the launch, cocked one eye on the boat-compass at his feet and stole occasional glances at the faint line in the mist that marked the Rügen shore. The surface of the water was as smooth as glass, disturbed only by the concentric and ever expanding rings that marked the progress of the oar blades as they propelled the boats along. Rogers led in the launch followed by Quilhampton in the red cutter, Lord Walmsley in the blue and Lieutenant Fraser in the barge.

Rogers was seconded by Mount and Midshipman Frey, and it was Mount's marines that made up the bulk of the launch's crew, apart from the oarsmen. In the boat's bow, mounted on its slide, a 12-pounder carronade was being fussed over by a gunner's mate.

The boats pulled on in comparative silence, moving in a world that seemed devoid of time or distance, so disorienting was the mist. It hung heavily, close to the water, discouraging speech, so that the only noises were the laboured breathing of the oarsmen, the dull regular knocking of oar looms against thole pins and the dip and splash of the oar blades. Under the bow of each boat a chuckling of water showed as they pulled on for mile after mile. After two and a half hours Rogers drew out his watch and consulted his chart. Then he stood in the stern of the boat and waved the others up alongside. The boats glided together, their oars trailing, their men panting over the looms, dark stains of sweat on the backs of their shirts.

'By my reckoning we must be bloody close to the French lines,' hissed Rogers. 'We'll move across the channel to the mainland side. If we sight a decent target we land and do our worst. Now you buggers keep in close contact. I'll give the order to attack. Understand?'

There was a general nodding of heads.

'Very well. Get your lobsters to fix bayonets, Mr Mount.'

Mount gave the order and the whispering hiss and click of the lethal weapons was accompanied by a sudden twinkling of reflected sunlight from the silver blades.

'There's a bit o' breeze coming up,' observed Fraser and, for the first time, dark, ruffled patches appeared on the water. The heat of the sun was warming the marshes and water meadows on either side of the strait, the rising air sucked in the sea-breeze, a strengthening zephyr which began to disperse the mist in patches.

'Very well, keep your eyes open then.' Rogers waved the boats onward. The oars began to swing again and the boats resumed their passage.

Rogers stared into the mist ahead. He felt the public shame of his recent humiliation like a wound and could still only half comprehend why Drinkwater had sanctioned Lallo's treatment. But he was pragmatist enough to know that, if nothing else, his future hung upon the day's events. He had under his command the greater part of the ship's marines and a large detachment of seamen. He was seconded by most of the officers and had left the frigate almost without boats. What was more, he was alone in a mist and was determined, at any cost, to make an impression upon the enemy. His mouth set in a grim line and, as he looked forward, the eyes of the men tugging at the oars avoided his own. Well, that was as it should be. He was the first lieutenant again, and by heaven they would feel his wrath if they did not do their utmost to secure him a paragraph in the Gazette!

'Boat, sir! Starboard bow!'

Rogers jerked from his introspection and looked to starboard. At the same instant a challenge rang out. A large boat, pulling a dozen oars a side with a huge-muzzled cannon in her bow and the blue and gold of Sweden lifting languidly over her stern, loomed out of the mist. It was a 'gunsloop' rowing guard in the supposedly neutral water of the strait.

Rogers swore and pulled the tiller over, turning to watch the other boats follow in his wake, and headed more directly for the southern bank. Astern he heard shouting and the splash of oars holding water, turning the big gunsloop after them. But after five minutes, despite the gradual dispersal of the mist, they had lost the Swedish boat.

A few minutes later the grey margin of Pomerania was visible ahead and then on the larboard beam as Rogers straightened their course parallel to it. A few cows, brindled black and white, stood hock-deep in the lush grass that swept down to the water. Ruminating gently they stared at the passing boats.

The appearance of the guard-boat had galvanised the oarsmen. Before, the stroke had been that leisurely and easy swing that a practised oarsman could keep up for hours, now the men tugged at their oars and the boats began to leap through the water. Then, quite suddenly, the mist lifted and at the same instant Rogers saw the means of realising his long awaited 'opportunity'.

'By God, Mount!' he said in a low and excited tone. 'See there, ahead! A whole bloody battery with its back to us!'

Ahead of them a sudden bend in the channel brought the Pomeranian shore much closer. A small, low bluff formed a natural feature, a patch of beaten earth which the French had taken advantage of and on it constructed a demi-lune with an earthen rampart reinforced by fascines and gabions. The rampart was pierced by crude embrasures and in each, facing away from the approaching boats towards the town of Stralsund, were eight huge siege guns and a pair of howitzers. A smaller field piece faced across the strait and commanded any approach from Rügen. In quieter times the little bluff had been used as a quay, for behind the battery was a small inlet, the estuary of a stream that wound, willow-lined, inland towards a village. The edge of the inlet was piled with rotten wood staithing from which local peasants had shipped their hay and other produce to the markets of Stralsund. It took but an instant for Rogers to perceive that the inlet and quay gave direct and undefended access to the rear of the battery.

He was standing now and he commanded his oarsmen to pull with greater vigour. Behind him the officers in the other boats had also seen the enemy position and acknowledged his frantic wave.

'Make ready, men,' said Mount quietly beside him.

Rogers looked again at the battery. He could see a pair of artillerymen, each carrying a bucket and wearing fatigues, walking slowly across the beaten earth of the compound. A group of men were gathered round one gun intent upon some task or another and one further man was lounging on the rampart, staring in the direction of Stralsund. Rogers could see quite clearly the puffs of smoke from the indolent sentry's pipe.

'We've got 'em, by God, Mount! The buggers are as good as asleep!'

Rogers put the tiller over and the launch swung in towards the inlet and the quay. He could not believe his luck. 'Come on you lubbers! *Pull!*'

'We are pulling . . .' someone muttered and Rogers's eyes narrowed and he scanned the boat for the insolent seamen. Perhaps he would have taken the matter further but at that instant emerging from the mist astern of them, the Swedish gunsloop hailed them. The cry made the sentry turn. He jerked upright and then began to shout, a hoarse bellow of surprise and alarm. The gunners carrying the buckets dropped them and ran; the group round the siege gun turned and ran also. More men were shouting and appearing from somewhere. Rogers was vaguely aware of trees, horse-lines and a row of limbers, ammunition-boxes and shot piles.

The sight of red coats and the glint of sunshine on bayonets swiftly raised the alarm. Even as the launch closed the last few yards to the quay the French artillerymen were dropping to one knee and levelling muskets fetched from the arms stacks.

'That gun ready?' roared Rogers at his gunner's mate forward.

'Aye, sir!'

'Then clear those bastards out of our way!'

The launch jerked and the carronade roared, recoiling up its slide and flinging its reek back over the gasping oarsmen. The marines were fidgeting and Mount was standing beside Rogers. Most of the canister splattered against the wooden piling, but sufficient balls raked the compound to knock down three or four of the defenders.

'That's the way!' yelled Rogers, drawing this sword.

The next moment the launch bumped alongside the staithe and, as the oarsmen dragged their oars inboard, Rogers leaped from thwart to thwart, closely followed by Mount. Rocking violently the launch spewed its cargo of marines onto the quay as the other boats arrived and more and more men poured ashore.

There were far more soldiers in the demi-lune than had at first been apparent. Hidden by the willows were the bivouacs of the eighty gunners that made up the complement of the battery. They were forming into a rough line, led by a pair of officers on foot. Behind them another officer was struggling into the saddle of a trace-horse.

'Drop that man!' Rogers screamed to Mount, pointing.

Mount turned to a marine who was already levelling his musket, but the shot missed and the officer escaped down a lane that ran alongside the little stream.

'Form line, platoon fire!' Mount was drawing up his men and they began to fire volleys at the enemy. Behind the marines the seamen milled, those of them who had been rowing still getting their breath back.

'Rush the bastards!' roared Rogers impetuously, waving his sword at the other lieutenants, but Mount ignored him. He was advancing his line of marines platoon by platoon.

'Come on, lads, charge them!' Rogers began to run, leading his men through the line of marines.

'Hold on, Rogers!' Mount shouted as the first lieutenant began to block his field of fire, but there was no stopping him. Only a few of the seamen had followed Rogers and there were murmurs among the others, murmurs that, overheard on board, would have earned their makers a dozen at the grating.

'Let the bastard go!'

'Hope he gets a ball in his brain-pan . . .'

'Better his balls . . .'

'Good riddance to him . . .'

Mount stood for a second, furious, and behind him Quilhampton suddenly divined the intentions of some of the men.

'Come on, Mount! Forward! Bayonets!'

'Bayonet charge!' bawled Mount as the artillerymen, taking advantage of the brief pause in the attack, loosed off a well timed volley. Several of the marines dropped, but Rogers, twenty yards from the French, was untouched.

'The devil looks after his own . . .'

They were all running forward now, marines and seamen mixed together, all mad with blood-lust and tripping over their fallen comrades. Then suddenly they clashed with the enemy. The fighting became hand to hand. The artillerymen dropped their muskets and lugged out short swords which each man had slung on a baldric over his shoulder. They were old faces, almost faces they knew, dark with campaigning, slashed by scars, as moustached as their attackers were clean-shaven. They grunted, swore, cut, thrust, killed and died as well as their opponents, but they fell back under the onslaught, out-numbered by the British who fought with a maddened ferocity. For a few blessed moments they were free of shipboard constraints and could swear and stab and hack at anything that stood in their path. With every slash and lunge they paid back the cheating of the purser, the heartlessness of the bosun's mates, the injustice of the lash and the venality of the Dockyard commissioners. In the merciless killing they found outlets for their repressed passions and frustrated desires. It was not the enforcers of Napoleon's Continental System that they killed, but the mere surrogates for the rottenness in their own.

Lieutenant Quilhampton knew this and kept his wits about him. He had heard of men shooting their own officers in the heat of battle and kept a weather eye on Rogers. He did not fear for himself, for the constraints of naval discipline, once they had been laid upon a man, could never be entirely thrown off, even under such circumstances. Intuition told him he was perfectly safe, for he had long ago learned the wisdom of consideration and justice towards the men in his own division. But Rogers was at risk although he seemed safe now, surrounded by Mount and his marines as they swept the last of the gunners out of the battery at the point of the bayonet. The British did not pursue beyond the limit of the rampart. A few of the marines got up on the rough parapet and took pot-shots at the retreating Frenchmen as they ran stumbling over the tussocks of grass and boggy marshland of the water meadows beyond.

'Keep an eye on 'em, Mount. That bloody officer will have gone for reinforcements!'

'Very well!'

All around men panted for their breath. The dead and wounded lay in heaps, their blood soaking darkly into the dry earth. Little Frey with his toy dirk was trying to bandage a cut arm. Other men were attending to the wounded.

'Tom's lost his bonus, then,' said one man, staring down at a dead messmate. Quilhampton recalled the bonus Drinkwater had promised the men.

'You lads start getting the wounded back to the boats now.'

'Aye, aye, sir.'

Rogers was still bawling orders.

'Mr Fraser, bring a party over here! You too, Mr Q! I want those three limbers over to the guns. We'll blow the wheels off! And see here, these Frog bayonets are thinner than ours. You, Walmsley and Frey, gather 'em up and stick 'em in the touch-holes of these guns. Look . . .'

Rogers picked up a French bayonet and stabbed it downwards, into the touch-hole in the breech of the nearest gun. Then he jerked his hand sideways and the narrow blade snapped, leaving the hole neatly blocked. 'See, that should fuck 'em up for a while . . . and stuff those shell carcases under the guns and they'll blow the whole bloody shebang to kingdom come.'

Officers, marines, midshipmen and men ran about at his bidding, fetching and carrying. Kegs of powder, shell cases and combustibles were placed under each of the siege guns. The field gun close to the strait was rolled into the water and every gun was rendered at least temporarily useless by spiking.

At the height of this activity a strange officer was seen walking slowly across the open space behind the guns. Everyone had forgotten the Swedish gunsloop.

'Excuse . . . you are British, yes? I must protest very much. There is no fighting . . . truce, between the forces of His Majesty King Gustavus and the army under Marshal Mortier.' He approached

Rogers who, from his activity and lively direction of affairs, was clearly the senior officer.

'Will you get out of my way . . . hey, you! More powder over here . . . no, no, a keg if you've got one . . .'

'You must not fight . . . not break the truce . . .'

'Will you get out of my way?' Rogers turned on the Swedish officer who suddenly understood he was being rebuffed and drew himself up.

'I am a Swedish officer.'

'I don't give a damn if you're the Grand Turk, fuck off!' snarled Rogers, shoving the Swede aside. The man spun round and reached for his sword, as angry as Rogers.

Quilhampton hurried up. 'Come, sir,' he said civilly to the Swede, 'I know you have a truce with the French, but regrettably we do not. I am sure you understand that we mean no offence to yourself.'

The Swedish officer looked down at his sleeve. The point of the iron hook that this tall, gangling English officer wore in the place of a left hand, had caught in the fabric of his uniform. It was covered in blood.

Shrugging his shoulders he allowed himself to be led away with as much dignity as he could muster. Quilhampton had hardly seen the intruder into his boat than another crisis occurred. On the rampart a sudden shout from Mount brought both the first lieutenant and Quilhampton running across the compound. Flinging themselves down on the earth beside him, they followed the marine officer's pointing finger.

Jogging towards them, their pennons gay in the sunshine, was a squadron of lancers.

'Jesus Christ!' whispered Rogers and a thrill of pure fear ran through the three men. The thought of being speared by one of those lances was hideous.

'I think it's time for a tactical withdrawal . . .'

'Get your men back to the boats to cover us, Mount,' snapped Rogers.

'I can keep some here and pick a few of those fellows off . . .'

'Do as you're fucking well told!'

'Very well.'

'Mr Q, get the men back in the boats, load up the carronade, tell Fraser . . . where the hell is he?'

'I don't know but I'll find him.'

Rogers ran across the open space. 'Hey, Walmsley, get that last powder keg and lay a trail back towards the boats. Make sure no stupid turd runs in it . . .'

'Aye, aye, sir.' Lord Walmsley picked up a keg and knocked out the bung. He bent over and scuttered backwards, spreading a liberal trail across the earth. 'Mind your confounded feet, damn you!' he shouted at some marines.

'Into the boats, you men!' Quilhampton was shouting at the seamen. 'Get to your oars!'

'They're coming!' Mount was yelling, running back from the rampart. 'One volley, sergeant,' he called, 'then tumble into the boats as quick as you can!'

'Sah!' Sergeant Blixoe lined his men up. 'Steady now, lads. Take partiklar aim and shoot the lubbers' horses in the chest . . . make ready . . .'

The boats were a confusion of legs and oar looms as men tried to sort themselves out. They were stumbling on the wounded whose shrieks and curses lent a nightmare panic to the scene. Somehow the word had spread that they were about to be ridden down by lancers. Round shot and cutlass slashes were one thing. Lances and horses quite another.

Walmsley's powder trail had stopped several yards short of the quay. Rogers stood over him as he tipped the last of the powder out of the keg. 'Get to the launch. Back it off the quay and point the carronade ashore. Leave your cutter alongside for me.' Rogers drew a pistol from his waistband and looked quickly round him. He could feel the earth shaking under the advancing hooves of the horses.

'Get down, Rogers, let me fire over your head,' Mount was shouting at him.

'Damn you, be silent! Fire and get your men in the boats.'

A wild and magnificent feeling swept over Rogers. He stood alone in the middle of the enclosed space. Behind him the boats were full of men and the edge of the quay was lined with Mount's marines, their muskets pointing at the end of the rampart where the little track wound round the battery's defences. All eyes were on him. The humiliation of his confinement, the long-standing and corrosive effects of disappointment and missed opportunity seemed to coalesce in one moment of sublime defiance. Like the men, action had given Lieutenant Rogers the means of defying the system whose injustices had tormented him in proportion to his rank. He was filled with a hysterical disregard for the danger he was in.

The cavalry swept into the battery. Confined to a narrow front of six or seven horses they spread out, their red and white lance pennons lowering. They were in green, wearing tall crested brass helmets, and their horses snorted and plunged as they advanced across the compound.

'Fire!' yelled Mount and then waved his men backwards. A cutter pushed off, so did the barge.

'Come on, sir!' yelled Quilhampton.

Rogers turned. 'Fire that boat gun!' he roared as though bawling out the topmen in a gale. The lancers came on, only yards separating them from Rogers. Mount's men had only succeeded in knocking over one horse, so distracted had they been by the defiant spectacle of Lieutenant Rogers.

'What is the silly bastard *doing?*' agonised Mount as he turned and watched from the safety of a boat.

'Bein' a fuckin' hero, sir,' a man muttered.

'Gettin' 'is name fair an' square in the Gazette,' said another, but Mount ignored them.

In the launch the gunner's mate jerked the lanyard of the carronade. Full of men aft and backed off from the quay, the gun took better effect than it had when they had made their approach. The canister tore through the cavalry and threw back three lancers who were within feet of Rogers.

'It's bloody unbelievable,' muttered Mount, half in admiration of the madness being displayed by an apparently fearless Mr Rogers. As if knowing the three men who most nearly threatened his life would be blown away by the shot from the carronade, Rogers bent over the pile of powder, levelled the cocked pistol and pulled the trigger. The spark landed on the powder, grew dim and then suddenly the powder trail took fire. There was a brief searing light but Rogers felt nothing from the burn on his hand. He stood for a second staring at the leaping flame and then seemed aware of the danger round him. He dodged the next lancer who was trying to rein in his horse as he approached the edge of the quay. Rogers ran for the cutter, bending low as the marines stood in the boats and fired over his head. Behind him the powder fired and sputtered and the horses jibbed at the demon under their hooves. There were shouts and plunging horses and then the launch carronade got off another shot. Rogers leapt for the cutter which backed swiftly off the quay.

The cheated cavalrymen were pulling their horses up at the edge of the water. An officer had jumped off his horse and was trying to stamp out the burning train. Some of his men had slung their lances and were levelling their carbines. The little sputter of flame could no longer be seen. Perhaps it no longer threaded its way over that patch of beaten earth.

The shouts and popping of carbine and musket were suddenly eclipsed by the deafening roar which broke into several subsidiary explosions as limbers and carcases and powder kegs took fire. The redoubt was suddenly transformed into a lethal rocketing of wood, iron and flame among which horses reared in terror and men fell amid the stamping of hooves. Heavy axle-trees, wheels and spokes, even the massive barrels of the cannon themselves were hurled into the air. Pieces of shell-case whistled into the blue sky, then the boats were being showered by black debris which fell into the water alongside them with a hiss.

The boats were swinging into the channel now, the men settling into the rhythm of the long pull back to the ship. They swept past the Swedish gunsloop and Rogers stood and raised his hat in a gesture of arrogant and exaggerated courtesy.

'Bye the bye,' he said to no one in particular as he sat down again, 'did any of you fellows catch a glimpse of Stralsund?'

Nielsen

Drinkwater sat in his cabin in a happier frame of mind than he had enjoyed for weeks. Although the butcher's bill for the boat action was heavier than anticipated, there was no doubt that the attack had been a success. The real damage to Marshal Mortier's Army Corps was not great, but the unexpected destruction of a battery showed the long arm of the British Admiralty, and could not fail to have its effect upon the general morale of the French corps.

There had been a little necessary diplomacy at the protest they had received from a Swedish officer who had come on board as *Antigone* entered Sassnitz Bay; but it had been passed off easily enough with a glass or two. Most important to Drinkwater was the effect the action had had upon Rogers and the people. He had heard several versions of the affair and gathered that a sneaking admiration had been aroused for Rogers, on account of his coolness under attack. It was undoubtedly only a temporary lull in the hostility between the lower deck and the first lieutenant, but it was a lull nevertheless, and Drinkwater was relieved to see that Rogers himself seemed to have recovered some of his old self-possession.

But it was not merely the raising of the morale of his own ship's company that occasioned Drinkwater his present good humour. On their return to Sassnitz Bay and the Swedish fleet, they had found a flying squadron of British frigates. Supposing at first that he was to place himself under the orders of the senior captain, Drinkwater found to his delight that special orders awaited him. Taking the opportunity to send mails home, including a highly laudatory report on the affair before Stralsund, he had hurried back to *Antigone* to digest the import of his written instructions. It was clear that Horne of the *Pegasus* was somewhat jealous of Drinkwater's independence and had wished to include *Antigone* in his flying squadron.

'You seem to enjoy a kind of privilege,' Horne had lisped. 'I have to give you written orders of your own.' Reluctance was written plain on the man's face and even discernible in the way he handed over the sealed package.

'The forward berth ain't always the most pleasant,' Drinkwater replied, happy to escape from the constraints of serving under someone young enough to be his son. Horne would be a rear-admiral by the time he reached Drinkwater's age, but that was not Drinkwater's concern at the moment; he was more interested in the other news newly arrived at Sassnitz Bay.

'I heard one of your officers mention Dantzig when I came aboard,' he prompted.

'Dantzig? Oh, damn me yes, the place has fallen to the French.'

It seemed inevitable that, failing a major Russian victory, the French would mop up the resistance in their rear. Making his excuses as early as he could, Drinkwater had returned to *Antigone*, set a course to the eastward and retired to his cabin to open the package Horne had given him. Slitting the fouled anchor seal of the Admiralty Office, he unfolded the papers and began to read.

His instructions from Mr Barrow, Second Secretary at the Admiralty, were a mere repeat of those he had left the Nore with. The same stock phrases: *You are requested and required to cruise against the enemy . . . to examine all vessels and in particular those of neutral nations . . . detaining those whose cargo is of advantage to the enemy . . .* and so on. In short, there was nothing to suggest that he had earned Horne's envy or that his 'independence' had much advantage to it. But appended to Mr Barrow's formal instructions was another letter, similarly sealed but not signed by the Admiralty's civil administrator; this document bore the scrawled and familiar name of the Director of the Secret Department. It was brief and undated, typical of the writer's economy of style when using plain English.

My dear Drinkwater,

Until you are able to ascertain the outcome of military operations in East Prussia, you are to cruise to the eastward of the Gulf of Dantzig and inform London the instant you learn anything of significance. You should afford any assistance required by persons operating on the instructions of this Department.

Yours &c

Dungarth

Drinkwater laid the letter down and turned his chair to stare through the stern windows and watch *Antigone*'s furrowing wake, where the sea swirled green and white from under the frigate's stern.

He saw nothing of the gulls dipping in the marbled water; his mind was turned inwards, contemplating the full implication behind Dungarth's instruction, and it seemed that his independence was no coincidence. That last sentence, that he should afford assistance to persons operating on the instructions of Lord Dungarth's Secret Department, was a clear order. And both Dungarth and Drinkwater knew that one of those 'persons' was Drinkwater's own brother, Edward. Drinkwater's frigate was cruising independently for reasons beyond the arbitrary processes of normal Admiralty planning. Dungarth knew that Drinkwater was the one post-captain on the Navy List who would take more than a passing interest in 'persons operating on the instructions of this Department' in East Prussia, where the Tsar's armies were in the field.

Drinkwater sighed. Surely this was only a partial truth, and one that was engendered by his own long-held guilt over the whole affair of his brother. Colonel Wilson, whose presence in the area would be well known to Lord Dungarth, had given him almost identical advice, mentioning in particular a certain Mackenzie. Nevertheless that strange and fleeting feeling of presentiment could not be denied. Brief and passing though it was, it had the reality of one of those glimpses of the hungry gulls quartering their wake.

Drinkwater mused on the likely outcome of those military operations that were obviously preoccupying Dungarth and, by implication, His Majesty's Government. Horne had told him of the fall of Dantzig to the French on 26 May. Dungarth could not have known of that when he had written his letter. Yet Drinkwater knew, as Wilson had told him, the coming weeks of the new campaigning season were vital to the outcome of the long and increasingly bitter war. *Antigone* was to be, for the foreseeable future, the Government's eyes and ears; to learn of the outcome of what promised to be a crucial clash of arms between France and Russia somewhere in East Prussia, Poland or Kurland.

There was a knock at the cabin door; Drinkwater folded Dungarth's letter and slipped it into the drawer.

'Enter!'

Midshipman Wickham's face peered into the cabin. 'Beg pardon, sir. Mr Quilhampton sends his compliments and we shall have to tack, sir. The island of Bornholm is two leagues distant.'

'Very well. Thank you.'

'Aye, aye, sir. And I'm to tell you, sir, that Mr Rogers is on deck.' There was more than a hint in this last remark. It annoyed

Drinkwater that a youngster like Wickham should be privy to such innuendo. He frowned.

'Very well, Mr Wickham. Be so kind as to give Mr Rogers *my* compliments and ask him to take the deck and tack ship.'

'Mr Rogers to tack ship . . .' There was a slight inflection of doubt in Wickham's voice.

'You heard what I said, Mr Wickham,' Drinkwater said sharply. 'Be so kind as to attend to your duty.'

The little exchange robbed Drinkwater of some of his former sense of satisfaction. He swore under his breath and, determined not to lose the mood entirely, he reopened the drawer beneath the table, pushed aside Dungarth's letter and drew out the leather-bound notebook and unclasped it. He also took out his pen-case and picked up the steel pen Elizabeth had given him. Uncapping his ink-well he dipped the nib and began to write in his journal.

It would seem that Ld Dungarth's Interest has influenced their L'dships to appoint us to this Particular Service. I am not inclined to enquire too closely into his L'dship's motives . . .

He paused as the pipes twittered at the hatchways. The muffled thunder of feet told where the watches below were being turned up. There was no need for him to go on deck. Rogers would benefit from any public demonstration of the captain's confidence, though there would doubtless be a deal too much in the way of starting. Drinkwater sighed again. He regretted that, but there was a deal too much of it in the naval service altogether. Shaking his head he continued to write.

I therefore directed our course to the eastward, as far as the wind would admit, intending to try for news at Königsberg; for, with Dantzig capitulated to the Enemy, what news there is will surely be discovered there.

He sanded the page, blew it and put book and pen-case away. Flicking the cap over his ink-well he rose, took his hat from the peg and went on deck.

Antigone was turning up into the wind as he emerged onto the quarterdeck. Rogers was standing by the starboard hance. He looked at Drinkwater but the captain shook his head. 'Carry on, Mr Rogers.'

Clasping his hands behind his back, Drinkwater affected to take little notice of what was going on on deck. Ahead the jib-boom pointed towards the long, flat table-land of Bornholm. Dark with fir trees, it impeded their making further progress to the north-east, and they were in the process of going about onto the larboard tack, to fetch a course of south-east until they raised the low coast of East Prussia, fifty miles away.

'Mains'l haul!'

Rogers's order was given with every appearance of confidence and the hands obeyed it willingly enough. He was not sure that his presence on deck had not toned down the usual activity of the bosun's mates with their rope starters. The frigate paid off on the new tack.

'Fore-yards there! Heads'l sheets! Leggo and haul!'

The fore-yards came round, the sails filled and the ship began to drive forwards again. 'Steer full and bye!'

'Full an' bye it is, sir . . . Full an' bye steering sou'-east three-quarters south, sir.'

'Very well. Mr Frey!'

'Sir?'

'Move the peg on the traverse board, Mr Frey . . . course sou'-east three-quarters south.'

'Sou'-east three-quarters south, sir. Aye, aye, sir.'

A comforting air of normality attended these routine transactions and, much heartened, Drinkwater crossed the deck.

'Very well, Mr Rogers.' He smiled and added with less formality, 'Will you join me for dinner, Sam?'

Rogers nodded. 'Thank you, sir.'

It proved an odd meal. They dined alone and Drinkwater avoided serving wine, drinking the thin small beer that was usually drunk in the cockpit. Its very presence seemed an obstruction to any form of conviviality. Indeed, serving small beer and avoiding any reference to Rogers's recent unhappy experience only seemed to emphasise the matter. Drinkwater tried to fill the awkwardness and attempted an appraisal of the complex state of affairs among the Baltic States. But Rogers was not a man to interest himself in anything beyond the confines of the ship and such had been the mental disturbance he had so recently undergone that he was quite incapable of anything beyond the most subjective thinking. At the end of ten minutes of monologue, Drinkwater's lecture foundered on the first lieutenant's apathy.

'Well, Sam, that is the situation as I comprehend it. Now it remains to be seen who will outmanoeuvre whom. D'you understand?'

'Yes, sir,' said Rogers mechanically, avoiding Drinkwater's eyes.

There was a silence between the two men. It was not the companionable silence of contentment between friends. Drinkwater could sense the hostility in Rogers. Once, long ago on the brig *Hellebore*, it had been open and obvious; now it was concealed, hidden behind those downcast eyes. Drinkwater could only guess at its origins but that letter from Lord Dungarth made it imperative that Rogers suppressed it. He changed the subject.

'You did very well at Stralsund, Sam.'

'Didn't you think I'd be up to it?' Rogers jibbed at the patronisation. 'Look, if you're implying they didn't put up a spirited fight . . .'

'I'm implying nothing of the kind, Sam,' Drinkwater said with a weary patience he was far from feeling. Silence returned to the table. Then Rogers seemed to come to a decision. He pulled himself up in his chair as though bracing himself.

'Did you order Lallo to put me in a strait-jacket?'

Drinkwater looked directly at Rogers. To deny such a direct question would put poor Lallo in an impossible situation and give Rogers the impression that he was dodging the issue.

'I gave orders for the surgeon to restrain you with such force as was necessary, yes. It was for your own benefit, Sam. Now that you are weaned off the damnable stuff and have been recommended in a letter to the Admiralty – oh, yes, I sent it off with Captain Horne's dispatch boat – you have a much better chance of . . .' Drinkwater paused. He knew Rogers craved promotion and the security of being made post. Yet of all his officers Rogers was the one he would least recommend for command. Rogers would turn into the worst kind of flogging captain.

'Advancement?' said Rogers.

'Exactly,' Drinkwater temporised.

Rogers sat back, apparently appeased, looking at Drinkwater from beneath his brows. Drinkwater had told Rogers nothing of the real reason for their new station. The prevailing political situation was one thing, the complexities of secret operations quite another. Nevertheless it was not inconceivable that Rogers might wring some advantage out of their situation. Drinkwater would feel he could encourage Rogers if he could also avoid the man commanding a ship.

'Sam,' he said, 'I have a trifling influence; suppose I was able to get you a step in rank. What would you say to a post as Commander in the Sea-Fencibles?'

Rogers frowned. 'Or of a signal station?' he said darkly.

'Just so . . .'

But Drinkwater had miscalculated. Rogers rose. 'Damn it,' he said, 'I want a ship like you!'

'Damn,' muttered Drinkwater as Rogers withdrew without further ceremony and, reaching for the hitherto untouched decanter, he poured himself a glass of wine.

The waters of the eastern Baltic which two months earlier had presented a desolate aspect under pack-ice, were alive with coasting and fishing craft the following morning. Convention decreed that all fishing boats were free to attend to their business and Drinkwater was not much interested in stopping the small coasting vessels that crept along the shore. But mindful of the underlying task of every British cruiser, Drinkwater's written orders to his officers included the injunction to stop and search neutral vessels of any size. At two bells in the forenoon watch the look-out had sighted a large, barque-rigged vessel of some three hundred tons burthen. As Fraser eased his helm the barque set more sail and Drinkwater was sent for.

Coming on deck Drinkwater heard Rogers remark to Fraser, 'A festering blockade runner, eh?' with enough of his old spirit to dispel any worries as to permanent damage after the previous evening's conversation. He acknowledged the two lieutenants with a nod and a smile. Rogers's face was impassive.

Almost without any conscious effort on anyone's part, the news that the ship was in chase of a possible prize attracted every idler on deck. Gathering amidships were Mount and Lallo, with Pater the purser. Forward, on the triangular fo'c's'le, a score or so of seamen were crowding the knightheads to sight their quarry. James Quilhampton ascended the quarterdeck ladder and touched his hat to the captain.

'Morning, sir,' he said.

'Morning, James,' Drinkwater replied, dropping the usual formalities since Quilhampton not only was a friend but was not on duty. Fraser looked anxiously at the captain. He was eager to crack on sail for all he was worth.

'D'ye wish that I should set . . .?'

'Carry on, Mr Fraser, carry on. You are doing fine. Just forbear carrying anything away if you please.'

Drinkwater raised his Dollond glass and levelled in on the chase. 'Now what nationality do you guess our friend is, James?' He handed the glass to Quilhampton who studied the quarry.

'Er . . . I don't know, sir.'

'I think he's a Dane, Mr Q; a neutral Dane with a cargo of . . . oh, timber, flax, perhaps, and bound for somewhere where they build ships. We shall have to exercise our right of angary.'

'Of *what*, sir?'

'Angary, Mr Q, angary. A belligerent's right to seize or use neutral property: in our case temporarily, to ascertain if he is bound for a port friendly to the French,' Drinkwater took back his glass and again looked at the barque. Then he turned to Fraser. 'You are coming up on him hand over fist, Mr Fraser. Let us have a bow-chaser loaded, ready to put a shot athwart his hawse!'

In the brilliant sunshine and over a sparkling sea the *Antigone* soon overhauled her deep-laden and bluff-bowed victim. A single shot across her bow forced the barque to bring-to and an hour and a half after they had first sighted her, the blockade runner lay under *Antigone*'s lee.

'Very well done, Mr Fraser, my congratulations.'

'Thank you, sir.' Mr Fraser, looking pleased with himself, acknowledged the captain's compliment.

Drinkwater turned to Quilhampton. 'Do you board him, Mr Q. Examine his papers and, if you think it necessary, his cargo. Take your time. If you consider the cargo is bound for a port under French domination or of use as war material we are authorised to detain him. D'you understand?'

'Perfectly, sir. Angary is the word.' And he went off to the quarter, where the lee cutter was being prepared for lowering.

Rogers and Hill were active about the deck as, aloft, the flogging topgallants were dropped onto the topmast caps and the big maintopsail was backed in a great double belly against the mast. Both courses and spanker were brailed in and *Antigone* pitched, reined in and checked in her forward dash.

'Lower away!' There was a loud smack as the cutter hit the water and a few minutes later she was being pulled across the blue sea towards the barque, her dripping oar-blades flashing in the sun.

Drinkwater settled down to wait patiently. The hiatus occasioned by Quilhampton's search could be long, depending upon the degree of co-operation he received from the vessel's master. Drinkwater watched idly as a fishing boat crossed the stern, her four-man crew standing up and watching the curious sight with obvious interest.

'She's Danish, sir,' said Fraser suddenly. Drinkwater looked up and saw that the barque was hoisting the colours that she had studiously avoided showing before. That very circumstance had made her actions sufficiently suspicious to Drinkwater.

'Hm. I thought as much.'

'This'll annoy the Danes,' added Rogers joining them, and Drink-water recalled the incident off Elsinore. It seemed an age ago.

'Yes, they are somewhat sensitive upon the subject of Freedom of the Seas,' Drinkwater remarked. 'At least they ain't escorted by a warship.'

At the turn of the century British men-of-war had detained an entire Danish convoy escorted by the frigate *Freya*. The incident had almost caused open hostilities and had certainly contributed to the rupture that had resulted in Nelson's victory at Copenhagen a year later.

'Well, to be neutral during such a war as this carries its own penalties and entails its own risks,' Drinkwater remarked. 'I feel more pity for others whose lives are more deeply affected by French imperialism than a few profit-mongering Danish merchants.'

Fraser looked sideways at the captain. Did Drinkwater refer to the widows and orphans they themselves had made in the destruction of the battery at Stralsund? Or was he alluding to the families of the pressed men that milled in the ship's waist?

'Boat's returning,' said Rogers, recalling Fraser from his unsolved abstraction.

'Yes,' said Drinkwater peering through his glass. Beside Quilhampton in the cutter was another figure who seemed, by his gesticulations, to be arguing.

'Damnation,' muttered Drinkwater, 'trouble.'

'Capten, I protest much! Goddam you English! Vy you stop my ship?'

'Because you are carrying a cargo proscribed by the Orders in Council of His Majesty King George, to the port of Antwerp which is invested by ships of King George's Royal Navy.'

Drinkwater studied the papers Quilhampton had brought him, then looked up at the Danish master. 'The matter admits little argument, sir; Anvers, Antwerpen, Antwerp, 'tis all the same to me.' He held up the papers and quoting from them read, '*Der Schiff* Birthe, *Captain Nielsen, von Grenaa, Dantzig vor Antwerpen* . . . your cargo is, er, sawn timber, flax turpentine. They make excellent deals in Dantzig, Captain, and with such deals they make excellent ships at Antwer-pen. About a dozen men o' war a year, I believe.'

'And vot vill you do now, eh, Capten English?'

'Detain you, sir,' Drinkwater said, folding the *Birthe*'s papers and tucking them in his tail-pocket, 'and send you in as a prize.'

'A prize! *Å for helvede!*'

'To be condemned in due form according to the usages and customs . . .'

'No! Goddam, no!'

Drinkwater looked at the man. He had expected anger and despised himself for hiding this unpleasant necessity behind the jumble of half-legal cant. The Danish mariner could scarcely be expected to understand it, beyond learning that he and his ship were virtually prisoners.

'A disagreeable necessity, Captain, for both of us,' Drinkwater spread his hands in a gesture to signify helplessness. Oddly, the man seemed to be considering something. This suspicion was almost immediately confirmed when Nielsen stepped forward, taking Drinkwater by the elbow and saying in his ear:

'Capten, ve go below and talk, yes?'

'I think that will not be necessary.'

Nielsen's grip on his arm increased. 'It is important . . . ver' important!' He paused then added, 'Before Dantzig I was in Königsberg, Capten . . .' and nodded, as if this added intelligence was of some significance. Nielsen suddenly stepped back and gave a grave nod to Drinkwater. Frowning, Drinkwater suspected he was to be made a bribe, but something in the man's face persuaded him to take the matter seriously. After all, Königsberg was a Prussian port and Dantzig now a French one. Was Nielsen trying to placate him with some news?

'Mr Rogers, take the deck. Watch our friend carefully. Mr Fraser, this man wants to talk to me privately. I'd be obliged if you'd come as a witness.' And leaving the deck buzzing with speculation, Drinkwater led them below.

'Now, sir,' he said to Nielsen the instant Fraser had closed the cabin door, 'what is it you want?'

The Danish master put his hand up to his breast and reached under his coat.

'If you intend to offer me money . . .'

'*Nein* . . . not money, Capten . . . this', he drew a package from his breast, 'is more good than money, I tink. I come from Königsberg, Capten, plenty Russians Königsberg.' He handed Drinkwater the sealed packet.

'What the devil is it?'

'It is, er . . .' Nielsen searched for a word, '. . . er, secret, Capten . . . for London from Russia . . . for many times I, Frederic Nielsen, carry the secret paper for you English.'

Drinkwater turned the package over suspiciously. 'You intended taking this where? To Antwerp?' Drinkwater fixed the Dane with his eyes, searching for the truthful answers to his questions. Any fool could wrap up an impressive bundle of papers scribbled in a supposed 'cipher' and try it as a ruse. 'Together with your cargo for the French, eh, Captain. Is that how you trade first with Königsberg and then with Dantzig, eh?'

Nielsen shrugged. 'A man must live, Capten . . . but yes. To Antwerpen. In two days from Antwerpen it can be to London – by Helvoetsluys or Vlissingen – who know? This is not for me. I only make my ship go ver' fast.' He shrugged again. 'Now it is stop by you.'

'Are you paid?'

'Yes.'

'How?'

Nielsen hesitated, reluctant to admit his private affairs. He looked first at Drinkwater then at Fraser. He found comfort in neither face. 'How?' Drinkwater repeated and Fraser stirred menacingly.

'Ven the paper to London, den is money made to me, to Hamburg.'

Drinkwater considered for a moment. 'If I undertake to deliver this, will you get your money?'

A look of alarm crossed Nielsen's face.

'Have a look at the thing, sir,' said Fraser, unable to remain silent any longer. 'He's trying to get you to let his cargo through on the pretext o' this cock-and-bull story.'

'What is the news in here, Captain Nielsen?' Drinkwater tapped the packet.

Again Nielsen shrugged. 'I do not know. Is some good news for London I hear at Dantzig.'

'Good news! At Dantzig?'

'Yes. French have battle at Heilsberg. Russian ver' good.'

Drinkwater frowned. 'You say the Russians beat the French at Heilsberg?'

Nielsen nodded. Drinkwater made up his mind, turned to the table and picked up the pen-knife lying there.

'No, Capten, I tell good. if you cut paper I not get money! *Gott!*'

It was too late. Drinkwater had slit the heavy sealing on the outer, oiled paper and unfolded the contents. They consisted of several sheets of handwriting at the top of which was a prefix of seven digits. The message was meaningless in any language and was either in cipher or an imitation cipher. Drinkwater looked up at Nielsen.

'Any damned fool could write a few pages of gibberish,' said

Drinkwater. He lifted the final sheet. At the bottom was a signature of sorts. At least it was a series of signs in the place one would write a signature. They seemed to be in Cyrillic script whereas the body of the thing was in Roman handwriting; Drinkwater could make nothing of them, but then his eye fell on something else that stirred a memory of something Colonel Wilson had said. When he had mentioned Mackenzie, the British agent to whom he should offer assistance, he had also spoken of a Russian officer, a lieutenant whose name he had forgotten. Were those Cyrillic letters this man's signature? Both men used a cryptogramic code, Wilson had said, and both sent their reports to Joseph Devlieghere, Merchant of Antwerpen. He did not have to recall the Flemish name: it was written at the bottom of the page.

'Capten, if you take my ship prize, you make London ver' angry. Frederic Nielsen help you English . . .'

'For money!' said Fraser contemptuously.

'No!' Nielsen was angry himself now and turned on Fraser. 'Why you not to trust Nielsen, eh? You English not like business of oder people! Only for English it is good. Yes! But I tell you, Capten,' here he rounded on Drinkwater, 'if Nielsen not bring paper, sometimes London not know what happen in Russia, Sweden an' oder place. You English send gold . . . much gold . . . but not keep it good . . . Ha! ha! Ver' funny! You English crazy! You lose much gold but stop poor Frederic Nielsen to take some deals to Antwerpen . . . bah!'

Drinkwater had only the haziest notion of what Nielsen meant and was only paying partial attention to the Danish master for there was something else about the papers he held that was odd; not merely odd but profoundly disquieting. Something had tripped a subconscious mechanism of his memory. Now he wanted Nielsen and Fraser out of his cabin.

'Take Captain Nielsen on deck, Mr Fraser. I want a moment to reflect.'

'Don't be misled by such a trick, sir,' Fraser said anxiously.

'Cut along, Mr Fraser,' Drinkwater said with sudden asperity, waiting impatiently for the two men to leave him alone. When they had gone he sat and stared at the document. But he could not be certain and gradually the beating of his heart subsided. He cursed himself for a fool and began to fold the letter, then thought better of it and opened his table drawer, drew out journal, pen-case and ink-well. Very carefully he copied into the margin of his journal the strange exotic letters of the document's 'signature': NCЛAHﬅ .

Then he stowed the things away again, stuffed Nielsen's dispatch into the breast of his coat, strode to the cabin door and took the quarterdeck ladder two steps at a time.

'Mr Rogers!'

'Sir?'

'Be so kind as to have Captain Nielsen returned to his ship.' Drinkwater turned to the Dane. 'Captain, I apologise for detaining you.' He handed the dispatch back. 'You must re-seal it and please tell Mynheer Devlieghere the news of the defeat at . . .'

'Heilsberg,' offered Nielsen, visibly brightening.

'Yes. Heilsberg. Good voyage and I hope you have good news soon from Hamburg.'

Nielsen's face split in a grin and he held out a stubby hand. 'T'ank you Capten. You English are not too much friend with Denmark, but this,' he wagged the dispatch in the air, 'this is good news, yes.' He strode to the rail where a puzzled Quilhampton waited.

'You are not going to let the bugger go are you?' asked Rogers with some of his wonted fire, seeing a plum prize slipping once again beyond his grasp.

'Yes, Mr Rogers,' said Drinkwater, fixing the first lieutenant with a cautionary eye, 'for reasons of state . . .' Then he turned to the master. 'Mr Hill, be so kind as to resume our course for Königsberg when the boat returns,' he said and added, by way of a partial explanation, 'we must investigate the nature of a French defeat at a place called Heilsberg.'

'Aye, aye, sir,' replied the imperturbable Hill.

'And Mr Mount?'

'Sir?'

'Can we locate Heilsberg on that atlas of yours?'

'I should hope so, sir,' said the marine officer with enthusiasm as Drinkwater led him below.

Lieutenant Rogers strode to the lee rail and watched the boat pulling back towards *Antigone*.

'Reasons of state!' he hissed under his breath, and spat disgustedly to leeward as the Danish barque made sail.

Friedland

'No, Mr Rogers, no wine, I beg you.' Lallo put out a restraining hand.

Rogers, his fist clamped around the neck of the decanter which he had ordered the negro messman to bring, looked from one to another of the gunroom officers. They returned his stare, watching his pale face with its faint sheen of perspiration showing in the dim light of the gunroom.

'God damn and blast you for a set of canting Methodicals,' he said. 'God damn and blast you all to hell,' and drawing back his arm he sent the decanter flying through the air. It smashed on the forward bulkhead and in the silence that followed they could hear Rogers's laboured breathing.

'Mr Rogers . . .' began Fraser, but he was instantly silenced by Lallo. They watched as Rogers calmed himself. After a pause Rogers ceased to glare at them all, picked up his knife and fork and addressed himself to his plate. In an embarrassed silence the others dutifully followed suit. For fifteen minutes no one said a word and then Rogers, flinging down his utensils, rose from the table and stumped out. His exit provoked a broadside of expelled breath.

'Phew! How long will he go on like this?' asked Fraser. 'If he isn't damned careful he'll end up with the other irredeemable toss-pots in Haslar Hospital.'

'That was what I tried to tell you, Mr Fraser,' said Lallo, 'when you interfered.'

'I'm damn sorry, Mr Lallo, but I couldna tolerate him being trussed like a chicken for the table.'

'I was not aware', said Lallo archly, 'that there was any love lost between you.'

'Nor there is, but . . .'

'The captain ordered me to restrain him. It was out of kindness, to avoid too public a humiliation for the man.'

'But was all that really necessary?'

'In my opinion yes. Despite being anorexic, which was attributable to his reliance on strong drink, he was quite capable of doing himself and myself a great deal of damage in his ravings. The aboulia . . . the loss of will-power associated with addiction, disturbs all the natural processes and inclinations of the body. He was by turns lethargic and extremely violent. At times he was almost cataleptic, but at others his strength was amazing.' Lallo paused, then added, 'I'd say the treatment, though drastic, was successful.' He turned and looked down on the deck where the broken decanter lay amid a dark stain on the planking. 'At least he resisted the stuff.'

'Well, it was a damnable thing . . .' said Fraser.

'It was a damnable thing that you had a man gagged yourself for the use of strong language the day before yesterday . . .'

'That's preposterous . . .'

'And furthermore,' Lallo interrupted, 'I'd diagnose your own condition . . .'

'For goodness sake, gentlemen,' put in Quilhampton, raising his voice to overcome the rising argument, 'I conceive Mr Rogers to be upset because we let the Danish ship go. He has never enjoyed much luck in the way of prize-money.'

'There would have been nothing very certain about making any out of that Dane,' snapped Fraser. 'Condemning neutrals usually turns upon points of law. It isn't the same thing as taking a national ship or a privateer.' Lallo was grateful for the changed mood of the conversation. 'What *did* happen in the cabin, Mr Fraser? Did the scoundrel offer the captain money?'

'No,' said Fraser after a pause. 'The Dane, Frederic Nielsen, claimed he was carrying secret papers for London, or some such nonsense. The fellow was adamant and I don't think the captain believed him. Then . . .'

'Go on . . .'

Fraser shrugged. 'Well, he suddenly looked closer at the papers and appeared to change his mind. Bundled Nielsen and myself out of the cabin and a few minutes later came up, handed the papers back to the Dane and let him go.'

'Just like that?' asked Lallo.

'Yes. Or that is how it seemed to me.'

'I wonder . . .' mused Quilhampton, attracting the attention of the other two.

'You wonder what, James?' asked Fraser. 'Have you any idea what's afoot?'

'The captain's been mixed up in this sort of thing before.'

'What sort of thing?' asked Fraser.

'*This* sort of thing?'

'*What* sort of thing, for God's sake?' Fraser repeated in exasperation.

'Well, secret operations and such like.'

'*Secret operations?*' said Lallo incredulously. 'Are we bound on a secret operation? I thought we were on a cruise against blockade runners.'

'Can't you be more specific, James?' Fraser's curiosity was plain and almost indignant.

Quilhampton shrugged. 'Who knows . . . ?' he said enigmatically.

'Oh, for Heaven's sake, James!'

'Well, ask Hill. They were both on the cutter *Kestrel* years ago, doing all sorts of clandestine things . . . Oh, my God!' Quilhampton jumped up.

'What the devil's the matter?'

'It's Hill! I've forgotten to relieve him again!' Quilhampton grabbed his hat and trod in the broken glass from the smashed decanter.

'Damn! Hey, King! Come and sweep up this damned mess, will you?'

Drinkwater paced up and down the deck as the hands went aloft to stow the sails. *Antigone* rocked gently in the swell that ran in over the Pregel Bar. The desolation of two months earlier was scarcely imaginable in the present lively scene. The sea, now clear of ice, was an enticing blue. The distant line of coast was a soft blue-green and, above the long yellow spit that made it a lagoon, the Frisches Haff was dotted with the sails of coasting craft and fishing vessels. There were others in the open sea around them and the activity seemed to indicate that events ashore were having little effect on the lives of the local population who were busy pursuing their various trades. Perhaps Nielsen had been right and the French had been badly mauled at Heilsberg. Perhaps another battle had been fought and the Russians had flung back the Grand Army. Perhaps the French were in headlong flight, a circumstance which would explain all this normality! Drinkwater checked his wild speculation. He was here to gather facts without delay. He would have to send to Königsberg as soon as the ship was secured and a boat was prepared. He contemplated going himself. Properly it was Rogers's prerogative to command so important an expedition but, despite his success at Stralsund, Rogers's lack of interest in political matters did not recommend him for the service. On the other hand, if he sent Fraser, the next in seniority, a slight would be imputed to Rogers. He did not wish to risk a reversal to the first lieutenant's progress back to normality. But that left Hill or Quilhampton, and Hill could not be sent because the same imputation attached to the dispatching of the sailing master as the second lieutenant. It would have to be Quilhampton.

Drinkwater, irritated by all these trivial considerations, swore, consoled himself that Quilhampton was as good a man as any for the task, and made up his mind. He passed orders for the preparation of the launch for a lengthy absence from the ship and summoned the third lieutenant to his cabin.

'Now, Mr Q,' he said, indicating the chart and Mount's borrowed atlas. 'See, here is Königsberg. You are to take the launch which is being provisioned for a week, and make the best of your way there. I shall provide you with a letter of accreditment to the effect that you are a British naval officer. Your purpose is to ascertain the truth and extent of a report that the French suffered a defeat at Heilsberg.' Drinkwater placed his finger on a spot on a page of the atlas. 'You *must* get the best information you can and try to determine if anything else has occurred. Was the French army routed or merely checked? Have there been any further engagements? That sort of thing. Do you understand?'

'Yes, sir.'

'Very well. Now, I suggest that initially you search out a British merchant ship. There will almost certainly be at least one in the port. Do that first. Do not land until you have made contact and obtained advice from a British master. The port is Prussian and there may be Russian troops there. You would do well to avoid any problems with language and your best interpreter will be the master of a British ship who will have an agent and therefore someone acquainted with local affairs.' Drinkwater remembered Young and Baker and added, 'Sometimes, I believe, these fellows have quite an effective intelligence system of their own.'

'What force will I take, sir?'

'Twenty-four men, James; no marines, just seamen.'

'Very well, sir . . . May I ask a favour?'

'Well?'

'May I take Tregembo, sir?'

'Tregembo?' Drinkwater frowned. 'You know I dare not expose him to any unnecessary danger, I shall never hear the last of it from his wife . . .' Drinkwater smiled.

'Well Königsberg is supposed to be a friendly port, sir. I cannot see that he can come to much harm.'

'True. Why do you want Tregembo?' Drinkwater paused and saw Quilhampton's hesitation. 'Is it because you do not trust the temper of the men?'

Quilhampton shrugged, trying to pass his concern off lightly. 'One or two may try and run, sir. They are still somewhat mettlesome. With Tregembo there they will be less inclined to try. Besides, I shall have to leave the launch.'

'You will take two midshipmen, Dutfield and Wickham.'

'I should still like Tregembo.'

Drinkwater raised his voice. 'Sentry! Pass word for my coxswain!'

A minute or two later Tregembo arrived. 'You sent for me, zur?'

'Aye Tregembo. Mr Q here wants you go to in the launch with him to Königsberg. To be particular, he has requested you go. I'd like you to accompany him.'

'Who'll look after you, zur?' Tregembo asked with the air of the indispensible.

'Oh, I expect Mullender will manage for a day or two,' Drinkwater replied drily.

Tregembo sniffed his disbelief. 'If you'm want me to go, zur, I'll go.'

'Very well.' Drinkwater smiled. 'You had better both go and make your preparations.'

An hour later he watched the launch pull away from the ship's side. On board *Antigone* the men were coiling away the yard and stay tackles used to sway the heavy carvel boat up from its chocks on the booms in the frigate's waist and over the side. Half a cable away the men in the launch stowed their oars, stepped the two masts and hooked the lugsail yards to their travellers. An hour later the two lugsails were mere nicks upon the horizon, no different from half a dozen others entering or leaving the Frisches Haff. Drinkwater settled down to wait.

For two days *Antigone* swung slowly round her anchor. On board, the monotonous routines of shipboard life went on, the officer of the watch occasionally studying the low, desolate shore for the twin peaks of the launch's lugsails. Once a watch Frey or Walmsley climbed to the main royal yard and peered diligently to the eastward, but without seeing any sign of the ship's boat. Then, early in the morning of the third day, an easterly breeze carried with it the sound of gunfire. Sent aloft, Frey brought down the disquieting intelligence that there was smoke visible from the general direction of Königsberg.

All the officers were on the quarterdeck and Mount, as if disbelieving the boy's report, ascended the mast himself to confirm it.

'But what the devil does it mean, Mount?' asked Hill. 'Your atlas shows Heilsberg as to the south and west of Königsberg. If the Russkies threw the French back, what the hell is smoke and gunfire doing at Königsberg?' He crossed the deck and checked the wind direction from the weather dog-vane to the compass. 'That gunfire isn't coming from anywhere other than east.'

'It means', said Drinkwater, 'either that Heilsberg was wrongly reported or that the French have counter-attacked and reached Königsberg.'

'Bloody hell!'

'What about Quilhampton?'

And Tregembo, thought Drinkwater. Should he send another boat? Should he work *Antigone* closer inshore? He had no charts of the area accurate enough to attempt a passage over the bar and into the Frisches Haff, and did not relish the thought of grounding ignominiously within range of the shore. A picture of French batteries revenging themselves on him from the shingle spit enclosing the great lagoon presented itself to him. Napoleon would make much of such an event and *Le Moniteur* would trumpet it throughout Europe. No, he would have to give Quilhampton his chance. The man was not a fool. If he heard gunfire he would assume the place was under attack and, as it could only be attacked by one enemy, he would come off to the ship as his orders said. But the officers were looking at him, expecting some response.

'I think that we can do little but wait, gentlemen,' Drinkwater said, and turning he made his way below, to brood in his cabin and fret himself with anxiety. For two hours an uneasy silence hung over the ship, then Frey, suspended in the rigging with the ship's best glass, hailed the deck, his voice cracking with excitement.

'Deck there! Deck there! The launch, sir! It's in sight!' His frantic excitement promised to unseat him from his precarious perch and it was only with difficulty that Hill persuaded him that his own safety was more important than the precise bearing of the launch. But Frey would not desert his post and kept the image of the launch dancing in the lens by lying full length on the furled main-topgallant. It was he, therefore, who spotted the reversed ensign flying from the launch's peak as she approached the ship. 'She's flying a signal for distress, sir!'

Once again all were on deck; the waist and fo'c's'le were crowded with *Antigone*'s people straining their eyes to the eastward where the launch was now clearly visible.

'Mr Comley!' Rogers called sharply and with no trace of his former debility. 'Stir those idlers! Man the yard and stay tackles! Prepare to hoist in the launch!'

'Mr Lallo,' said Drinkwater lowering his telescope, 'as far as I can ascertain there is nothing amiss with the launch itself. I can only assume the signal of distress refers to the people in the boat. I think it would be wise if you were to prepare your instruments.' A chilling foreboding had closed itself round Drinkwater's heart.

The launch came running down wind, the men in her hidden behind the bunts of the loose-footed lugsails. She was skilfully rounded up into the wind and, sails a-flapping, came alongside *Antigone*'s waist. With an overwhelming sense of relief Drinkwater saw a dishevelled Quilhampton at the tiller, his iron hook crooked over the wooden bar. Then he saw wounded men amidships: one of them Tregembo.

The fit men clambered from the launch up *Antigone*'s tumblehome. With her sails stowed and masts lowered the boat was hooked and swung up and inboard onto the booms. Here eager arms assisted in lifting the wounded men out and down below to the catlings and curettes of Mr Lallo.

Drinkwater waited until Quilhampton reported. His eyes followed the inert body of Tregembo as, his shoulder slung in a bloodstained and makeshift bandage, he was taken below. He was therefore unaware of a dusty stranger who stood upon the deck ignored amidst the bustle.

'Well, Mr Q? What happened?'

James Quilhampton looked five years older. His face was drawn and he was filthy.

'I have your intelligence, sir, Königsberg has fallen to the French. There has been a great battle, just two days ago. It was disastrous for the Russians. There is chaos in the port . . .' He paused, gathering his wits. He was clearly exhausted. 'I made contact, as you suggested, with the master of a Hull ship. We went ashore to gather news at a tavern much used by British shipmasters. To my surprise Captain

Young was there, together with Captain Baker.' Quilhampton shook his head, trying to clear it of the fog of fatigue. 'To my astonishment their ships had still not discharged their lading . . .'

'Good God . . . but go on.'

'The fellows were debating what should be done, as the news had just arrived of the precipitate flight of the Russians. I said *Antigone* was anchored on the Pregel Bar and would afford them convoy. Most felt that with their cargoes not yet completed they could not stand the loss. They affirmed their faith in the garrison and the defences of the city. I tried to tell Young that his cargo *must* not fall into the hands of the enemy. He assured me it wouldn't. The men had had a tiring passage with the necessity of rowing up the river, so I judged that we should remain alongside Young's ship. Her chief mate offered us accommodation and I accepted, intending to see how matters stood in the morning and, if necessary, help to get the *Nancy* and the *Jenny Marsden* to sea. I thought, sir, that if the threat from the French persisted, I might better persuade Captain Young to change his mind. You see, sir, the evening before he had been somewhat in his cups and difficult to move . . .'

'I understand, James. Go on.'

'There is not much more to tell. I slept badly, the town was shaken throughout the night by artillery fire, and the bursting of the shells was constant. In the morning French cavalry were in the town. Young was not on board and I attempted to get his mate to sail and bring out Baker's ship as well. They would not move unless their respective masters were with them. I undertook to return to the tavern where it was thought they had lodged. I got caught in a cross-fire between some infantry, I don't know whether they were Prussians or Russians, and some French sharp-shooters. Tregembo and Kissel were with me. Kissel was hit and Tregembo and I went back for him. As we dragged him towards the *Jenny Marsden*'s jolly boat we were ridden down by French dragoons. They dispatched Kissel and wounded Tregembo . . .'

'Go on. What happened to you?'

'Oh, nothing, sir.'

'He unhorsed a dragoon, Captain, pulled the fellow clean out of his saddle . . .'

Drinkwater turned and was aware of an unfamiliar face.

'And who, sir, are you?'

The stranger ignored the question. 'Your officer unhorsed the dragoon with that remarkable hook of his. You see, sir, they were pursuing me. I had evaded them in an alley and they took their revenge on your officer and men. However, as I swiftly made him out to be a seafaring man as well as an Englishman, I made myself known to him and assisted him in getting his wounded comrade into the boat.'

'I doubt I could have done it alone, sir,' explained Quilhampton, 'before the other dragoon got me. Fortunately the fellow missed with his carbine and we were able to get to the *Jenny Marsden* without further ado, but I could not get either of them to unmoor and, with shot flying about the shipping and this gentleman here insisting on my bringing him off, I decided that discretion was the better part of valour . . .'

'What is the extent of Tregembo's wound?' Drinkwater cut in.

'A sabre thrust in the fleshy part of the shoulder, sir. I do not believe it to be mortal.'

'I hope to God it ain't.' Drinkwater turned on the stranger. 'And now, sir, who are you and what is your business?'

'I think, Captain,' said the stranger with that imperturbable coolness that was rapidly eroding Drinkwater's temper, 'that this should be discussed in your cabin.'

'Do you, indeed.'

'Yes. In fact I insist upon it.' His cold blue eyes held Drinkwater's in an unblinking gaze. The man made a gesture with his hand as if their roles were reversed and it was he who was inviting Drinkwater below. 'Captain . . .?'

'Mr Q, get below and turn in. You, Mr Frey, cut along to the surgeon and tell him to debride those wounds immediately or they will mortify.' He turned to the stranger. 'As for you, sir, you had better follow me!'

Drinkwater strode below and, shutting the door behind the stranger, rounded on him.

'Now, sir! Enough of this tomfoolery. Who the deuce are you and what the devil d'you mean by behaving like that?'

The stranger smiled cooly. 'I already have the advantage of you, Captain. Your lieutenant informed me that you are Captain Drinkwater. Captain Nathaniel Drinkwater, I understand . . .' A small and strangely threatening smile was playing about the man's mouth, but he held out his hand cordially enough. 'I am Colin Alexander Mackenzie, Captain Drinkwater, and in your debt for saving my life.'

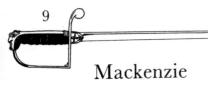

Mackenzie

Drinkwater felt awkward under Mackenzie's uncompromising scrutiny. He hesitated, then took the outstretched hand. Everything about the stranger irritated Drinkwater, not least his proprietorial air in Drinkwater's own cabin.

'Mr Mackenzie,' he said coldly, 'Colonel Wilson mentioned you.' Drinkwater was not ready to say the British Commissioner had urged him to offer this cold-eyed man as much assistance as he required. The manner of Mackenzie's arrival seemed to indicate he already had that for the time being.

'So,' Mackenzie smiled, 'you have met Bob Wilson. I wonder where he is now?'

Drinkwater indicated a chair and Mackenzie slumped into it. 'Thank you.'

'A glass?' Drinkwater asked.

'That is very kind of you. What did Wilson say?'

Drinkwater poured the two glasses of wine and handed one to the Scotsman. He did not hurry to answer, but observed the man as he relaxed. After a little he said, 'That I was to afford you such assistance as you might require. It seems we have already done so.'

The two men were still weighing each other up and Drinkwater's manner remained cool. Now, however, Mackenzie dropped his aloofness.

'I'm damn glad you did, Captain. I had to ride for my very life. I am almost sure those dragoons knew who I was ...' He shrugged, passing a hand over his dust-stained face. 'The Russians were smashed, you know, on the fourteenth, at a place called Friedland. Bennigsen got himself caught in a loop of the River Alle and, though the Russians fought like bears, the French got the better of them. Bennigsen was forced to retreat and Königsberg has fallen. The Russians are falling back everywhere to the line of the Nieman. I was lucky to get out ... and even luckier to find you.' He smiled, and

Drinkwater found himself feeling less hostile. However he did not pass up the opportunity to goad Mackenzie a little.

'What exactly is your function, Mr Mackenzie? I mean what was it you feared the French dragoons took you for?'

Mackenzie looked at him shrewdly, again that strangely disquieting smile played about his mouth, again Drinkwater received the impression that their roles were reversed and that he, in goading Mackenzie, was in some obscure way being put upon.

'I am sure you are aware of my function as a British agent.' He paused and added, 'A spy, if you wish.'

Drinkwater shied away from the dangerous word-game he felt inadequate to play. This was his ship, his cabin; he switched the conversation back onto its safer track.

'I heard that the French were defeated at a place called Heilsberg. After Eylau we were expecting that the Russians might throw Boney back, once and for all.'

Mackenzie nodded tiredly, apparently equally relieved at the turn the conversation had taken. 'So did I, Captain. It *was* true. The Russians and Prussians moved against the French at the beginning of the month when Ney's Corps went foraging. *Le Rougeard* was caught napping and given a bloody nose. But Napoleon moved the whole mass of the Grand Army, caught Bennigsen ten days later at Friedland and crushed him.'

'I see.' Drinkwater considered the matter a moment. He did not think that the news left him much alternative. The retreat of the Tsar's Army beyond the Nieman, the French occupation of Poland and East Prussia, the fall of Dantzig and now Königsberg, left Napoleon the undisputed master of Europe. In accordance with his orders, London must be informed forthwith.

'Well, Mr Mackenzie, having rescued you and rendered that assistance required of me, I must now take the news you bring back to London. I take it you will take passage with us?'

Mackenzie hesitated then said, 'Captain Drinkwater, how discretionary are your orders?'

'Those from their Lordships are relatively wide.'

'You have, perhaps, orders from another source?' Mackenzie paused. 'I see you are reluctant to confide in me. No matter. But perhaps you have something else, eh? Something from the Secret Department of Lord Dungarth?'

'Go on, Mr Mackenzie. I find your hypothesis .... intriguing,' Drinkwater prevaricated.

'The Russians are defeated; the shipments of arms in the two merchantmen at Königsberg have fallen into enemy hands. In commercial terms the Tsar is a bad risk.' Mackenzie smiled. 'Sweden is led by an insane monarch and on the very edge of revolution. Now, Captain, what is the victorious *Napoleone* going to do about it all? He has destroyed Prussia, driven the Russians back into Mother Russia itself, he is suborning the Swedes, threatening the Danes. He has the Grand Army in the field under his personal control, his rear is secured by Mortier at Stralsund and Brune's Corps of Hispano-Dutch on the borders of Denmark. Austria is quiescent but . . .' and Mackenzie paused to emphasise his point, 'he has not been in Paris for over a year. The question of what is happening in Paris will prevent him sleeping more than anything. He has a few more months in the field and then,' he shrugged, 'who knows? So what would you do, Captain?'

'Me? I have no idea,' Drinkwater found the idea absurd.

'I would conclude an armistice with the Tsar,' said Mackenzie evenly.

Drinkwater looked sharply at him. The idea was preposterous. The Tsar was the sworn enemy of the French Revolution and the Imperial system of the parvenu Emperor, and yet such was the persuasion of Mackenzie's personality that the cold, cogent logic of it struck Drinkwater. He remembered Straton's cautionary removal of the Tsar's subsidy, and his own now-proven misgivings. He said nothing for there seemed nothing to say.

Then Mackenzie broke the seriousness of their mood. His smile was unsullied and charming. 'But then, 'tis only a hypothesis, Captain Drinkwater . . . and it is my business to speculate, intelligently, of course.'

'And it's not my business to verify the accuracy of your speculations, Mr Mackenzie,' said the captain brightening, 'but to take this intelligence back to London as quickly as possible.'

'Have you heard of any preparations against the Baltic being made at home?'

'Yes,' said Drinkwater. 'Horne of the *Pegasus* mentioned some such expedition to be mounted this summer in support of Gustavus at Rügen. There were problems of command: the King of Sweden wanted to command British troops in person . . .'

'They would walk into a trap,' said Mackenzie, his voice a mixture of contempt and exasperation.

'Well then,' said Drinkwater, 'the sooner we prevent that, the better.'

'I think you are mistaken, Captain, to think our news would stop His Majesty's ministers from acting in their usual incompetent manner. Hypotheses are not intelligence. Lord Dungarth would be pleased with the news, but not ecstatic. They will know of the Battle of Friedland in London in a day or so, if they do not already. There are other channels . . .' Again Drinkwater was confronted by that strange, ominous smile.

'Well,' expostulated Drinkwater, feeling his irritation returning, 'what *do* you suggest I do?'

'I know what we *should* do, Captain Drinkwater. The question is, *can* we do it?' Mackenzie's eyes closed to contemplative slits, his voice lowered. 'I am certain that there will be an armistice soon. The French dare not over-extend themselves; Napoleon must return to Paris; yet, if he withdraws, the Russians will follow like wolves. There *must* be an accommodation with the Tsar.'

'And will the Tsar agree to such a proposal, particularly as it reveals Boney in a position of weakness?'

Mackenzie chuckled. 'My dear Captain, you know nothing of Russia. There is one thing you must understand, she is an autocracy. What the Tsar wills, is. Alexander professes one thing and does another. The Tsar can be relied upon to be erratic.'

Drinkwater shook his head, still mystified. 'So what do you advise I do?'

'You already asked that question.'

'But you did not answer it.'

'We should eavesdrop on their conversation.'

'Whose?' asked Drinkwater frowning.

'Alexander's and Napoleon's.'

'Mr Mackenzie, I am sure that you are a tired man, that your recent excitement has exhausted you, but you can scarcely fail to notice that this is a ship of war, not an ear trumpet.'

'I know, I know Captain, it is only wishful thinking.' Mackenzie's eyes narrowed again. He was contemplating a scene of his imagination's making. 'But a frigate could take me to Memel, couldn't it?'

'Is that what you want?' asked Drinkwater, the prospect of returning Mackenzie to the shore a pleasing one at that moment. 'A passage to Memel?'

'Yes,' said Mackenzie, seeming to make up his mind. 'That and somewhere to sleep.'

Drinkwater nodded at his cot. 'Help yourself. I must get the ship under weigh and see the wounded.'

Picking up his hat Drinkwater left the cabin. Too tired to move suddenly Mackenzie stared after him. 'Captain Drinkwater,' he muttered, smiling to himself, 'Captain *Nathaniel* Drinkwater, by all that's holy . . .'

In the dark and foetid stink of the orlop deck Drinkwater picked his way forward. *Antigone* listed over, and down here, deep in her belly, Drinkwater could hear the rush of the sea past her stout wooden sides. Here, where the midshipmen and master's mates messed next to the marines above the hold, Lallo and his loblolly boys were plying their trade.

'How are they?' he asked, stepping into the circle of light above the struggling body of a seaman. Lallo did not look up but Skeete's evil leer was diabolical in the bizarre play of the lantern. Drinkwater peered round in the darkness, searching for Tregembo, one hand on the low deck beam overhead. The prone seaman groaned pitifully, the sweat standing out on his body like glass beads. His screams were muted to agonised grunts as he bit on the leather pad Skeete had forced into his mouth. With a twist and a jerk Lallo withdrew his hand, red from a wound in the man's thigh, and held a knife up to the dim light. The musket ball stuck on its point was intact. Lallo grunted his satisfaction as the man slipped into a merciful unconsciousness, and looked up at the captain.

'Mostly gunshot wounds . . . at long range . . . spent . . .'

'They came under fire getting out of the river. Where's Tregembo?'

With a grunt, as of stiff muscles, Lallo got to his feet and, stepping over the body that Skeete and his mate were dragging to a corner of the tiny space, he led Drinkwater forward to where Tregembo lay, half propped against a futtock. Drinkwater knelt down. Tregembo's shirt was torn aside and the white of the bandage showed in the mephitic gloom.

'A sabre thrust to the bone,' explained the surgeon. 'It would have been easier to clean had it been a cut. It is too high to amputate.'

'Amputate! God damn it, man, I sent particular word to you to ensure you debrided it.'

Lallo took the uncorked rum bottle that Skeete handed him and swigged from it.

'I took your kind advice, sir,' Lallo said with heavy irony, 'but, as I have just said, the wound is a deep one. I have done my best but . . .'

'Yes, yes, of course . . .'

Tregembo opened his eyes. He was already on the edge of fever, slipping in and out of semi-consciousness. He made an effort to focus his eyes on Drinkwater and began to speak, but the words were incomprehensible, and after a minute or two it was plain he was unaware of his surroundings. Drinkwater touched his arm. It was hot.

'The prognosis?' Drinkwater rose, stooping under the low deck-head.

Lallo shook his head. 'Not good, sir. Uncertain at best.'

'They spent a long time in the boat after the wounding.'

'Too long . . .' Lallo corked the rum bottle and wiped his mouth with the back of his hand.

'Mr Lallo, I will risk the chance of offending you by saying that, when I was a prisoner aboard the *Bucentaure*, I observed a method of dressing a wound that was considered highly effective.'

'A *French* method, sir?'

'Yes.'

'Humph!'

'Soak a pledget in sea-water or camphorated wine and add a few drops of lead acetate. D'you have any lead acetate? Good. Bind the wound firmly with a linen bandage in which holes have been cut. Do not disturb the dressing but have the purulent matter which seeps through the holes wiped away. A compress of the same type is bound tightly over the first dressing and changed daily.' Drinkwater looked at the men groaning at his feet. 'Try it, Mr Lallo, as I have directed . . . and perhaps you will have less need of rum.'

He turned and made for the ladder, leaving Lallo and Skeete staring after him. On deck the fresh air was unbelievably sweet.

Mackenzie woke among unfamiliar surroundings. He tried to get out of the cot and found it difficult. When he got his feet on the deck *Antigone* heeled a little, the cot swayed outboard and in getting out he fell, sending the cot swinging further. Disencumbered of his weight the cot swung back, fetching Mackenzie a blow on the back of the head.

'God!' He got to his feet and stood unsteadily, feeling the bile stirring in his gullet. Casting desperately about he recalled the privy and reached the door to the quarter-gallery just in time. After a little while he felt better, and being a self-reliant and resourceful man he diverted his mind from his guts to the matter in hand. He carefully crossed the cabin and stood braced at Drinkwater's table, staring down at the chart and the open pages of Mount's Military Atlas. The latter attracted his interest and he swiftly forgot his seasickness.

'By God, that's providential,' he murmured to himself. After a moment or two his curiosity and professional interest turned itself to Drinkwater's desk. The left-hand of its two drawers was slightly open. Mackenzie pulled it out and lifted Drinkwater's journal from it. He flicked the pages over and, on the page on which the neat script ceased, he noticed a strange entry in the margin. It consisted of a short word in Cyrillic script: НСЛ АНfi.

'So, I was right . . .'

'What the devil d'you think you're doing?'

Mackenzie looked up at Drinkwater standing in the doorway, his hat in his hand. He was quite unabashed.

'Is this how you abuse my hospitality?' Drinkwater advanced across the cabin, anger plain in his face. He confronted Mackenzie across the table; Mackenzie remained unruffled.

'Where did you come across this?' He pointed to the strange letters.

In his outrage Drinkwater had not seen exactly what Mackenzie had found. He had assumed the spy had been prying. Now the sudden emphasis Mackenzie put on those strangely exotic letters recalled to his mind his own, intensely personal reasons for having written them. He was briefly silent and then suddenly explosively angry.

'God damn you, Mackenzie, you presume too much! That is a private journal! It has nothing to do with you!'

'Be calm, Captain,' Mackenzie said, continuing in a reasonable tone, 'You are wrong, it has everything to do with me. What do these Russian letters mean? Do you know? Where did you learn them?'

'What is that to you?'

'Captain, don't play games. You are out of your depth. This word and the hand that wrote it are known to me.' He paused and looked up. 'Do you know what these Cyrillic letters mean?'

Drinkwater sank back into the chair opposite to his usual one, the chair reserved for visitors to his cabin, so that their roles were again reversed. He shook his head.

'If you transpose each of these letters with its Roman equivalent you spell the word *island*.'

Drinkwater shook his head. 'I do not understand.'

'If you then translate the word *island* back into Russian, you have the word *Ostroff*. It is a passably Russian-sounding name, isn't it?'

Drinkwater shrugged, 'I suppose so.'

'Do you know who *Ostroff* is?'

'I haven't the remotest idea.'

'Oh, come, Captain,' Mackenzie remonstrated disbelievingly.

111

'You went to the trouble of making a note of his name and in a book that was personally significant.'

'Mr Mackenzie,' Drinkwater said severely, 'I do not know what you are implying, but you have obviously invaded my privacy!'

But Drinkwater's anger was not entirely directed at Mackenzie, furious though he was at the man's effrontery. There *had* been a reason why he had noted that incomprehensible Russian lettering down in his journal; and though he did not know who Ostroff was, he had his suspicions. He resolved to clear the matter up and settle the doubts that had been provoked by the sight of Nielsen's dispatch.

'Who the devil *is* this Ostroff then?'

Mackenzie smiled that tight, menacing smile, and Drinkwater sensed he knew more than he was saying. 'A spy. An agent in the Russian army. And now perhaps you will trade one confidence for another. Where did you get these letters from? Are you in correspondence with this man?'

Drinkwater's heart was thumping. Mackenzie's words closed the gap between speculation and certainty.

'From a dispatch intercepted in the possession of a Danish merchantman which I stopped a week or two ago.'

'What was the name of the ship?'

'The *Birthe* of Grenaa, Captain . . .'

'Nielsen?' interrupted Mackenzie.

'Yes. Frederic Nielsen.'

'And what did you do with Nielsen and his dispatch?'

'I let him go with it. I was satisfied that he and it were what they said they were.'

'But you copied out the name by which the dispatch was signed?'

'Yes.'

'Why?'

Drinkwater shrugged.

'Captain, you say you were sure of the authenticity of a dispatch carried by a neutral and you let the vessel go. Yet you were not sure enough not to note down the signatory. Odd, don't you think? Where was the dispatch bound?'

'I do not think that a proper question to answer, Mackenzie. I am not sure I should be answering any of these questions. I am not sure I ought not to have you in irons . . .'

'Captain,' said Mackenzie in a suddenly menacing tone, 'mine is a dangerous trade in which I trust no one. I am curious as to whom you thought this man was; why you copied out this signature. It is almost inconceivable that any obviously trusted servant of their Lordships of the Admiralty should behave traitorously . . .'

Drinkwater was on his feet and had leaned across the table. He spat the words through clenched teeth, beside himself with rage:

'How dare you, you bastard! You have no right to come aboard here and make such accusations! Who the hell are you to accuse me of treason? Get out of my seat! You stand *here* and make *your* report to *me*, before I have this ship put about for The Sound and confine you in the bilboes!'

'By God, Captain, I apologise . . . I see I have misjudged you.' Mackenzie stood and confronted Drinkwater. 'I think you have reassured me on that point at least . . .'

'Have a care . . .'

'Captain, you *must* hear me out. It is a matter of the utmost importance, I assure you. I know you have had previous contact with Lord Dungarth's Secret Department; I assume from what you implied earlier that you have some freedom in the interpretation of your orders, perhaps from his Lordship. I also assume that you let Frederic Nielsen proceed because he had a dispatch addressed to Joseph Devlieghere at Antwerp . . . Ah, I see you find that reassuring . . . Tell me, Captain, did you ever know a man called Brown?'

'I saw the Dutch hang him at Kijkduin.'

'And do you think the Dutch were responsible?'

Drinkwater looked sharply at Mackenzie, but he did not answer.

'Come, Captain, have you not come across a French agent named Edouard Santhonax?'

Drinkwater strode across the cabin, pulled out his sea-chest and from it drew a roll of frayed canvas. He unrolled it.

'Identify this lady and I'll believe you are who you say you are.'

'Good God!' Mackenzie stared at the cracking paint. The portrait showed a young woman with auburn hair piled upon her head. Pearls were entwined in the contrived negligence of her classical coiffure. Her creamy shoulders were bare and her breasts just visible beneath a wisp of gauze. Her grey eyes looked coolly out of the canvas and there was a hint of a smile about the corners of her lovely mouth. 'Hortense Santhonax, by heaven!'

'A celebrated beauty, as all Paris knows.'

'Where the devil did you get it?'

Drinkwater nodded at the portrait of Elizabeth that had not been done with half as much skill as that of Madame Santhonax. 'It used to hang there. This ship, Mr Mackenzie, was once commanded by

113

Edouard Santhonax when she was captured in the Red Sea. I was one of the party who took her.' He rolled up the portrait. 'I kept it as a memento. You see, I rescued Madame Santhonax from a Jacobin mob in ninety-two . . . before she turned her coat. She was eventually taken back to France. I was on the beach with Lord Dungarth when we released her . . .'

'And he didn't shoot her,' put in Mackenzie, shaking his head. 'Yes, he has told me the story.' He looked about him. 'It's incredible . . . this ship . . . you. Captain, I am sorry, I acted hastily. Please accept my apologies.'

'Very well. It is of no matter. I think you have provided proof of your identity. We had better sink our differences in a glass of wine.'

'That is a capital idea.' Mackenzie smiled and, for the first time since meeting him, Drinkwater felt less menaced, more in control of the situation. He poured the two drinks and behind him he heard Mackenzie mutter 'Incredible' to himself.

'This man Ostroff,' said Drinkwater conversationally, seating himself in his proper place at last, 'is he of importance to you?'

'He will be invaluable if my hypothesis proves accurate.'

'You mean if an armistice is concluded between Alexander and Napoleon?'

'Yes. Whatever terms are agreed upon, they will clearly be prejudicial to Britain. Ostroff is the one man in a position to learn them. Now, with the loss of Königsberg, Ostroff's communications are cut. The situation is serious but not fatal. We still have access to Memel, at least until the two Emperors meet, hence my request that you carry me there. You see, I am Ostroff's post-boy. I forwarded his dispatch through Nielsen.'

'You . . . you know him well then, this Ostroff?' Drinkwater's heart was thumping again; he felt foolishly vulnerable, although Mackenzie's manner towards him had so drastically altered.

'Oh yes, I know him, Captain Drinkwater. That is why I could not understand your attitude.'

'I do not understand you.'

Mackenzie frowned. 'You mean you really do not know who Ostroff is?'

'No,' he said, but he felt that his voice lacked conviction.

'You share the same surname, Captain Drinkwater . . .'

The blood left Drinkwater's face. So, he had been right! Despite the cipher, despite the years that had passed, he *had* recognised the hand that had penned Nielsen's dispatch.

114

'So Ostroff is my brother Edward,' he said flatly.

'It is a chain of the most remarkable coincidences, Captain,' said Mackenzie.

'Not at all,' replied Drinkwater wearily, rising and fetching the decanter from its lodgement in the fiddle. 'It is merely evidence of the workings of providence, Mr Mackenzie, which rules all our fates, including those of Napoleon and Alexander.'

The Mad Enterprise

'How did you discover the connection between us?' Drinkwater asked at last, after the two men had sat in silence awhile. 'I understood my brother to be living under a *nom de guerre.*'

'Oh, it isn't common knowledge, Captain Drinkwater; you need have no fear that more than a few men know about it. Dungarth does, of course, and Prince Vorontzoff, your brother's employer and a man sympathetic to the alliance with Great Britain, knows him for an Englishman. But I think I am the only other man who knows his identity, excepting yourself, of course.'

'But you have not said how you knew.'

'It is quite simple. He told me once. He was sent to me from Hamburg. I introduced him to the elder Vorontzoff and, one night, shortly before I left St Petersburg, we got drunk . . . a Russian custom, you see,' Mackenzie said and Drinkwater thought that Mackenzie had probably ensured Edward's loose tongue by his own liberality. 'He had reached a turning-point. A man does not put off the old life overnight and he seemed over-burdened with conscience. He made some thick allusions to drinking water. The joke was too heavy for wit and he was too drunk to jest, yet his persistence made me certain the words had some significance . . . but it was only when I learned your name from Lieutenant . . .'

'Quilhampton.'

'Just so, that I began to recall Ostroff's drunken pun. Then, having had my professional curiosity aroused, I felt it was necessary to,' Mackenzie shrugged with an irresponsible smile, 'to invade your privacy, I think you said. And my effrontery was rewarded; you had inscribed Ostroff's Russian signature in your journal. *Quod erat demonstrandum.*'

'I see.' It was very strange, but Drinkwater felt an enormous weight lifted from him. Somehow he had known for years that he must atone for his own crime of aiding and abetting Edward's escape from the gallows. It was easy to excuse his actions, to disguise his motives under the cant of reasons of state. The truth was that his own rectitude made him feel guilty. Edward was a man who drifted like a straw upon the tide and who, through some strange working of natural laws, managed to float to the surface in all circumstances. To Edward, and probably Mackenzie, his own misgivings would seem utterly foolish. But he knew himself to be of a different type, a man whose life had been dogged by set-backs, wounds and hardships. Perhaps the atonement would still come, but he could not deny the relief at Edward's identity no longer being quite so hermetic a secret.

He looked at Mackenzie. A few moments earlier he had been ready to consign the man to the devil. Now they sat like old friends sipping their wine, bound by the common knowledge of Ostroff's true identity. It occurred to Drinkwater that, yet again, Mackenzie had a superior hold over him; but he found the knowledge no longer made him angry.

'I knew my brother to have found employment with Prince Vorontzoff, on account of his abilities with horses, but I do not fully understand how he serves you and Lord Dungarth.'

'He is a brilliant horseman, I believe, and on account of this he formed a close friendship with Vorontzoff's son. Good horsemen are much admired in Russia and the younger Vorontzoff, being appointed to the army in the field, got some sort of commission for Ostroff. That sort of thing is not difficult in the Tsar's bureaucracy. Ostroff was at Austerlitz and attached to the Don Cossacks at Eylau, though what he has been up to lately I do not know. I was trying to make contact with him and Wilson when I was chased into Königsberg by those French dragoons.'

'And now you want to make another attempt at reaching him through Memel?'

'Yes. And I would wish you to wait there for my return.'

'And then convey you to London with all dispatch?'

'I see, at last, that we are of one mind, Captain Drinkwater,' Mackenzie smiled.

'Then we had better drink to it,' Drinkwater said, rising and fetching the decanter.

'A capital idea,' replied Mackenzie, holding out his glass.

Drinkwater woke sweating and staring into the darkness, trying to place the source of the wild laughter. He had been dreaming, a nightmare of terrifying reality, in which a white-clothed figure loomed over him to the sound of clanking chains. The figure had been that of Hortense Santhonax, her beauty hideously transformed. The Medusa head had laughed in his face and he had seemed to drown below her, struggling helplessly as the laughter grew and the breath was squeezed from his lungs.

In the darkness of the cabin, surrounded by the familiar creaking of *Antigone*, he found the laughter resolve itself into a knocking at the cabin door. He pulled himself together. 'Enter!'

'It's Frey, sir.' The midshipman's slight figure showed in the gloom. 'Mr Quilhampton's compliments, sir, and we've raised Memel light.'

'Very well. I'll be up shortly.'

Frey disappeared and he lay back in the cot, seeking a few minutes of peace. The nightmare was an old one but had not lost its potency. Usually he attached it to presentiment or times of extreme anxiety, but this morning he managed to smile at himself for a fool. It was the unburdening of the secret of Edward that had brought on the dream; a retrospective abstraction haunting his isolated imagination while he slept.

'Damn fool,' he chid himself and, flinging back the blankets, threw his legs over the edge of the cot. Five minutes later he was on deck.

'Mornin', Mr Q.'

'Morning, sir. Memel light three leagues distant, sir.' Quilhampton pointed and Drinkwater saw the orange glow. 'It's supposed to rival the full moon at a league, sir.'

'I'm pleased to see you have been studying the rutter, Mr Q,' said Drinkwater drily, amused at Quilhampton.

'To be fair, sir, it's Frey who has studied the rutter. I merely picked his brains.'

'Tch, tch. Most reprehensible,' Drinkwater laughed. 'Incidentally, Mr Q, I will want you to put our guest ashore later.'

'Mr Mackenzie, sir?'

'Yes.'

Drinkwater could almost hear Quilhampton's curiosity working. He considered the wisdom of revealing something of Mackenzie's purpose. On balance, he considered, it would not hurt. It was better to reveal a half-truth than risk stupid speculation growing wild. He had known a silly rumour started on the quarterdeck reach the fo'c's'le as a hardened fact magnified twentyfold. It had caused a deal of resentment among the hands, and even a denial by the first lieutenant had failed to extinguish it. The old saw about there being no smoke without fire was murmured by men starved of any news, whose days were governed by the whims of the weather and the denizens of the quarterdeck, and by whom any remark that intimated yet greater impositions upon them was accepted without question. In the end it was better that the people knew something of what was going on.

'I expect you are wondering exactly who, or what, Mr Mackenzie is, eh, James?'

'Well, sir, the thought had crossed my mind.'

'And not just yours, I'll warrant.'

'No, sir.'

'He's an agent, Mr Q, like some of those mysterious johnnies we picked up in the Channel a year or two ago. We shall put him ashore in order that he can find out what exactly the Russians are going to do after Boney beat 'em at Friedland.'

'I see, sir. Thank you.'

Drinkwater fell to pacing the quarterdeck as, in the east, the light grew and the masts, rigging and sails began to stand out blackly against the lightening sky. By the time the people went to their messes for breakfast they would know all about Mr Mackenzie.

A few hours later the barge was swung out and lowered as, with her main-topsail against the mast, *Antigone* hove to. It was a bright summer morning and the port of Memel with its conspicuous lighthouse was no more than four miles away. Mackenzie came aft to make his farewells.

'I rely upon you to cruise hereabouts until my return, Captain,' he said.

'I shall maintain station, Mr Mackenzie; you may rely upon it. I may chase a neutral or two for amusement,' Drinkwater replied, 'but my main occupation will be to ensure the ship is in a fit state for a swift passage home.'

Beyond Mackenzie, Drinkwater saw the word 'home' had been caught by a seaman coiling down a line. That, too, would not hurt. It would brighten the men's spirits to know the ship was destined for a British port.

'Do you wish me to keep a boat at Memel to await you, Mr Mackenzie?'

'No, I think not, Captain. In view of the possible results of our . . . hypothesis, I think it unwise. I can doubtless bribe a fishing boat to bring me off.' He smiled. The cupidity of fishermen was universal.

Mackenzie held out his hand and moved half a pace nearer. 'Do you have a message for Ostroff?' he asked in a low voice.

'Yes . . . wish him well for me, Mackenzie . . . and ask him if he is still afraid of the dark.'

Mackenzie laughed. 'He does not strike me as a man who might be afraid of the dark, Captain.'

Drinkwater grinned back. 'Perhaps not; but he was once. Good luck, Mackenzie.'

'*A bientôt*, Captain . . .'

For two days Drinkwater kept *Antigone* under weigh. He was merciless to the entire crew, officers and men alike. The British frigate stood on and off the land, first under easy sail and then setting every stitch of canvas she possessed. When ropes parted or jammed, he chastised the petty officers and midshipmen responsible with verbal lashings from the windward hance. It brought him a deep inner satisfaction, for junior officers were rarely blamed for the many small things that went wrong on board. They buried such failings more often than not by starting the unfortunate hands, a practice that usually assuaged the quarterdeck officers. Midshipmen had the worst name for these minor malpractices which caused such resentment among the men, and it did them good to be chased hither and thither and called to account for their failures in full view of the ship's company.

As the studdingsails rose and set for the eighth or ninth time, as the topgallant masts were struck and the yards sent down, the men worked with a will, seeing how at every misfortune it was a midshipman, a master's mate or a petty officer that was identified as being the culprit. The hands were in high glee for, with the captain on deck throughout the manoeuvres, there was little revengeful starting carried out by the bosun's mates who well knew Drinkwater's aversion to the practice. It was one thing to start men aloft in an emergency or when faced with the enemy, when the need to manoeuvre was paramount; but quite another to do it when the ship was being put through her paces.

Even the officers bore their share of Drinkwater's strange behaviour, Rogers, as first lieutenant, in particular. But he bore it well, submitting to it as though to a test of his recovery. At the end of the second day, as the men secured the guns from a final practice drill, Drinkwater pronounced himself satisfied, ordered a double ration of three-water grog served out to all hands and brought the ship to anchor a league from Memel light.

'Well, Mr Rogers, I think the ship will make a fast passage when she is called upon to do so, don't you?'

'Yes, sir. But a passage where, sir?' asked Rogers, puzzled.

'Well, if we get the right slant of wind, we shall make for London River!'

Rogers's smile was unalloyed. 'Hell's teeth, that's good news. May I ask when that might be?'

'When Mr Mackenzie returns, Sam, when Mr Mackenzie returns.'

Mr Mackenzie returned shortly before noon three days later, hailing them from the deck of a fishing boat and obviously in a state of high excitement. Drinkwater was on deck to meet him and found Mackenzie had lost his air of cool self-possession. His dust-stained clothes flapping about him, he strode across the deck, his face lined with dirt which gave its expression a compulsive ferocity.

'Captain, your cabin at once,' he seemed breathless, for all that he must have been inactive during the boat's passage.

'Prepare to get under weigh, Mr Rogers,' Drinkwater ordered, turning towards Mackenzie, but the agent shook his head.

'No . . . not yet. There is something we must attend to first. Come, Captain, every second counts!'

Drinkwater shrugged at the first lieutenant. 'Belay that, Mr Rogers. Come then, Mr Mackenzie.' He led the way below and Mackenzie collapsed into a chair. Pouring two glasses of blackstrap Drinkwater handed one to the exhausted agent. 'Here, drink this and then tell me what has happened.'

Mackenzie tossed off the glass, wiped a hand across his mouth and stared at Drinkwater with eyes that glittered from red-rimmed sockets.

'Captain,' began Mackenzie, 'I need you to come with me. I have returned to persuade you. It is imperative. It is a mad enterprise, but one on which everything hangs.'

'Everything?' Drinkwater frowned uncertainly.

'Yes, everything,' Mackenzie insisted, 'perhaps the history of Europe. You are the one man who can help!'

'But I am a sea-officer, not a spy!'

Drinkwater's protest roused Mackenzie. 'It is precisely because you are a sea-officer that we need you . . . Ostroff and I. You see, Captain Drinkwater, my hypothesis has proved correct. Napoleon and Alexander are to meet in conditions of the greatest secrecy, and to gain access we need a seaman's skills.'

The British spy made out a desperate case for Drinkwater's help and he had to concede the justice of the argument. What Mackenzie demanded was incontrovertibly within the latitude of Dungarth's special instructions. Whatever the bureaucrats at the Admiralty might think of him leaving his ship, he felt he was covered by Lord Dungarth's cryptic order: *You should afford any assistance required by persons operating on the instructions of this Department.* Now he knew why the old, recurring dream had woken him 'a few mornings before; he had felt a presentiment and he knew the moment for full atonement had come.

'Damn these metaphysics,' he growled, and turned his mind to more practical matters.

Mackenzie had suggested they took a third person, someone with a competent knowledge of horses, for they had far to travel, yet one who would play up to the fiction of Mackenzie masquerading as a merchant and Drinkwater as the master of an English trading vessel lying in Memel. For this there was only one candidate, Midshipman Lord Walmsley, the only one of *Antigone*'s people who was familiar with horses, and who spoke French into the bargain. His lordship showed a gratifying willingness to volunteer for a 'secret mission' and was ordered to remove the white patches from his coat collar and to dress plainly. His preparations in the cockpit spread a sensational rumour throughout the ship.

For himself Drinkwater begged a plain blue coat from Hill, leaving behind his sword with the lion-headed pommel that betrayed his commissioned status. Instead he packed pistols, powder and ball in a valise together with his shaving tackle and a change of small clothes.

'You will not need to worry about being conspicuous,' Mackenzie had yawned, 'the countryside is alive with travellers all going wide-eyed to see their little father the Tsar meet the hideous monster Napoleon.'

The hours of the afternoon rushed by. He had left instructions with Quilhampton to execute his will should he fail to return, and had attempted to write to Elizabeth but gave the matter up, for his heart was too full to trust to paper. Instead he went to the orlop to see Tregembo who was recovering well, and passed on a brief message to be given in the event of his disappearance. It was inadequate and ambiguous, but it was all he could do.

'I wish I could come with 'ee, zur,' the old man had said, half rising from the grubby palliasse upon which he lay. Drinkwater had patted his unhurt shoulder.

'You be a good fellow and get better.'

'And you look after yourself, boy,' Tregembo had said with a fierce and possessive familiarity that brought a sudden smile to Drinkwater's preoccupied face.

Finally, he had written his orders to Rogers, placing him in temporary command. Should he fail to return within ten days, Rogers was to open a second envelope which informed their Lordships of the state of affairs Mackenzie had so far discovered and his own reasons for leaving his ship. As the dog-watches changed, Mackenzie woke, and half an hour later they left the ship.

Lieutenant Quilhampton commanded the boat, making his second trip to Memel to land agents and scarcely imagining why the captain found it necessary to desert them like this. The mood in the boat was one of silent introspection as each man contemplated the future. Drinkwater and Mackenzie considered the problems ahead of them while James Quilhampton and the oarsmen gazed outboard and wondered what it would be like to be under the orders of Samuel Rogers. The only light heart among them was Lord Walmsley who had a thirst for an adventurous lark.

The long northern twilight offered them no concealment as they pulled into the river, past the lighthouse tower and its fire. The quays of Memel were still busy with fishing boats unloading their catches. Drinkwater tried to assume the character of Young, master of the *Jenny Marsden*, as typifying the kind of man he was trying to ape. He tried to recall the jargon of the merchant mariners, mentally repeating their strange terms in time with the oars as they knocked against the thole-pins: loss and demurrage; barratry and bottomry; pratique and protest; lagan and lien, jetsam and jerque notes, flotsam and indemnity. It was a bewildering vocabulary of which he had an imperfect knowledge, but in the event there were no Custom House officers to test him and with a feeling of anti-climax Drinkwater followed Mackenzie up a flight of slippery stone steps onto the quay, with Walmsley bringing up the rear.

There were no farewells. Quilhampton shoved the tiller over and the bowman bore off. Ten minutes after approaching the quay the barge was slipping seawards in the gathering darkness. Quilhampton did not look back. He felt an overwhelming sense of desolation: Drinkwater had deserted them and they were now to be subject to the arbitrary rule of Samuel Rogers.

Lieutenant Samuel Rogers sat alone at the captain's desk. His eyes looked down at the table-top. It was clear of papers, clear of Mount's long-borrowed Military Atlas, clear of everything except a key. It was a large, steel key, such as operated a lock with four tumblers. A wooden tag was attached to it and bore the legend: SPIRIT ROOM.

Rogers stared at the key for a long time. He was filled with a sense of power quite unattached to the fact that he was now in effective command of the *Antigone*. This was something else, something strange stirring in a brain already damaged by alcohol and the horrible experience of being lashed in a strait-jacket. Rogers was quite unable to blame himself for his addiction. He blamed fate and bad luck and, in a way, that obligation to Drinkwater which had become a form of jealousy. And Lallo's justification for his treatment had rested on Drinkwater's own instructions. He had been 'confined quietly' . . . the meaning was obvious. That it had been done for his own good, Rogers did not dispute. Disagreeable things were frequently done for one's own good and a streak of childishness surfaced in him. Perhaps it was a weakness of his character, perhaps a by-product of his recent chronic alcoholism, but it was to darken his mind in the following days, worsened by the isolation Drinkwater's absence had placed him in and the position of trust that he now occupied. That, too, was attributable to Drinkwater, and it was this sense of being in his place and having to act in his stead that suffused Rogers with an extraordinary sense of power. In this peculiar and unbalanced consummation of a long aggrieved and corrosive jealousy, Rogers found the will to reject his demon.

With a sweep of his hand he sent the spirit room key clattering into a dark corner of the cabin.

PART TWO

The Raft

"I hate the English as much as you do!"

Alexander to Napoleon, 25 June 1807

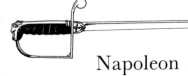

Napoleon

General Edouard Santhonax, aide-de-camp to His Imperial Majesty Napoleon, Emperor of the French and Commander-in-Chief of the Grand Army, completed his verbal report. He watched his master pace slowly up and down the beaten earth floor of the low wayside inn which was serving briefly as Imperial Headquarters. The Emperor's polished half-boots creaked slightly as he walked between the two crude tables and their attendant benches at which sat his secretaries and crop-headed Marshal Berthier, the Grand Army's Chief-of-Staff. Their heads were bent over piles of documents taken from dispatch boxes.

The Emperor was dressed in the dark green undress uniform coat of the Horse Chasseurs of the Guard and his plump hands were clasped in the small of his back. He spun round at the end of the tavern, his head bowed, the fine brown hair swept forward in a cow-lick over the broad forehead. He paced back, towards the waiting Santhonax.

Santhonax stood silently, his plumed hat beneath his arm, the gold lace on his blue coat a contrast to the Emperor's unostentatious uniform. Napoleon stopped his pacing a foot in front of the tall officer and looked up into Santhonax's eyes.

'So, my General, we have an emissary from the Tsar, eh?'

'That is so, Sire. He waits for your command outside.'

Napoleon's face suddenly relaxed into a charming smile. His right hand was raised from behind his back and pinched the left cheek of General Santhonax, where a livid scar ran upwards from the corner of his mouth.

'You have done well, *mon brave.*'

'Thank you, Sire.'

Napoleon turned aside to where a map lay spread on the rough grey wood of the table. He laid a plump finger on the map where a blue line wound across rolling country.

'Tilsit.'

A shadow of hatching lay under the ball of the Emperor's finger, indicating the existence of a town that straddled the River Nieman.

'You say the bridge is down?'

Santhonax stepped forward beside the Emperor. 'That is so, Sire, but there are boats and barges, and the transit of the river is not difficult.'

'And you are certain that Alexander seeks an armistice, eh?'

'That is what I was led to believe, Sire.'

The Emperor hung his head for a moment in thought. At the end of the table Berthier stopped writing, pushed aside a paper and sat poised, as though sensing his master was about to dictate new movements to the Grand Army. A silence hung in the long, low room, disturbed only by the scratching of the secretaries' pens and the buzzing of a pair of flies in the small window of the inn, for the June heat was oppressive.

'Very well!' The Emperor made up his mind and began to pace again, more rapidly than before. Santhonax stepped back to make way for him.

'Write, Berthier, write! The town of Tilsit is to be declared a neutral zone. On the acceptance of our terms by the Tsar, orders are to be passed to the advance units of the Grand Army that have already crossed the Nieman, that they are to retire behind the line of that river. An armistice is to be declared. General Lariboissière of the Engineers is to requisition boats and to construct a pontoon or raft surmounted by pavilions, two in number, one to accommodate their Imperial Majesties, the other their staffs.' The Emperor paused and looked at Santhonax.

'It is fortunate, General, that you were formerly a frigate-captain. We shall put your maritime expertise to good account.' Napoleon smiled, as if pleased at some private joke, then he addressed himself to Berthier again. 'General Santhonax is to liaise with General Lariboissière as to the method of mooring this raft in midstream and to be responsible for the complete security and secrecy of the meeting between ourself and the Tsar.'

The Emperor swung suddenly round on Santhonax and his eyes were ice-cold.

'Is that clearly understood, my General? Secret, utterly secret.'

'Perfectly, Sire.'

'The Russian court is a sink of iniquitous intrigue, General Santhonax, a fact which should be uppermost in your mind.' The

Emperor's mood had mellowed again; he seemed suddenly in an almost boyish good humour.

'Of course, Sire,' replied Santhonax dutifully.

'Very good! Now you may show in this Russian popinjay and let us set about the wooing of Alexander!'

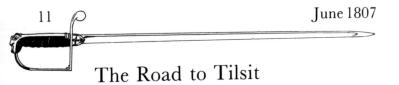

The Road to Tilsit

Captain Drinkwater woke from a deep sleep confused and disoriented. For several moments he did not know where he was. The unfamiliar smell of his bedding, the white-washed ceiling and the chirruping of sparrows outside the small window all served to perplex him. Slowly he recalled the rapid train of events that had taken place since they landed from the barge and took their unceremonious farewell of Quilhampton.

Led in silence by Mackenzie, Drinkwater and Walmsley had walked swiftly into a maze of small, narrow streets reminiscent of an earlier age, with overhanging buildings and rickety roofs. Despite a lingering light in the sky, the omnipresence of the shuttered houses threw them into darkness as they followed the spy. Then abruptly they stopped and Mackenzie knocked imperiously on a nail-studded door. After a moment it opened, there was a quick exchange of what Drinkwater took for sign and counter-sign, and then he and Walmsley were drawn inside, the door was closed behind them and they stood in a large, partially lit room, their presence and necessities being explained by Mackenzie to the occupant of the house. A sense of curiosity filled Drinkwater. The street smells of Memel had been odd enough, but those of the house seemed almost diabolical and this impression was heightened by what he could see of the room. Low and overhung with beams, it was largely lined by shelves, drawers and cupboards. On the drawers he could see vaguely familiar lettering and in the cupboards, behind glass, the owner's lantern shed highlights on jars and sorcerers' retorts. On the shelves, however, were even more sinister exhibits: a monstrous foetus, a coiled snake and a diminutive mermaid. Beside him he felt Walmsley shudder with apprehension and utter a low expression of repulsion. Drinkwater recognised the lettering on the little wooden drawers as the abbreviated Latin of the Pharmacopoeia.

'We are the guests of an apothecary, I believe,' Drinkwater

whispered to the midshipman. Both men were fascinated by the ugly mermaid whose wrinkled, simian face stared at them, the dancing light of the lantern flame reflected from her glass pupils.

Mackenzie and their host turned at this moment. 'Ah, so you like my little mermaid do you, gentlemen?' The apothecary was of middle age and held the lantern for them to see the piece of cunning taxidermy. His accent was thickly Germanic, but his command of English appeared good. Mackenzie smiled.

'Well, gentlemen, our host will show you to your rooms. It is already late. I advise you to retire immediately. I have some business to attend to and we must make good progress tomorrow.'

There were no introductions and in silence Drinkwater and Walmsley followed the apothecary to an attic bedroom where two low beds were prepared by a silent and pretty blonde girl with a plait like a bell-rope down her back. The two Englishmen stood awkwardly with the apothecary while the girl bustled about. Then, as she left, he gestured to the beds.

'Thank you,' Drinkwater said. The man bowed and withdrew. Mackenzie had already disappeared and as the door closed Drinkwater heard the lock turned. 'It seems we are prisoners for the night, Mr Walmsley,' he remarked with an attempt at a reassurance he was far from feeling. To his surprise Walmsley grinned back.

'Perhaps it's just as well, sir.'

'Eh?' Drinkwater was puzzled, then he remembered the blue eyes of the girl and her last, frankly curious glance as she bobbed from the room. 'Ah, yes . . . well, I think we must sleep now.' And despite his misgivings, despite a gnawing reaction of having deserted his post, Drinkwater had fallen into a deep, dreamless and wonderful slumber.

His confusion on waking was less comforting. He lay for a long time wondering if he had made the right decision in leaving *Antigone*; his thoughts alternated in a wild oscillation between a patient argument in favour of co-operating with the mysterious Mr Mackenzie, and a swift panic that he had acted with insanely foolish impetuosity. In the opposite corner Midshipman Lord Walmsley still snored peacefully, sublimely unconcerned and probably dreaming of the blonde girl.

There was a sudden grating in the lock and the door opened. The apothecary came in and wished them good morning. The girl followed, a tray in her pink hands from which coffee, fresh bread and a species of black sausage sent up a pungent and appetising aroma. Drinkwater saw Walmsley stir and open his eyes. He looked at the pretty face, smiled and sat up.

'Herr Mackenzie requests that you be ready in half an hour, gentlemen,' the apothecary said, then chivvied the girl out and closed the door.

'I will shave while you pour the coffee,' Drinkwater said in an attempt to preserve a little of the quarterdeck dignity in the awkward and enforced intimacy with the midshipman. While this curious little ritual was in progress Mackenzie made his appearance.

'Good morning, gentlemen. You must forgive me for having deserted you last night. There were certain arrangements to make.'

He waited for the two naval officers to complete their preparations and when they were both ready said, 'Now, gentlemen, when we leave here we assume our new identities. I am a merchant, a Scotsman named Macdonald. You, Captain, are a merchant master. I leave you to choose your own name and that of your ship. Mr Smith here', he nodded at Walmsley, 'is a junior mate. I have a chaise below.' He smiled at Drinkwater, 'by great good fortune you are not compelled to ride. Lord Leveson-Gower arrived here last night. He is no longer persona grata at the Tsar's court. Fortunately the chaise he used for amusing himself in St Petersburg bears no arms. I have the use of it.' He made a gesture to indicate the door. 'Come, we must be off. We have twenty leagues to cover before night.'

They clattered down the stairs and emerged into the apothecary's room which looked less terrifying in the daylight that slanted in through the narrow windows. The mermaid was revealed as a hybrid sham, a curiosity of the taxidermist's art designed to over-awe the ignorance of the apothecary's customers. They passed through into the street.

'The box please, Smith.' Mackenzie nodded Walmsley to the driver's seat and opened the door of the chaise for Drinkwater. 'A steady pace,' he said to the midshipman. 'We don't want the horses blown.'

Walmsley nodded and vaulted up onto the seat. Drinkwater climbed in and settled himself. Mackenzie lifted their meagre baggage in with them and then climbed in himself. He tapped Walmsley's shoulder and the chaise jerked into motion. Drinkwater turned to take his farewell of the apothecary, but the studded door was already closed. Only a small, pretty, blue-eyed face watched their departure from a window.

For the first quarter of an hour Drinkwater attended to the business of settling himself in comfort as the chaise moved over the uneven road. Mackenzie was kneeling up on the front seat, giving the midshipman directions as they drove the equipage through the narrow streets, round innumerable corners and out onto what passed in Lithuanian Kurland for a highway.

'A sea of mud in the autumn, a waste of ice and snow in winter, a mass of ruts in the spring and a damnable dust-bowl at this time of the year,' explained Mackenzie at last, 'like every damned road in the Tsar's empire.'

In the June heat the dust clouds rose from the horses' hooves and engulfed the chaise so that Drinkwater's view of the countryside was through a haze. The road ran parallel to the wide and shining expanse of the Kurische Haff, the huge lagoon which formed the ponded-back estuary of the Nieman. On either side, slightly below the level of the highway, the marshy grassland was grazed by cattle.

'A somewhat monotonous landscape, Captain,' observed Mackenzie conversationally, 'but I assure you, you are seeing it at its best.'

'You know it well?' prompted Drinkwater, enforced leisure making him anxious to discuss with Mackenzie more than the appearance of the hinterland of Memel.

Mackenzie, with an infuriating evasion, ignored the question. 'I believe that it was the great Frenchman De Saxe that wanted this country for his own. A bastard aspiring to a dukedom, eh? And now, in our modern world, we have an attorney's son aspiring to an empire . . . That, my dear Captain, is progress.'

'He has done more than aspire, if what you are saying is true.'

'You prefer "acquire" then?'

'It would be more accurate . . . Mackenzie.'

'Macdonald.'

'Macdonald, then. This chaise, you say it belongs to our ambassador, Lord Leveson-Gower, and that he arrived in Memel last night?'

'Yes. The Tsar let it be known that his lordship was no longer welcome about his Imperial Majesty's person. He confirms what I had already learned, that emissaries have been received with every appearance of cordiality from French Headquarters and that Prince Czartoryski has left for a preliminary interview with the French Emperor to arrange a secret meeting.'

'So your worst fears are indeed justified.'

Mackenzie nodded. 'And now we have the leisure, I can offer you a full explanation of what has happened, and how your help is essential.'

'Anything that lessens my doubts about the folly of this journey would be welcome,' said Drinkwater grimly, suddenly clutching at the side of the chaise as it heeled over, its offside wheels running off the road while they overtook a heavily laden ox-cart trundling slowly along. He gestured at the pair of plodding peasants who trudged at the head of the team and the man and woman who sat on the cart.

'I am still unconvinced about your lack of secrecy,' he said frowning. 'I am at a loss . . .'

Mackenzie laughed. 'This business of spying', he said, still smiling, 'is not always a matter of cloaks and daggers. I move about quite openly for the most part. For me the subterfuge of disguise is of little use. I am well known in high places in Russia. The Tsar himself might recognise me, for I have served in the Caucasus with a commission from himself.'

Mackenzie's eyes drifted off, over the flat landscape that was such a contrast to the precipitous peaks of those distant mountains. 'General Bennigsen knows me too. In fact we shall be sharing lodgings with him.'

'Good Lord!'

'Let me explain, Captain. There is no hurry, we have a long way to go. To allay your fears of being discovered you will observe before we go very much further that the whole country is turning out. Tilsit, the town on the Nieman whither we are bound, is attracting all the country gentry for miles about. It has been declared a neutral zone and will be seething with soldiers and squires by tonight. It was already filling when I left. Nothing like this has happened in this backwater since De Saxe came to Mitau to wrest Kurland from the Tsars. We shall be like a drop in the ocean. Sometimes a bold front is the best concealment.' He nodded at Walmsley's back. 'I have told our young friend there to cluck to his horses in French, and am glad that he knows enough of the tongue to manage tolerably well.'

'You think of everything.'

'It is my business to. Now, as for me, I proceeded directly towards Tilsit when your lieutenant landed me the other day. As soon as I encountered the outposts of the Russian army I made my way to the bivouac of the Hetman's Don Cossacks and found Ostroff. Together we went off to Piktupohen where the Imperial Russian headquarters lay and located Vorontzoff. The Prince is as staunch a believer in a British alliance as his old father and distrusts the French. He told me at once that Alexander has agreed to a secret meeting with Napoleon. Both Vorontzoff and Ostroff undertook to supply whatever information they might learn as to the outcome of this secret conclave, as I told you yesterday. By a stroke of luck, Vorontzoff, in his capacity as an Imperial aide, was ordered into Tilsit to commandeer lodgings for the Tsar and his Commander-in-Chief, General Bennigsen. As a result, I was able to apply a little influence and General Bennigsen and his staff will be quartered in a large house on the Ostkai, having a good view of the Nieman and the French across the river. It is an ancient house, built round a courtyard, and the ground floor consists of stables and a large warehouse. The owner is an old Jew who proved characteristically amenable to gold. I secured a tiny attic, locked and barred from the inside and obviously a well-used hiding place during the frequent persecutions of the Hebrews. Here I prepared to hole-up until it became clear what had been arranged between Alexander and Napoleon. I was ideally placed. If my hypothesis proved true and Alexander and Napoleon combined, then it was likely that Bennigsen would fall from grace. He is already in disfavour, having lost at Friedland. Such are the suspicions at the Tsar's court that the fact that he was born a Hanoverian and hence a subject of our own King George is held against him, and there is, in any case, a rising tide of resentment against German officers, who are held largely responsible for the recent military disaster.'

'But I thought the Tsar owed Bennigsen some obligation due to the part he played in the murder of his father,' put in Drinkwater, as Mackenzie drew breath.

Mackenzie smiled with a sardonic grin. 'There is little honour in this world, least of all among thieves and murderers, despite the proverb,' he said. 'No, I think Bennigsen will be quietly sacrificed when the time comes. Alexander is unpredictable in the extreme, and an autocrat's foreign policies are apt to be as erratic as the tacking of your own frigate.'

It was Drinkwater's turn to grin at the simile. 'So, you were ensconced in the attic of the Jew's house,' he prompted.

'Yes. And I could rely upon Bennigsen's disaffection and consequent disloyalty if things went against us. Part of Bennigsen's staff arrived, a coterie of drunken young officers whose behaviour would disgrace a farmyard. But they brought with them some of the finest bloodstock in Russia, stabling them in the warehouse. My own mount was quartered some distance away and this ready form of transport further satisfied me in my choice of post.'

'And yet you deserted this secure bolt-hole, risked everything and returned to Memel to fetch me. Yesterday you mentioned boats and secret meetings and the presence of a seaman as being vital.'

'My dear Captain, I spavined a good horse because, without

136

exaggeration, you are truly the only man who can help effect this thing.'

'That much you already said, but you also said my brother . . .'

'Ostroff.'

'Ostroff, then, was not likely to be able . . .'

'Not without you, Captain, hence your unique importance in the matter. You are, as it were, of a dual value.'

'I do not follow.'

Mackenzie leaned forward, his face a picture of urgency. Gone were the traces of yesterday's exhaustion. 'Captain,' he said, 'Napoleon has ordered that his meeting with Alexander shall take place exactly midway between their two armies, in conditions of such secrecy that no one shall be privy to the settlement between them.'

'I understand that; and that you intend, with my help, to eavesdrop on them.'

'Exactly, Captain. You will help devise the method by which it shall be done, but there is also the question of who shall do it. I myself cannot undertake the task since it is for me to ensure that the intelligence is got out of this benighted land and back to London. Vorontzoff is out of the question since he has his duties to attend to, is of more use in other ways and is far too well known to be passed off in disguise. The only candidate for the post of danger is Ostroff, but Ostroff protests it is impossible, despite the money he has been offered, and only you, as his brother, will be able to persuade him of the absolute necessity of attempting this coup.'

Drinkwater sat for some moments in silence. The whirring of the wheels on the road, the heat and the dust suggested an illusion of peace, yet every revolution of those soothing wheels took them nearer a situation as desperate and risky as any he had yet faced in his life. He was penetrating deep into territory that would soon be abruptly hostile, dressed in plain clothes on a mission of such danger that he might end his life before a firing squad, shot as a spy. He passed a hand wearily over his face and looked up at Mackenzie.

'You have me on a lee shore,' he said ruefully as Mackenzie smiled thinly. 'So I have to convince Ostroff that he must spy on the two Emperors as well as devise a means by which it may be done?'

'Exactly,' replied Mackenzie, leaning back against the buttoned leather of the chaise, his face a picture of satisfaction.

'Has it occurred to you that the thing might indeed be impossible?'

'No. Difficult, yes, but not impossible.'

'You have a great deal of faith in my inventiveness . . . something I'm not sure I share with you.'

'Come, come, Captain, I'm certain that you have sufficient resourcefulness to devise a means of concealing a man in a raft!'

The morning rolled by in a cloud of dust. The broad and shining Nieman wound its way through increasingly undulating country of low hills. Here and there the river ran close to the road, undercutting a red clay cliff before it swung away in a great loop. The coppices of willow gave way to birches and scattered elms that reminded Drinkwater of home and they passed through the occasional village with its low steadings and slow, incurious peasants. Above the noise of the horses, the creak of harness and the thrum of wheels on the dirt road, the soaring song of larks could still be heard. At one point, where the river swung close to the road, Mackenzie bade Walmsley pull over and into a side lane which led down to a ferry.

'We'll water the horses and take a bite to eat,' he said and they pulled up beside a sunken hovel and a box-like pontoon provided with chains that formed a crude ferry across the Nieman.

As Walmsley tended the horses and Mackenzie provided black bread, sausage and a bottle of kvass from his saddlebags, he nodded to the ferry.

'Take a look at it,' he muttered. 'They've one just like it at Tilsit, hauled out on a slipway and being prepared for the secret meeting.'

Drinkwater walked casually down to the rickety wooden jetty alongside which the ungainly craft lay moored. He ignored the ferryman who emerged from the hovel and approached him, concentrating his attention on the raft. It was a 'flying bridge', or chain ferry of large size, clearly intended to transport cattle and carts across the broad river and he spent several minutes studying the thing intently. Mackenzie shouted something incomprehensible at the ferryman which made the Lithuanian swear and retire gesticulating behind a slammed door.

Twenty minutes later they resumed their journey. Mackenzie had briefed Walmsley as to the dangers they might now encounter, leaving Drinkwater to consider the problem of the raft. When they were fairly on their way Mackenzie leaned forward.

'Well, can it be done?'

Drinkwater nodded. 'In theory, yes . . . but we need to consider tools, how we get to the thing . . . you must let me think . . .'

Mackenzie leaned back, permitting himself a small, secretive smile of satisfaction. From time to time he cast a surreptitious glance at Drinkwater, but for the most part he dozed as the chaise rolled on. Ahead of them smoke blurred the horizon and there were an increasing number of travellers on the road. The carriages and open chaises of the gentry, blooming with the light colours of women's dresses and hats, were moving towards Tilsit, while coming in the contrary direction a thin stream of peasants accompanied by the occasional bandaged soldier made their weary way. Mackenzie roused from his nodding.

'The wealthy and curious travel with us,' he said, 'the indigent poor escape the rapacity of the military who will be busy consuming every hidden bushel of stored grain, every chicken and pig in every poor steading, and requisitioning every house, hovel and pigsty for their billets.'

As the afternoon wore on, Mackenzie's assertion was proved true. For now, along the road were encamped green-and-grey-clad infantry, milling in bivouac, their cooking fires sending the smoke pall up into the blue sky. Lines of tethered cavalry horses stood patiently as troopers distributed fodder, and the regimental smithies stood by the roadside and made good the ravages of the campaign. Here and there lines of unlimbered guns were pulled off the road, their gunners sitting on the heavy wooden trails smoking, drinking or playing cards. Along the riverside a party were duck-shooting and, at one point, they were over-taken by a wild group of young officers racing their Arabs, to the complete disregard of all other users of the highway.

They passed through a village deserted by its inhabitants. In the duck-pond an entire battalion of nakedly pink Russian soldiers splashed and skylarked, bathing themselves clean of the red dust. The plain was filled with men and horses, and it seemed impossible that this vast multitude had suffered a defeat. Such numbers seemed to Drinkwater to be invincible.

They breasted a low hill and were met by a great wave of sound, that of hundreds of deep voices intoning the chants of the Russian Orthodox liturgy. Amid the gaudy trappings of war the summit of the knoll was crowned with the gilded panoply of the church. The priests' vestments gleamed in the sunshine as they moved through a long line of bare-headed men beneath banners of gold and red. The gilded chasubles, the waving banners and the sacred images borne aloft by acolytes, were accompanied by wafts of incense and the intense, low, humming song of the soldiers of Tsar Alexander at their devotions.

Mackenzie leaned over and tapped his knee: 'You see now why

Napoleon wants them for allies, and why we must not let them go. I know them, Captain, I have served with them.'

As they slowed to force their way through the worshippers, Drinkwater thought that at any moment their progress would be challenged. But nothing happened. There seemed to be hardly a man posted as a sentry. In company with other equipages they travelled on, Walmsley on the box, making sheep's eyes at the prettier of the women in the neighbouring conveyances.

The sun was westering when Mackenzie pointed ahead and Drinkwater craned around to see.

'*Voilà*, Tilsit.'

The Nieman was narrower now, and wound less wildly between the water-meadows of lush green that were dotted with the bright gold of buttercups. More cows grazed its banks and stood hock-deep in its waters among the reeds, their tails lazily flicking off the flies and mosquitoes that abounded. On the rising ground to their left the ripening wheat and rye was trampled, but ahead of them the red roofs and towers of a substantial town lay hazy in the sunshine.

'And look there!' said Mackenzie suddenly, pointing again, but this time across the river.

A score of horsemen were watering their horses. They wore rakish shakoes and pelisses, their two vedettes clear against the skyline.

'French hussars!' Mackenzie declared.

Drinkwater's curiosity was terminated abruptly when Walmsley pulled back on the reins and applied the brake, so that the wheels locked and the chaise skidded. He turned in his seat as Mackenzie put a cautionary finger on his knee.

'I'll do the talking,' he said, nodding reassuringly as Walmsley looked round anxiously from the box.

Ahead of them, drawn up in a rough line across the road, was a dark mass of cavalry; shaggy men on shaggy horses whose fierce eyes glared at the passengers in the carriages and moved over reluctantly to let the gentry through. Drinkwater looked at them with undisguised curiosity, for these were undoubtedly the Cossacks of which he had heard. They scarcely looked like cavalry; they wore baggy blouses and their trousers were stuffed into boots, it was true, but their waistbands and sheepskin saddles were strung about with the products of looting and plunder. Those few who were on foot waddled bow-legged with a rolling gait that reminded Drinkwater of grotesque seamen. Wicked-looking lances were slung across their backs and sabres gleamed in metal scabbards at their hips.

One great bearded giant, whose legs seemed to drag low on either side of his diminutive pony, kicked his mount close to the chaise. Peering at Drinkwater he made some comment which excited laughter from his compatriots. Drinkwater smelt the animal odour of the man, but Mackenzie, undaunted, riposted in Russian. The Cossack's face altered and his friends roared again at the man's obvious discomfiture.

The man was about to reply when his pony was shoved aside by a magnificent bay horse ridden by an officer. He appeared to recognise Mackenzie.

'Ah, Alexei, where the devil did you spring from?' he said in the French that was the lingua franca of the Russian nobility. 'I thought you had gone into Tilsit with Ostroff.'

Drinkwater recognised the last word and felt his heart hammering painfully under his ribs.

'Indeed, Count, I did, but I returned to Memel to fetch this gentleman here,' Mackenzie said in the same language, gesturing towards Drinkwater. 'He is the master of an English brig.'

'An Englishman, eh?' The Cossack officer stared at Drinkwater. 'I doubt he'll be welcome in Tilsit. But, to you merchants and the English, business is business, eh?'

'If the rumours are true, Count, and an armistice is declared, the Captain here wants his cargo out of Tilsit and Memel. But the rascally Jews won't sell at the prices they had agreed because the place is stuffed full of fools who might buy at a higher rate.'

'Tell him to hurry then,' said the Cossack officer and added, 'you'll be lucky to find lodgings in the town unless, like the Blessed Virgin, you are satisfied with a byre.' He crossed himself as he laughed at his blasphemous joke, then he peered into the chaise.

Drinkwater looked with sudden apprehension at Mackenzie, but the 'merchant' grinned and reached under the seat.

'Would a bottle be welcome to help us past your unspeakably stinking ruffians, Count?'

'As the Blessed Virgin herself, M'sieur Macdonald.' The officer grinned and caught the bottle of vodka. 'I shall toast you, Alexei, when I rest my ignoble centaurs tonight. He turned and shouted something to the great bearded Cossack who had taken such an interest in Drinkwater. 'Hey, Khudoznik . . .!'

The man was looking curiously at Lord Leveson-Gower's horses in the shafts. At the Count's remark he looked up and growled something in reply, at which the whole squadron, its commanding officer included, roared with laughter.

'On your way, Alexei, and *bon voyage*, Captain!' he said, and Walmsley, seeing the road ahead clear, whipped up the horses.

Drinkwater wiped his face with relief. 'Who the devil was that? You seemed uncommonly intimate.'

Mackenzie laughed. 'That, believe it or not, was Ostroff's superior officer, Count Piotr Kalitkin, commander of two squadrons of the Hetman's Don Cossacks. He knows me for a Scottish merchant, Alexander Macdonald, and we have been drunk several times in each other's company. He thinks you are going to Tilsit . . .'

'Yes, I got the drift of it: to find out why my cargo has not been brought down river to Memel.'

'Excellent!' laughed Mackenzie, in high good humour after the incident.

'What was that exchange between the Count and that malodorous fellow?' asked Drinkwater.

'It was an obscenity. The Count asked the man, Khudoznik, if he wanted to bugger our horses before he stood aside and let us through. Khudoznik replied there was no need for he had found a farm where the farmer had a wife, a daughter and forty cows!'

'Good God!'

'I doubt they're any worse than your own seamen . . .'

'Or some of the officers,' agreed Drinkwater, jerking his head in Walmsley's direction, 'but those fellows looked born in the saddle.'

'Indeed. Their Little Father, the Tsar, exempts them from taxation in exchange for twenty to forty years of military service. And they will literally steal the shirt from your back, if you let them.' Mackenzie nodded at Drinkwater's open coat.

'It seems I had a lucky escape in several ways,' remarked Drinkwater.

It was dark by the time they reached the town and here they encountered sentries. They were the third in a little convoy of carriages that had bunched together on the road, and by the time the sergeant had got to them he paid scant attention to the pass Mackenzie waved under his nose.

'I doubt if the fellow can read,' Mackenzie said, as Walmsley urged the exhausted horses forward, 'although, if he could, he would find the pass in order and signed by Prince Vorontzoff.' Mackenzie stood and tapped Walmsley on the shoulder. 'Pull in over there,' he ordered in a low voice, and the chaise passed into the deep shadow of a tall building. Mackenzie and Walmsley exchanged places and the chaise rolled forward again.

'How do you do?' Drinkwater asked Walmsley in a low voice.

'Well enough, sir,' replied the midshipman, stretching tired muscles. 'Where are . . .?'

'No questions until we are safe.'

'Safe, sir?'

'In hiding.'

'I don't think I'll feel safe until I'm back on the old *Antigone*.'

'We are of one mind then. Now be quiet.' They had pulled into a side turning which bore no resemblance to what Drinkwater had imagined the Jew's house looked like even in the darkness. Mackenzie dropped from the box, opened the door and motioned them down. Taking the saddle-bags from the chaise he handed them to Drinkwater.

'Wait here,' he said and moved round to the horses' heads. He led the chaise off, and left the two Englishmen standing in the darkness. They pressed back into the shadows and listened to the noises of the night.

Kalitkin's news of an armistice was affirmed by the noise of revelry around them. Every window they could see was ablaze with candlelight. The strains of violins and balalaikas, of bass and soprano voices were added to raucous laughter and the squeals of women. Beside him Drinkwater heard Walmsley snigger nervously and their proximity to a bawdy house was confirmed by Mackenzie who approached out of the shadows without horses or chaise.

'The more people, the easier the concealment,' he whispered. 'I've left the chaise at a brothel full of officers' horses.' He led them back the way they had come and into the comparative brilliance of the town square.

The place was full of people milling about, women giggling on the arms of officers, the curious gentry and their outraged womenfolk hurrying past the licentious soldiers. Beggars and whores, vendors and street musicians filled the open space and occasionally a horseman would ride through, or a carriage escorted by lancers trot by to be wildly cheered in case it was the Little Father, the Tsar.

Drinkwater began to see what Mackenzie meant. The crowd, hell-bent on pleasure, took no notice of them. Within minutes they had entered beneath a low arch, reminiscent of an English coaching inn, and found themselves in a courtyard. Two or three orderlies lounged about, smoking or drinking, but no one challenged them. Even the tall sentry at the door snapped to attention as Mackenzie, walking with an air of purpose, threw open the door and led the trio inside.

Crossing the courtyard Drinkwater had been aware of stable doors and upper windows flung open, from which candlelight and the noise of drunken revels poured in equal measure. Inside, the stairs were littered with bottles, an officer in his shirt sleeves, his arm round the waist of a compliant girl, lounged back and ignored them. A half-open upper door revealed a brief glimpse of a mess-dinner, a table groaning under food, bottles, boots upon the table cloth and a whirling dancer kicking out the *trepak* to the wild and insistent beat of balalaika chords.

On the next floor the doors were closed. A woman's chemise and a pair of shoes and stockings lay on the landing. Above the shouts and cheers from below, the shrieks of drunken love-making came from behind the closed doors and were abruptly drowned by the concerted tinkle of breaking glass as, below, a toast was drunk to the dancer.

A flight higher they encountered the Jew, his family behind him, peering anxiously down from an upper landing. Mackenzie addressed a few words to him and he drew back. Drinkwater saw the dull gleam of gold pass between them.

They passed through a further door, dark and concealed in the gloom. It shut behind them and they stumbled up bare wooden steps in total darkness. At the top Mackenzie knocked on a door; three taps and then two taps in a prearranged signal. There was the noise of a bar being withdrawn and a heavy lock turning. He followed Mackenzie into a tiny attic, the rafters meeting overhead, a dormer window open to the night and from which the quick flash of lamplight on water could be glimpsed. Mackenzie stood aside, revealing the single occupant of the attic.

'Let me introduce you, Captain, to the man called "Ostroff".'

Ostroff

'By God, it *is* you . . .' Edward came forward, holding up a lantern to see his brother. 'Mackenzie said he would force the issue one way or another. It never occurred to me he would bring *you* back. You've come a damned long way to collect your debt.'

Edward's poor joke broke the ice. Drinkwater held out his hand and looked his brother up and down. The jest about money was characteristic; Edward was still the gambler, the opportunist. He was heavier of feature than Drinkwater remembered, his face red with good living and hard drinking, and he wore a Russian uniform unbuttoned at the neck. His feet were stuffed into soft boots and he had the appearance of a man who was about to leave. As if to confirm this he took off his tunic and loosened his stock.

'By God, it's hot up here, under the eaves. 'Who's this, Mackenzie?' He indicated the midshipman.

'Our driver, who has done a fine job and deserves some reward. Have you a bottle?'

Edward reached under a truckle bed and produced a bottle of vodka. 'There are glasses on that chest.'

They drank and Drinkwater performed the introduction, explaining that Ostroff was a British officer in the Russian service. Fortunately the looks of the two brothers were too dissimilar to excite suspicion as to the true nature of their relationship and Walmsley, tired and slightly over-awed by the situation he found himself in, maintained a sensible silence. As they finished the vodka Mackenzie motioned to the midshipman.

'You and I will go and forage for something to eat, and leave these gentlemen to reminisce over their last encounter.

They clattered down the steps and left a silence behind them. Drinkwater peered cautiously from the window, but he could see little beyond the black and silver river, the tall houses of the quay opposite and the sentries pacing up and down in the lamplight.

'You can't see much, but the raft is to the right. You'll see it clearly in daylight.'

'You know why I'm here, then?'

Behind him Edward sighed heavily and Drinkwater turned back into the attic. Edward had sat himself on the truckle bed and Drinkwater squatted on the chest.

'Yes. Mackenzie, a remarkable wizard, assured me he would bring back the one man who could accomplish this thing.'

'You sound doubtful.'

'It's impossible, Nat. Wait until you see the bloody raft. They've got one of those flying bridges . . .'

'I know, I saw one lower down the river.'

'And you think it can be done?' Edward asked doubtfully.

Drinkwater shook his head. 'I don't know yet. Let us make up our minds in daylight.'

'Here . . .' Edward held out the bottle and refilled their glasses. 'To fraternity.'

Their eyes met. 'Do you remember my taking you aboard the *Virago?*'

'I found the life of a seaman far from pleasant.'

'I'm sorry,' said Drinkwater curtly, 'I had no option. You recall Jex, the purser who discovered who you were?'

'Christ yes! What happened to him?'

'He was providentially killed at Copenhagen . . . But tell me about yourself. You look well enough. Mackenzie tells me that you live *chez* Vorontzoff.'

Edward smiled. 'Oh yes. The life of an exile is a good one when well-connected. Your Lord-at-the-Admiralty pays me well enough and I still trifle a little at the tables . . . I'm very comfortable.'

'Are you married?'

Edward laughed again. 'Married! Heavens, no! But I've a woman, if that's what you mean. In Petersburg, in Vorontzoff's palace . . . I do very well, Nat, that's why you will find me unwilling to risk myself under that raft.'

'I understand that Mackenzie has promised you a very handsome sum if you can pull it off.'

Drinkwater saw the expression of greed cross Edward's face; a small narrowing of the eyes, the quick lick of the tongue across the lips. He had always been a slave to money, easy money in large amounts. Edward suddenly looked askance at Drinkwater.

'You haven't come to reclaim your debt, have you?' The irrelevant question revealed the extent of Edward's corruptibility. Drinkwater smiled sadly.

'Good heavens, Ned, I cannot remember how much I loaned you.'

'Neither can I,' Edward replied with dismissive speed and occupied himself with refilling the glasses. 'You know, Nat,' he continued after a moment, 'I owe neither you, nor Mackenzie, nor Great Britain any allegiance . . . Despite my association with Vorontzoff, I am my own man . . .'

'That begs the question of whether you will get under this raft,' said Drinkwater, the problem vexing him again and intruding into his mind so that he half-stood, cracked his head on the eaves and sat down again. 'Besides, did you know who you killed at Newmarket?'

A shadow passed over Edward's face.

'I have killed since,' he said with sudden aggression, 'mostly Frenchmen . . .'

'It was a pity about the girl, Ned, but the man was a French agent.' Dawning comprehension filled Edward's face.

'Is that how you managed to protect me?'

Drinkwater nodded. 'And myself . . . and if you were to carry out this task, Ned, I fancy that I might persuade my "Lord-at-the-Admiralty" to obtain a Royal Pardon for you.'

Edward stared at his brother, his expression of incredulity gradually dissolving to amusement and cracking into stifled laughter. 'My dear Nat, you do not change! For God's sake . . . a Pardon! I would rather have two thousand pounds in gold!'

Mackenzie woke Drinkwater from his place of honour on the truckle bed at dawn. Drinkwater's head ached from the vodka and his mouth was dry. Mackenzie indicated a jug of water and, as Drinkwater vacated the bed, he rolled into it. Walmsley still slept, rolled in a blanket, on the rough boards of the attic floor. Edward was not there.

'Where's . . . Ostroff?'

'Don't worry,' muttered Mackenzie, his eyes already closed, 'he'll be back.'

Drinkwater stared for a moment at the extraordinary man. Edward had called him a wizard and doubtless had good reason for doing so. Mackenzie's quick-wittedness had clearly proved invaluable and he was as at home in the presence of the Tsar as on this present strange campaign. For Drinkwater himself, separation from his ship, the horrible responsibility of his task and the risk of capture filled him

147

with fretful gloom. But he addressed himself to the matter in hand. Edward had said the raft was visible . . .

He fished in the tail-pocket of Hill's coat and brought out his Dollond glass. Cleaning the lenses carefully with a pocket handkerchief whose stitched monogram brought a painfully poignant reminder of his wife, he peered from the dormer window whose casements stood open against the summer dawn.

The Nieman was perhaps a hundred yards wide. On the opposite bank a stone quay, similar to the one on which the Jew's house stood, was lined with tall old buildings, their storeys rising up above the storage for merchandise at ground level. They had Dutch gables and mansard roofs pierced by dormers such as the one from which he peered. On the quay, the Westkai, he could see the blue and white figures of the sentries, French sentries!

The thought made him ease forward gently so that he could see almost directly below him. Their Russian counterparts lounged on their muskets along the Ostkai and he withdrew into the shadow of the room. Then he saw the raft.

It was drawn up on a gravelled hard where the Westkai was recessed to facilitate the repair of the river barges. Drinkwater levelled his glass and studied it. It was identical to the flying bridge he had examined the day before, except that upon its rough boarded surface the railings had been removed and carpenters had begun the erection of a framework. He made his examination carefully, his heart beating with a mounting excitement as the possibility of success grew. Every supposition he had made after his examination of the chain ferry seemed borne out by the scrutiny of the pontoon opposite. It was impossible to be sure at this distance, but, as he went over and over his plan, he could find no major flaw in it. It would be difficult, but if he could lay his hands on some simple tools and a little luck . . .

He pulled back into the attic and put away his glass. 'The game *must* be worth the candle,' he muttered to himself. He cast a look at the extraordinary man who snored softly on the truckle bed and who had so disrupted his life.

'You could be the instrument of my undoing, damn you,' he murmured ruefully. When he turned again to the view of the Westkai the rising sun was gilding the gables opposite and a clock in Tilsit was striking five.

The day that followed was one of an intolerable imprisonment. The June heat upon the roof tiles made that attic an oven. Mackenzie left

148

them during the forenoon to glean what news he could, and to see if he could acquire the few tools that Drinkwater wanted. Behind him, forbidden to show himself near the window, Walmsley fretted and fussed like a child. Ostroff made no appearance and Drinkwater became increasingly worried. From time to time he watched the raft. French engineers, under the direction of an officer of high rank, were assisted by local craftsmen. The pavilion rose steadily during the morning and began to be draped during the afternoon.

Drinkwater's anxiety reached fever-pitch when he realised there was one vital matter that, in his study of the pontoon, he had completely overlooked. It was a piece of the most idiotic stupidity yet, after his realisation that he had overlooked it, the desperate need for quick improvisation was a solace for his over-active mind.

Drinkwater's problem was simply how to get across the river. To swim was too risky; besides it exposed Edward to a long period of immersion. The rowing-boats on the river had all been withdrawn to the French side, apart from a large barge moored almost directly below their window. A solution defied him until about mid-afternoon when, after a shouted parley across the Nieman, a small boat put off from the west bank. In its stern sat two officers. Disembarking just out of sight, Drinkwater heard the sound of talking men striding below the window. He guessed the two French officers had been met by some Russians. Unable to see much he realised the group had stopped directly underneath them. Wriggling back from the window he beckoned Walmsley. The bored young man came forward.

'I want you to see if you can hear what they are saying below,' Drinkwater whispered, pointing frantically downwards. Walmsley nodded and eased himself up under the sill of the open window. Drawing back into the attic Drinkwater stood and stretched. For perhaps ten minutes the hum of voices came up to them and Walmsley's face was contorted with concentration, but at last the impromptu conference broke up and Walmsley moved back into the room.

'Well?'

'I couldn't hear well, sir; but it was something about getting the barge across the river tonight . . . something about . . .' he frowned.

'Go on!'

'Well, I thought he said a "pavilion", a "second pavilion" . . . but I don't understand what that had to do with a barge . . .'

'Never mind, Mr Walmsley,' said Drinkwater suddenly grinning like a fool, 'you do not know what a signal service you have just rendered your country, by God!'

'Indeed, sir, I do not . . .'

'Never mind. When we return to the ship I shall tell you, but for the time being I must urge you to be patient and . . .'

He never finished the sentence, for the coded knock came at the door. Drinkwater motioned Walmsley to unlock it and lift the bar, while he picked up and cocked the loaded pistol left by Mackenzie when he had departed.

Mackenzie slid inside, his eyes shining with excitement.

'Bennigsen's below. The Tsar's given him the devil of a drubbing, and in public too. Bennigsen's furious at the humiliation and muttering God knows what . . . and there's more,' he took a draught at the vodka Walmsley passed him and unhooked his coat. 'The meeting is set for tomorrow.'

Kicking off his boots, Mackenzie padded cautiously to the window and stared at the raft. He gave a low whistle. '*Le théâtre de Napoleon*,' he said with an appreciative grin. It occurred to Drinkwater that Mackenzie throve on such high excitement. 'Hullo, what have those fellows been over for?' He nodded across the river and Drinkwater eased himself alongside. The small boat had returned to the Westkai and the two French officers were disembarking up an iron ladder.

'General officers,' murmured Mackenzie, 'by the look of them.'

The two men exchanged remarks, the sunlight reflected off their highly polished thigh-boots, and began to stroll along the quay towards the slipway and the bedizened raft. They were resplendent in the blue and gold of field officers, their great, plumed bicorne hats tucked under their arms. One of them, the taller of the two, wiped his forehead with a handkerchief. Some primaeval instinct beyond curiosity prompted Drinkwater. He drew out the Dolland glass again and focused it on the two officers. He drew his breath in sharply and Mackenzie turned.

'What the devil is it?'

'God's bones,' said Drinkwater, his face drained of colour. 'Santhonax!'

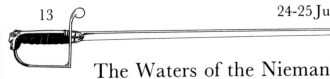

The Waters of the Nieman

Mackenzie snatched the glass from him. 'By God, you are right!'

'It's uncanny,' Drinkwater said, his mouth dry. He accepted the glass of vodka Mackenzie held out. 'Our paths have crossed so many times . . .'

'No matter,' said Mackenzie, suddenly resolute, 'I have brought the things you wanted. A farrier's axe was the nearest I could manage to a hammer and it can be used instead of a spike.'

Drinkwater looked at the axe which was similar to a boarding axe with a blade and spike. 'What about nails?'

'Here,' Mackenzie fished in his pocket, 'horse-shoe nails.'

'It reminds me of the nursery rhyme,' Drinkwater said, regaining his composure. It was quite impossible that Santhonax posed a threat to the success of the enterprise. 'Now what about Ostroff? Where the hell is he? I want to move at dusk, if not before . . . and Mackenzie, have you been in contact with Bennigsen's staff?'

Mackenzie nodded and both men listened to the hubbub that floated up from lower in the house. 'Somehow you've got to find out which of them met those two over there,' he jerked his head towards the window. 'They'll be detailing someone off to move that barge across the river. Local watermen, I expect. You're a merchant, an ingratiating fellow. Tell them you'll arrange it.'

'I'll get the Hebrew to do it. It's his barge.'

'No, Ostroff and I will get the barge over.'

Comprehension dawned in Mackenzie's eyes and he smiled appreciatively.

'And get us some rags and soot from the Jew.'

'I see I was not mistaken in you, Captain,' Mackenzie said.

'It'll come to naught if Ostroff ain't found!' said Drinkwater sharply. 'And now I want some food!'

'I shall attend to those matters forthwith.'

*   *   *

Midshipman Lord Walmsley heard the departing footsteps of Captain Drinkwater and Ostroff fade down the stairs. The strange Russian officer had returned only a few minutes earlier, in time to receive his instructions from an impatient Drinkwater. He had protested a little and was then coerced by the captain and Mr Mackenzie into agreeing to change into loose-fitting peasant's trousers, felt boots and a coarse cotton blouse. Both men put on hats and were given tobacco tubes such as were smoked by the Lithuanian peasantry. Walmsley had heard Captain Drinkwater mention that his capture in such clothing would guarantee his being shot as a spy and Ostroff, in a curiously unaccented English, denied it, saying the smell would drive off the most officious French officer. The grim joke shared between the two men sent a shiver of fear for his own safety up his spine. And then they had gone, leaving Walmsley hot, bored, yet strangely fearful, alone with the enigmatic Mr Mackenzie who ignored him in his eagerness to observe the departure of the barge from the Ostkai.

Walmsley lolled back in his corner of the attic and gave his mind up to the only thing a young man of his tastes and inclination could think of in such stultifying circumstances: women. The apothecary's daughter and the pretty young women in the carriages that had accompanied them on their journey had awakened desires which had been further titillated by the occasional squeals of pleasure or protest from below. He lay imagining the activities of the young bloods on Bennigsen's staff and brooded on his own long deprivation.

At last he could tolerate inactivity no longer.

'Do you mind, sir,' he hissed at the back of Mackenzie's head, 'if I take the opportunity to empty the bucket and get a breath of air?'

Mackenzie turned from the window and wrinkled his nose at the pail they had been using as a privy. 'If you are careful, no. You may walk about a bit . . . seek crowds, you are safer in a crowd.' He turned again to look down into the river.

Walmsley could scarcely contain his excitement and, picking up the bucket he unbarred the door.

Drinkwater forced himself to resist the nausea that swept over him as he tried to master the art of smoking tobacco. The nausea was replaced by an odd lightheadedness. The disgusting import brought back by Russian armies serving in the Caucasus revolted him almost as much as the filthy workman's clothing in which he was clad. He cleared his throat and spat with unfeigned gusto into the brown waters of the River Nieman. Above their heads the westward-facing glazings of the dormer window blazed with the reflected sunset, masking entirely the watching face of Mackenzie.

Edward, similarly malodorous but smoking with ease, came up to him. 'This is bloody ridiculous!' he muttered in English.

'We've no alternative,' his brother replied. Drinkwater was terrified of the need to speak, despite an hour's coaching in a few words of Lithuanian by Mackenzie. Edward, for whom languages presented little difficulty and who had learned sufficient patois from his campaigning, was to speak if speech were necessary. Drinkwater began to cast off the mooring ropes under the curious gaze of a tall Russian sentry.

As the semi-darkness of the northern twilight began to close over them, Drinkwater handed the end of the rope to his brother. He had told Edward exactly what to do: to hold on with a single turn until he gave the word. Drinkwater walked aft to where the sweeps poked their blades outboard, their looms constrained by grommets round single thole pins on either quarter. Drinkwater bent and ran the long sweeps out. It was going to be far from easy. He gritted his teeth, braced his feet and called '*Los!*'

Edward cast off and pushed the stone facing of the Ostkai with a booted foot. The current began to move the barge as the bluff bow fell slowly off the quay. Drinkwater began to move the sweeps.

Edward came aft. 'Can I help?'

Drinkwater shook his head. Edward was no expert and it was only necessary to get a little headway on the barge and let the current do the rest.

'I'll get the line ready then.'

Drinkwater nodded and strained with the effort necessary to make an impression on the massive inertia of the barge. He stared down into the hold, thankful that it was empty, as he thrust at the oar looms with every sinew he possessed.

He began to get the swing of it. They were thirty yards out from the Ostkai now, but fifty downstream. He threw his weight back and dragged the blades out of the water, dipped them and fell forward, his breast against his fists, his calf muscles bulging as he heaved his body forward against the resistance. The blades drove through the water slowly and he dragged them out again to repeat the process over and over, keeping the barge pointing upstream, angled outwards slightly against the current, so that they crabbed across the river.

The sweat rolled off him and he felt his head would burst. He clenched his eyes shut to prevent the perspiration stinging them. He drew breath in great rasping gasps and the unaccustomed effort set his muscles a-quiver. He became blind to everything but the need for constant effort and it seemed that he had been doing this for ever.

Then, through eyes that he opened briefly, he glimpsed the looming gables of the houses of the Westkai. Ten long minutes later, Edward jumped ashore with the bow line. The gentle nudge with which the barge brought up against the quayside almost knocked Drinkwater off his feet as he dragged the sweeps inboard. Breathing heavily and his heart thumping painfully, he caught the stern line through a heavy ring and walked forward to see that Edward had secured the bow. In accordance with their plan, and in view of the sentries on either bank, they sat down on the hatch-coaming of the barge and broached a bottle of vodka. Both men took a small swig themselves and let some dribble down over their chins and onto their clothes. Edward lit another of the disgusting cheroots while Drinkwater sat and scratched himself. The red haze was beginning to disperse from his eyes when suddenly they focused on the French sentry who came forward to stare down at them.

Edward looked up and said something in Russian. Weakened from his strenuous exertion Drinkwater sat panting, trying to still the thundering of his pounding heart. He felt quite powerless to confront the danger they were in and left the matter to his brother. The Frenchman shrugged uncomprehendingly so Edward held out the bottle. The soldier hesitated, looked round and then grabbed it and swigged at it twice before handing it reluctantly back. Edward laughed and made a guttural comment and the two men grinned, the soldier wiping a hand across his mouth. Suddenly the sentry turned, as though hearing something, and disappeared from view. A few seconds later two French officers gazed down at them and enquired what they were doing.

Edward embarked on a pantomime of pretended explanation, gesturing first to the east bank of the Nieman and then to the west, interspersed with grunted interrogatives aimed at the two officers. At their lack of understanding he launched into a repeat of the whole thing until one of them cut him short.

'*Très bien, mon vieux, nous savons . . .*' He turned to his compatriot and Drinkwater heard the name General Santhonax used twice. He felt his blood run cold and prayed to heaven that it was not their intention to verify the arrival of the barge with Santhonax. Not that he thought Santhonax would recognise him, unshaven, dirty and so totally

154

unexpected in such a place, but the very presence of the man filled him with apprehension. His heart had stilled now but the worms of anxiety were writhing in his guts.

Edward managed a loud belch and ostentatiously swigged the vodka again. Passing the bottle to Drinkwater he reached up and dragged himself up onto the quay. His sang-froid seemed to dispel any remaining suspicions the French officers might have had. They drifted away and Edward bent to give his brother a hand up.

'Phew!' Drinkwater grunted his thanks and Edward replied by giving an exaggerated and pointed belch, reminding him of the necessity of appearing tipsy. They approached the end of the quay where the small gravel slip-way ran into the river. Another sentry stood on the corner of the quay.

'*Qui va là?*'

They both began babbling incoherently, pointing down at the slipway, and indicating their intention to sleep on the pontoon that lay there.

'*Non.*'

Edward uttered an obscene dismissal. The sentry, a young man, cocked his musket but Edward slapped him on the shoulder and hung upon his arm. The man shrugged him off, wrinkling his nose in disgust, and nodded them past. They slid down onto the gravel and settled themselves under the growing shadows of the raft, lolling together and allowing their heartbeats to slow.

Twice the young sentry came to look at them but they lay still, two drunks inert and indistinguishable from the surrounding gloom. The clock in the town struck eleven, then midnight. There was a crunch of boots as a patrol, led by a corporal, came by to change the guards. Words were spoken as the man going off duty indicated the two pairs of felt boots that were just visible from the quay. The corporal spat, an eloquent attestation of the superiority of the French military over a pair of drunken Kurlanders, and the patrol marched on. The silence of the night settled over them, the noises of debauch muted beneath the low chuckle of the River Nieman as it made its way to the Baltic Sea.

'Let's begin,' whispered Drinkwater as soon as the sound of the marching feet had faded. Edward eased himself up and located the new guard. He was a more experienced soldier and had made himself comfortable against a bollard on the corner of the quay. A cloud of tobacco smoke was faintly illuminated from the red glow of his pipe bowl. Edward leaned down and tapped the all clear on Drinkwater's shoulder, remaining on the look-out while his brother crawled under the pontoon to begin work.

The flying bridge, or *pont volant*, was built on a heavy timber frame. The main members of the sides ran the length of the craft. These were crossed by beams on which the rough planking of the decking was laid. Such a craft would have floated very low without proper buoyancy and this was provided by two large box-like floats to which the main members were fastened. Watching the preparations from the attic window Drinkwater had observed some attention being paid to one section of these flotation chambers and had suspected one of them was giving cause for concern. Almost immediately he found fact and conjecture had spliced themselves neatly. Beneath the pontoon the new planks were identifiable by their slightly lighter colour and the rich smell of resin from them. The raw wood was unpayed and Drinkwater investigated further. His heart leapt for he was in luck.

Reaching down to his waistband he drew out the farrier's axe. His eyes were adjusted to the darkness and he worked the spike of the axe under the end of the upper plank and began to lever it off. The rot that had necessitated the renewal of the planks had already spread into the frame so the nails drew quite easily. He got the top plank off and then the next and then he dragged himself through the gap and slumped inside. The raw pine resin could not disguise the stench of the rotten wood and stagnant water which seeped into his clothes and felt cold against his sweating skin. Twisting round, he felt about in the roof of the chamber for any opening which would allow a man to receive sufficient air to breathe and, most important, to hear. He discovered a split between two planks and enlarged it with the axe. Rubbing his hand in the foul slime of the bottom, he smeared it over the raw wood to hide his work from a casual glance. When he had finished, he drew himself out of the chamber. Even beneath the pontoon the night air smelt sweet. He lay on the damp gravel, panting heavily; the clock in the town struck two.

Dragging himself along he pulled himself out from beneath the pontoon close to his brother. Edward was shivering from the chill. 'Well?' he hissed.

'Get under when you can. It's all ready.'

Edward cast a look round and Drinkwater sensed his reluctance, but the hesitation was only momentary. The two brothers crawled below the pontoon and Drinkwater tugged Edward until he was aware of the opening. He put his mouth close to Edward's ear. 'You won't drown, even if it fills partially with water. I have cut holes in the top, you should have no trouble breathing or hearing.'

Drinkwater patted Edward's shoulder and drew back. He felt Edward shudder and then begin to work his way through the narrow gap, which gave him more trouble than his slimmer brother. A hiss of disgust told that Edward had discovered the stink and damp of his prison.

'Christ, this is madness. Why did I let you talk me into it?'

'You can get out by kicking away the ends of the planks.'

'Leave me the axe.'

'I need it for hammering home the nails.' Drinkwater paused. Edward's face was a pale, ghostly oval in the stygian darkness. 'Do you have your bottle?'

'Of course I bloody well do.'

'Good luck.' Drinkwater moved to put the first board into place, fishing in his pocket for the stock of nails provided by Mackenzie. Holding the head of the axe he had Edward grip the bottom plank, found the nail hole with some difficulty, inserted a nail and pushed it with the end of the axe. He felt the nail drive part way into the rotten framework. Then he drew back his right hand and smacked it hard with the open palm of his left. After repeating this process a few times he felt the nail drive home. He managed the next nail at the other end of the plank in a similar fashion, but the third proved less easy. He knew he would have to give several hard bangs with the whole axe haft. He rolled quickly across and peered from under the pontoon. There was no sign of the sentry.

With feverish impatience he returned to the hole and, holding his breath, gave a few quick, sharp taps with the axe. In seconds the plank was secure. Edward's face peered from the narrowed gap as Drinkwater returned from a second look for the sentry. There was still no sign of the man. He must have strolled off to the far end of his beat. Drinkwater lifted the second plank. Edward resisted it being put into place.

'Nat.'

'What is it?' Drinkwater asked in a desperate whisper.

'Will you get me out of here if I cannot make it myself?'

Drinkwater remembered a small boy who was afraid of the dark and the shadows in the corner of the farmhouse bedroom. 'You'll have no trouble, I promise you,' he hissed reassuringly. 'Brace your back and simply kick outwards with your heels.'

'But promise.'

'For God's sake, Ned, of course . . .'

'Your word of honour.'

'My word of honour.' He pushed the plank and Edward vanished behind the faint grey of the new wood. As he tried to locate a nail, his hands shaking with the tension, the plank was pushed towards him. He choked down an oath with difficulty. 'What?'

'We may never meet again.'

'Don't be foolish. We shall meet when you get out, at the Jew's house tomorrow.'

'But it will not be the same.'

'For God's sake . . .'

'I *must* tell you something. I want you to know I repent of the murder . . . not the man, but I loved the girl . . .'

Drinkwater expelled pent up breath. 'I am sorry, Ned . . . Now for God's sake let me finish.'

'And I know I owe my life to you.'

'No matter now.'

'But all debts will be paid when this thing is done, eh?' Edward's voice was barely a whisper now, but Drinkwater was beside himself with anxiety. Once again he bore the burden of an elder brother. He comforted Edward's fear of a greater darkness.

'All paid, Ned, all paid.'

To Drinkwater's infinite relief Edward withdrew and Nathaniel began to fasten the last plank. It was the upper one and the nails went home with difficulty. In the end he was forced to bang hard, several times. The noise seemed deafening and as he drew back he heard the scrape of boots on gravel as a man jumped down onto the hard from the quay. He uttered a silent prayer that Edward would not react and rolled away from the buoyancy chamber, retreating further into the blackness beneath the raft.

As he lay inert, his eyes closed, trying to still his breathing, he could hear the sentry move round the pontoon, the crunch of his boots close beside him on the wet gravel. Beyond the shadow of the raft Drinkwater was aware of the first flush of dawn, a pale lightening of the river's surface. He could hear the man muttering and knew that he would be looking for the two drunken Kurlanders. For a second Drinkwater hesitated. Then, knowing he must leave Edward in no doubt of his successful escape, he acted.

Rolling from under the raft he found himself suddenly at the feet of the sentry.

'*Qui va là?*' snapped the astonished man unslinging his musket.

With one eye on the lowering bayonet Drinkwater grunted and rose on one knee. Tucked in the filthy breast of his blouse he gripped the boarding axe more firmly and staggered to his feet. If he allowed himself to be kept at bayonet point he was lost. The sentry growled at him.

Sucking in his breath he tore the axe from his breast and then, expelling air for all he was worth, he swung his arm with savage ferocity, twisting his body at the same time. With such sudden impetus the axe whirled and struck deep into the skull of the French soldier. With a dull thud the man fell, stone dead.

Drinkwater paused for an instant to catch his breath again, then he rounded on the raft and pressed close to the timber side of the float.

'Can you hear me?' he hissed.

'Yes,' he heard Edward's low reply.

'You're quite safe. I'm going now.'

Edward tapped twice and Drinkwater turned back to the gravel slipway and the dead sentry that lay beside the lapping water of the river. Slinging the musket he grabbed the man's heels and dragged him quickly into the water beneath the overhang of the quay. After the gloom beneath the raft it seemed quite light, but the dawn was delayed by rolling banks of heavy clouds and no cries of alarm greeted his panting efforts. He let the man's feet go and pushed the body out into the river. Unslinging the musket he let it fall to the muddy bottom of the Nieman. In the town the clock struck a half hour as he lowered himself into the water. He paddled out into the stream, nudging the body of his victim until he felt the current take it, then let it go. The water bore the thing away from him and he rolled on his back and peered back at the Westkai. He could see a party of sentries marching with a corporal, bringing the relief guard: he had left not a moment too soon. He began to swim with more vigour, the freedom of the river almost sensual after the strain and activity of the night. A light rain began to fall. Drinkwater rolled onto his back and let the gentle drops wash over his face.

By the time he floundered ashore on the opposite bank the rain had become a steady downpour.

The Meeting of Eagles

Drinkwater found himself in shallow water a mile below the town where the Nieman's banks were reeded. Lush green water-meadows lay beyond, rising slowly to low hills clear in the grey light. A windmill surmounted one of these and he remembered passing it as they had approached Tilsit. He lay for some time, gathering his strength and no longer sustained by the vodka. The rain had drawn a heavy veil of cloud across the sky and a smoking mist hung over the river. He had come a long way downstream, to be met by a herd of piebald cows whose steaming muzzles were turned suspiciously towards him. He would have to make for the road and knew that the next hour was, for him, the most dangerous. He had been unable to think out any strategy for his journey back, hoping that he would land in darkness only a short distance below the Ostkai.

'You are grown too old for this lunatic game,' he muttered wearily to himself and rose to his feet. Squelching through the reeds he reached a place where the river bank was trodden down by countless cattle hooves. The raindrops plopped heavily into each tiny lake and the mud dragged at his feet. He struggled through cow-pats and sodden grass, making towards the windmill and the road. He was within a few yards of the mill when the bugle sounded reveille. With a sudden panic he realised the place was a billet and full of soldiers. He fell back towards a ditch on his left. Then he saw the boat.

With ineffable relief he turned to it. It was a crude, flat-bottomed punt, meant only for river work, but it had a pair of oars across the thwarts and offered Drinkwater the only satisfactory means of re-entering Tilsit. He was dressed as a lighter-man and here was a boat, presumably belonging to the mill, and a downpour to explain his soaking condition. With renewed heart he clambered aboard and untied the frayed painter from a rotten stake. He got out the oars and worked the boat out of the dyke. Ashore he could hear shouts as men assembled for morning roll-call. He entered the main river, the rain hissing down, the smooth grey water an infinity of concentric circular ripples. Keeping close to the bank he found the counter-current and pulled easily upstream. Despite his lack of sleep he found his lassitude evaporate; the demands of pulling the boat sent new life into his chilling limbs and the rain seemed warm upon his tired muscles.

Edward Drinkwater lay on his back in the solitary darkness and fought successive waves of panic that swept over him, manifesting themselves in reflexive spasms of nausea. Despite the pale sliver of sky that showed through the slits his brother had opened in the float, the surrounding darkness had a threatening quality, a sentient hostility that caused him to imagine it was contracting upon him. So strong was this awful sensation that twice he found himself stuffing a fist into his mouth to prevent himself from screaming, while a cold sweat broke out all over his body. But these periods of terrifying panic waned and were replaced by a slow acceptance of his situation which was aided by the bottle of vodka. After an hour or two he floated in a kind of limbo: the stinking bilge-water and the damp clothes that wrapped him seemed bearable.

He was jerked from his reverie by the noise of approaching feet scrunching the gravel and his heartbeats thundered in the clammy darkness as men resumed work on the raft. The hammering and sawing went on for what seemed hours, resonating throughout the float so that his former silence seemed heavenly by comparison. He lay on his back, twisting about from time to time to keep his circulation going, watching the narrow strip of sky periodically obscured by the boot-soles of the French soldiers and diverting himself by practising eavesdropping on their conversation. Sometime later he smelt a curious smell and recognised it as it grew stronger for the odour of Stockholm tar. He knew then that it was almost time for the pontoon to be dragged down the slipway and into the river.

'They are heating tar,' observed Lord Walmsley, taking his eye from Drinkwater's telescope and turning towards Mackenzie lying on the truckle bed. 'D'you think the Captain and Ostroff are all right?'

'Uh?' Mackenzie rubbed the sleep from his eyes and rolled off the bed to join Walmsley at the window. 'I hope by now Ostroff is – what d'you sailors say? – *battened down* in that *pont volant* and the Captain already in the stable below. What o'clock is it?'

'Seven has struck, and the half hour. D'you want me to look in the stable?'

161

'Yes, take my cloak. Bennigsen's lot sleep late; they gave a dinner last night for some French officers. Just act boldly, there are too many comings and goings for anyone to take any notice, and the sentries are too ignorant to stop anyone with an air of authority.' Mackenzie gave a short, contemptuous laugh. 'Good men in a fight but deprived of any initiative . . . the Jew will notice you . . . take a rouble from the gold on the bed and slip it to the burgher if you see him.' Mackenzie's voice became weary, as though the corruptibility of men bored him. Behind him the door-latch clicked and the stairs creaked as Walmsley descended to the stables. Mackenzie focused his attention on the distant pontoon. The final touches were being put to the decorations, a wooden monogram placed over each of two draped entrances. He saw two men, wearing the regulation aprons of pioneers, emerge from under the pontoon with a steaming pot of pitch. The men worked doggedly but without enthusiasm as the rain continued to fall. He shifted his glass to the barge that the two brothers had moved across the river the evening before. Already a group of labourers had brought piles of sawn deals from an adjacent warehouse where they had been awaiting shipment, and were laying them across the lighter's open hatch to make a platform. Mackenzie took the glass from his eye and rubbed it, yawning. A movement on the extreme right of his field of vision caught his eye. A man was rowing upstream in a small boat. He would soon become involved with three other boats, anchored to moorings which they had been laying in mid-stream. There was more movement too, on the Westkai. They were changing the guard opposite. The sentries from a line regiment were being replaced by the tall bearskins and red plumes of the French Imperial Guard.

'*Grand tenue*, by Jupiter,' he muttered sardonically to himself. 'Pity about the rain.'

He peered cautiously below him where, on the Ostkai, a similar ritual was in progress. Instead of bearskins the Russian Guard wore great brass-fronted mitre-caps that had gone out of vogue in every other European army a generation earlier.

'*Touché*,' chuckled Mackenzie, almost enjoying himself, as the brilliance of the preparations was muted by the heavy downpour. The man in the small boat had pulled alongside and was making his painter fast.

Lord Walmsley could find no sign of Captain Drinkwater in the stable, but he found something else, something he had failed to find in

162

his walk of the previous night. The naked leg of a girl hung from the hayloft. Walmsley felt a stab of lust and cautiously peered through the gap in the stable doors. Several orderlies lounged under the overhanging roof of a balcony on the opposite side of the courtyard. They were smoking and drinking tea, and clearly unwilling to rush into the business of grooming officers' chargers while their owners slept off the excesses of the night. The stable was heavy with the smell of horses, dung and hay. The magnificent animals reminded him of his father's stables, and the naked ankle of a girl he had once laid in the straw there.

There was a ladder close to the bare foot and he climbed it, taking care not to wake its owner. The horses stamped and pawed the ground and whickered softly to each other, but he ignored them and climbed up to the sleeping girl. She was a maid in the Jew's service and lay prettily asleep, her red mouth half-smiling and her dreams full of the love-making of the Prince who had had her the night before. She had escaped when his drunkenness became violent, and found her refuge in the hayloft. Walmsley was aroused by the sight and scent of her. He slid a hand over her leg. She turned languidly, her body responding, and opened her eyes. Walmsley smothered her surprise with his kisses, his urgency meeting her own awakened lust half-way, and with the intemperate passion of their youth they were swiftly entwined in each other's arms.

Drinkwater flicked the painter through the ring set in the face of the quay, shipped his oars and steadied the boat at the foot of the steps. It was too late to turn back. The military activity on the Ostkai would have to be brazened out. He climbed the steps and found himself face to face with a giant of a man in a huge brass-fronted hat. The man stood immobile in the continuing rain and, without the slightest hindrance, Drinkwater shuffled past him. No one took the slightest notice of so disreputable and so familiar a sight as a dirty, stinking peasant. Even the orderlies smoking in the yard of the merchant's house ignored him. He was able to slip into the stable as arranged. From here Mackenzie was to arrange his return to the attic when the coast was clear.

He found Midshipman Lord Walmsley standing at the top of a ladder, buttoning his breeches. Wisps of straw clung to his clothing and beside him the face of a girl appeared. He caught the gleam of gold tossed to her, saw her bite it and lie back giggling. Neither of the lovers had seen the sodden beggar at the doorway. Then Walmsley turned and spotted Drinkwater, who scowled at the midshipman and, catching sight of Mackenzie's cloak that Walmsley had carelessly draped over one of the stalls, pulled it round himself. Walmsley joined him in silent embarrassment and led him into the house.

Mackenzie turned as they regained the attic. 'Ah, he found you all right. Good. Welcome back. Did everything pass as planned?'

'Well enough,' said Drinkwater shortly. He rounded angrily on the midshipman. 'What the hell are you playing at, you fool? Was that English gold you gave that trollop?' he asked savagely. 'If it was you'll likely have us all damned for your stupidity.'

'You gave that gold piece away? To a girl, or the Jew?' Mackenzie asked curtly.

Walmsley went pale under the inquisition of the two men.

'He gave it to a whore!'

'Who was she? That trull that skivvies for the Jew?'

Walmsley nodded.

Mackenzie chuckled. 'Calm yourself, Captain. It was Russian gold and I expect the trull has given him something for small change. It is of no account, she has been laid by most of Bennigsen's kill-bucks and I doubt she can tell the difference between an Englishman and a Russian in the throes of love!' Mackenzie dismissed the matter.

Drinkwater was dropping with fatigue. He sank on the low bed and, within moments was asleep.

It was past noon when Mackenzie shook him awake. 'You should come and look. Great events are in progress. There is some bread and sausage . . .'

Drinkwater rose with a cracking of strained muscles. His shoulder ached with a dull, insistent pain, but he stripped the filthy rags from his body and drew on his own breeches and shirt, joining Mackenzie at the window.

'You smell better in your own clothes,' observed Mackenzie, making way in the open casement. There was no need for conceal-ment now for nearly every window was occupied by a curious public. Both quays were lined by the massed ranks of the Imperial Guards of both Emperors, row upon row of splendid men in the impressive regalia of full-dress, their officers at their posts. A handful of staff-officers, more youthful than useful, dashed up and down on curvet-ting horses, their hooves striking sparks from the cobblestones. The heavy rain of the morning had stopped and a watery sun peeped occasionally through gaps in the clouds, lighting up bright patches of red roof tiles, the green leaves of trees and the gaudy splendours of military pomp.

But it was the river that was the cynosure for all eyes. A musket-shot from the watchers in the attic, roughly level with the slipway from which it had been dragged that morning and moored in the centre of the Nieman, the flying bridge lay at anchor. It was festooned with a profusion of drapery, red and blue and green, laced with gold tasselling, and on the side facing them the drapes had been looped back to form an entrance surmounted by the initial letter 'A'. Twenty yards downstream lay the less gaily appointed barge.

'Impressive, eh?' Mackenzie was grinning like a schoolboy on holiday and both knew a sense of triumph at their success. Two boats had now arrived, one on each side of the river waiting at the steps there. On the far quay a cavalcade of horsemen had appeared, riding through the ranks of soldiers. On a white horse sat the unmistakable figure of Napoleon Bonaparte, Emperor of the French, wearing the green and white of the Horse Chasseurs of the Guard. He was followed by a glittering bevy of marshals, one of whom ostentatiously caracoled his horse.

'That vainglorious fellow is Murat,' whispered Mackenzie.

They watched Napoleon dismount and walk to the steps. In the boat below him an officer stood and Drinkwater drew in his breath, for it was Santhonax. He pointed him out to Mackenzie and they watched the Emperor and some of his entourage embark. People on either bank were cheering. A minute later and the French marines were plying their oars as the boat swung out for the caparisoned raft. The distant batteries began the ritual discharge of the imperial salutes.

Mackenzie pointed downwards and they craned their necks. Almost exactly below them a similar scene was being enacted and another boat was pulling out from the Ostkai. Sitting in the stern were several officers of exalted rank.

'Ouvaroff and Count Lieven have their backs to us,' explained Mackenzie in a low voice, 'the gentleman with the unpleasant countenance is the Grand Duke Constantine, next to him is Bennigsen . . .' Drinkwater looked at the snub-nosed, stubborn features of the Hanoverian. He was answering a query from a fifth man, a tall, erect, red-haired officer in an immaculate, high-collared tunic.

'The Tsar.',

Drinkwater stared at the profile of the man who was said to be composed of a confusion of liberal ideals and autocratic inclinations.

Surrounded by the pomp of the occasion it was difficult to imagine that the handsome head knew anything but the certainty of its own will. A reputation for erratic decisions or total apathy seemed undeserved. The bizarre sight of the Tsar chatting to a man who had engineered the death of his own father, whom he had the day before humiliated in public and who, Mackenzie thought with his amazing prescience, might turn his coat in the next hour or two, reminded Drinkwater that he was in Kurland, a remote corner of a remote empire whose alliance with his own country was in jeopardy.

Beside him Mackenzie's mood ran in a lighter vein. 'Trust Boney to work for a meeting on equal footing and then upstage Alexander.'

The French boat arrived at the raft first. It pulled away to disembark the French staff on the barge, downstream. As the Russian boat arrived alongside the raft and Alexander stood to disembark, Napoleon appeared in the entrance on the Russian side, his hand outstretched. A great cheer went up from the massed soldiery on either bank. As the Russian boat dropped downstream, Napoleon let the curtains of the pavilion down with his own hands.

As if at a signal of the combined imperial wills, the concussions of the salutes faded into echoes and from a lowering sky the rain again began to fall.

In total secrecy, two men decided the fate of Europe.

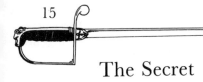

The Secret

Edward Drinkwater found the water rose no more than four inches about him once the pontoon had been launched. He found his situation uncomfortable but was less anxious once he felt the raft moored. He had suffered a brief, heart-thumping fear as the water rose about him, but his brother had been right, though to what properties of hydrostatics it was due, Edward was quite ignorant. The clumsy vessel found a sort of equilibrium, presumably supported by the other chambers, or perhaps due to its attitude to the stream of the river, once it had been moored. At all events the inrush of water soon ceased and he lay awash, awake and alert.

He heard the cannon and the cheers and the bumps of the boats. A few indistinct words of French, a rapid series of footsteps overhead, and then a voice asked: 'Why are we at war?'

It was quite distinct and clear, even above the rush and chuckle of the water to which his ears had become attuned, a question posed with some asperity and emotion. The reply was equally charged and candid: 'I hate the English as much as you do!' Edward recognised the Tsar's voice.

There was the small sharp slap of clapped hands and a brief barked laugh. 'In that case, my dear friend, peace is made!'

Lord Walmsley was denied much of a view of this historic event by Drinkwater and Mackenzie. The delights of the morning, despite the embarrassment of their conclusion, had not satisfied his desire. Mackenzie's gold still lay on the bed where it had been taken from the butt of one of his pistols. The girl might be a whore, as Captain Drinkwater and the mysterious Mr Mackenzie had alleged, but the captain was prone to a certain puritan narrowness. Walmsley had lain with whores before and he had been far too long without a woman. It was true he owed Captain Drinkwater a great deal, but not his moral welfare; that was his own business. Besides the girl had been good. Walmsley sat on the bed and supposed it had been hers before Mackenzie had seduced her Jewish master with his limitless gold. Desire pricked him again and he knew he would not be missed for a while. As the bellowing of the Guards again broke out, Walmsley slipped from the attic unnoticed. On the raft, the two Emperors had reappeared, smiling publicly. Renewed cheering greeted this concord and echoed through the streets of Tilsit.

General Santhonax dismounted from his horse and threw the reins to an orderly. It was already evening and the volleys from the two armies which signalled a general rejoicing had at last died away. He was tired, having been up since just after dawn, when the report of the missing sentry had been brought to him. It was the fourth such desertion of the night and with the armistice declared he was not surprised. He greeted a fellow officer with a tired smile.

'Ah, Lariboissière, His Imperial Majesty requires you to start immediately to throw a pontoon bridge across the river. He is desirous of impressing our late enemies with the superiority of our engineering. You may withdraw the rafts when you have finished.'

'*Merde!*' Lariboissière and his men were tired out, but an order was an order. 'Was His Imperial Majesty satisfied with today's arrangements, General Santhonax?'

Santhonax remounted and settled himself in the saddle. 'Perfectly, my friend,' he said urbanely, tugging his charger's head round. 'It went better than I anticipated.'

Edward had had enough. His head still buzzed with the news he had gleaned and he was eager to escape confinement. He had heard the town clock strike six and could wait no longer. Twisting round he got his shoulders against the plank-ends that Drinkwater had nailed down and pushed hard. He felt something give, and kicked. The plank-end sprang and light entered the chamber. He forced the other end free. The plank dropped into the water and he repeated the performance with the next. More water began to lap into the chamber. He took a deep breath and forced his body through the gap, rolled into the water and submerged. When he came up he was clear of the raft. Over his head arched the blue of the evening sky. He felt a supreme elation fill him and kicked luxuriously downstream.

General Santhonax pulled up his horse at the end of the Westkai and stared down at the slip where the *pont volant* had spent the previous night. The trampled gravel was covered with sawdust, wood offcuts and a few pieces of cloth where the drapery had been trimmed. One of the men had left a tool behind. The polished steel gleamed dully in the muck where it lay half-buried by a careless foot. It looked like a cavalry farrier's axe.

The professional curiosity of a former secret agent made Santhonax dismount and jump down onto the hard. He pulled the axe out of the mire and looked at its head. A feeling of disquieting curiosity filled him. He returned to his horse, tapping the grubby object thoughtfully with one gloved hand. Lithuanian workmen had been employed in raising the pavilion, but they had been civilians. What then was a Russian farrier's axe doing there? He looked down again. The thing had stained his white gloves with mud. But there was something else too: the spike on the vicious weapon was sticky with blood and hair.

A sudden alarm gripped General Santhonax. He recalled the post of one of the missing sentries and his eyes flew to the gaudy and deserted raft in midstream. A sudden flash came from just below the raft, a plank upflung and yellow with new wood reflected the low evening sunlight that had replaced the day's rain. And was that a head that bobbed and was gone behind the barge? He kicked his horse into motion, leaving the quay and riding along the raised bank that was topped by a narrow path. He fished in one holster for his glass.

Then he was sure. Downstream on the far bank he saw a man crawl out of the river. His blood ran cold. That man had to die, die secretly without the Emperor ever knowing that Santhonax had failed in his duty.

Tilsit was *en fête*, celebrating the peace. Candles lit every window again, the streets were thronged and cheers greeted every person of consequence who appeared. The Tsar was wildly applauded as he prepared to cross the river and dine with Napoleon. Edward made his way through the crowd to the rear of Jew's house unnoticed, for it was abandoned by Bennigsen and his suite, and the orderlies had taken themselves off to celebrate in their own manner, leaving only the sentries at the main entrance. Edward reached the attic and was helped out of his stinking rags while both Mackenzie and Drinkwater waited eagerly for his report. In the excitement no one was concerned by Walmsley's absence.

'Well,' said Mackenzie as Edward devoured a sausage and a quantity of vodka, 'our luck cannot last for ever, we are in hostile territory now by all accounts.'

'You are indeed,' said Edward swallowing the vodka, standing naked in a tin bath. 'But another thousand . . .'

'Damn you, Ned!'

'Five hundred,' said Mackenzie coolly, picking up the pistol from the bed, 'and not a penny more.' Mackenzie brought the pistol barrel up and pointed it at Edward's groin.

Edward realised he had chosen a bad moment to bargain; a man rarely impresses when naked. 'Very well, gentlemen,' he said grinning sheepishly and attempting to pass off the matter lightly.

'The truth, mind,' warned Mackenzie, the pistol unwavering.

'Yes, yes, of course,' agreed Edward testily, reaching for his breeches as if insulted that he was suspected of real perfidy.

'Well?'

'There are to be long negotiations, but Napoleon is a master of deceit; he played Alexander like a woman. I have never heard flattery like it. He sold his ally Turkey to the Tsar, promised him a free hand against the Porte, guaranteed him the same in Swedish Finland, told him that he was a true child of the liberating ideals of the French Revolution and that the two of them would release the new renaissance of a resuscitated Europe! I could scarcely believe my ears. Why such a tirade of flattery and promises should be made in such secrecy is for you to judge.'

'One always seduces in private,' observed Mackenzie, ironically, 'but go on. What of Great Britain?'

'That came last, though I distinctly heard Alexander declare his hatred of the English at the start, but he was much less easy to hear . . .'

'Go on, we have little time . . .'

'Britain is to be excluded from all trade with Europe or Russia. The Tsar agrees to chastise anyone who trades with a nation so perfidious as yours.' Edward paused, his choice of words significant. 'Your navy is to be destroyed by sheer weight of numbers. Napoleon said your navy is exhausted, your sources of manpower drying up, and that you cannot maintain a blockade for ever. He told the Tsar, who made some remark at this point, that your victory at Trafalgar was a narrow one and that this is proved by the death of Lord Nelson. He claimed the tide would have gone the other way but for the Spaniards deserting the French. Had the French had the Russian fleet with them that day the trident of Neptune would have been wrested from Britannia and with it the sceptre of the world!'

'What eloquence,' remarked Mackenzie.

'So the Russian fleet is to break out of the Baltic, eh?' asked Drinkwater.

'Yes. The Baltic is to be a *mare clausum* to Britain, supine under Russian domination, and to outnumber you the Portuguese fleet is to be seized at Lisbon and the Danish to be commandeered at Copenhagen.'

'God's bones!' exclaimed Drinkwater, his mind whirling with the news. With France and Russia allies, Napoleon's power in Europe would be absolute. The Russians would be free to expand into Turkey, the French to mass their great armies on the Channel shore once more for a final descent upon England. Napoleon would be able to summon the combined navies of every European power to add to his own. There were ships of the line building at Toulon, at Brest, at Antwerp; the Portuguese navy and the Danish navy would add a powerful reinforcement to the Russian squadrons already at sea, cruising as allies of Great Britain. Against such a force even the battle-hardened Royal Navy would find itself outgunned by sheer weight of metal! And, as Drinkwater well knew, the Royal Navy, that reassuring bulwark of the realm, was wearing out. Its seamen were sick of endless blockade, its officers dispirited by stalemate, its admirals worn with cares and its ships with sea-keeping. Such an outcome negated Drinkwater's whole life and he was filled with a sudden urgency to be off, to leave this stifling attic and regain the fresh air of his quarterdeck and a quick passage home with this vital intelligence.

'You have done well,' Mackenzie was saying, spilling into his palm a shower of gold. He held it out to Edward who was now fully dressed. 'Here, this is on account, the rest within the month in the usual way.'

Edward pocketed the cash. He was again the Russian officer, Ostroff. He held out his hand to Drinkwater. 'The parting of the ways, then Nat?'

Drinkwater nodded. 'Yes . . . it would seem so.'

'I have discharged all my obligations today.'

'With interest,' said Mackenzie drily as the two brothers shook hands.

'Where's Walmsley?' Drinkwater asked suddenly as their minds turned towards departure. The three men exchanged glances.

'He can't be far away,' said Mackenzie. 'It isn't the first time he's wandered off.'

'No, but it will be the last,' snapped Drinkwater anxiously.

'He's gone a-whoring,' said Edward as he bent to pick up his gear.

Mackenzie slung his saddle-bags over his shoulder and Drinkwater put a pistol in his waistband.

'We cannot wait,' said Mackenzie, looking at Drinkwater.' Perhaps he's down below.' Mackenzie unbarred the door and led them out down the steep and narrow stairs.

The only person they met in their descent through the eerie silence of the house was the Jew, who was on an upper landing. Mackenzie passed more money to him and the three men walked into the courtyard, shadowed by the late afternoon sunlight.

'I have a horse quartered here,' said Edward turning aside.

'Where do you go now?' asked Drinkwater.

'To Vorontzoff,' Edward replied, entering the stable. Drinkwater followed to see if Walmsley was repeating his performance of that morning: a brief look showed the hayloft empty.

'Come on . . .' said Mackenzie.

Drinkwater hesitated. 'I must have a look for Walmsley.'

Mackenzie swore and, for the first time since they had met, Drinkwater saw irresolution in his face. 'Damn it then, a quick look, but hurry!'

General Santhonax had searched the warehouses of the lower town as unobtrusively as possible. The thought that a soaking man could not vanish without accomplices beat in his brain. He reached the Ostkai with its tall houses where the previous evening he had selected the barge. Lariboissière's men, with whose help he had crossed the river, were already stretching the first cable of the bridge Napoleon had ordered thrown over the Nieman. Angrily he turned away. Perhaps the inns round the town square might have offered concealment.

Lord Walmsley smiled down at the girl. The bed of the Russian prince was rumpled by the wanton violence of their combined lust, but Walmsley knew he had to leave, to see if the strange, English-speaking Russian officer, Ostroff, had returned to the attic. He emerged onto the landing, hearing a noise on the stairs. Below him someone went out into the courtyard. From a window he could just see down into the deepening shadows of the yard. Captain Drinkwater was there and he was joined by Ostroff, leading a grey horse out of the stable. At the same time Mackenzie appeared, shaking his head. It was obvious that departure was imminent. Behind him the girl appeared and wound her arms around him.

*　　　　　*　　　　　*

Below in the courtyard the three men were holding a hurried conference.

'Nothing. It means we'll have to search the place thoroughly.'

'He may have wandered off anywhere,' said Mackenzie. 'I let him go for a while yesterday . . .'

'You'd best forget him,' said Edward, putting one foot in the stirrup. 'I will keep an eye out for him and spirit him away if I can.'

'And if you can't?' asked Drinkwater, at once furious with the midshipman for his desertion and in a quandary as to what to do.

'Come, this is no time to delay, we must make the best of our separate ways now,' Mackenzie said, taking Drinkwater's elbow. 'Come on, it is only a short walk to Gower's chaise and we have little to fear. It will not be very surprising if a Scottish merchant and an English shipmaster evacuate Tilsit in the wake of the day's events.'

Edward looked down from his horse. 'Goodbye, Nat, and good luck. Forget your young friend. I'll do what I can.'

'Very well, and thank you. Good fortune.'

The two men smiled and Edward dug his heels into the flanks of the grey and clattered out of the yard. At the arched entrance his horse shied, skittering sideways as a tall military officer almost collided with them. Edward kicked his mount forward.

As the big grey horse trotted away Santhonax looked under the arch. He saw two men walking towards him carrying bags over their shoulders; they had the appearance of travellers on the point of departure, yet he could see no reason for men to leave a town that was so full of wild celebration. With sudden caution he drew his pistol as they entered the covered passage and moved towards him.

Drinkwater saw the man under the arch and caught the movement of the drawn pistol.

'Look,' he hissed, sensing danger at the same moment as Mackenzie.

Drinkwater's hand went to his own pistol, Mackenzie strode forward.

'*Bonsoir m'sieur,*' he said. In the gloom the man turned and Drinkwater recognised Santhonax. Without a moment's thought he swung his heavy pistol butt: the steel heel of the weapon caught Santhonax on the jaw and he crashed against the wall. Drinkwater hit him a second time. Santhonax sprawled full length, unconscious.

'It's Santhonax,' hissed Drinkwater as both men stared down at the French general, their thoughts racing. 'Do you think he was looking for us?'

'God knows!'

'Do we kill him?'

'No, that might raise a hue and cry. Take his watch, make it look like a theft.' Mackenzie bent over the inert body and wrenched at Santhonax's waist. He straightened up and handed a heavy gold watch to Drinkwater. 'Here . . .' Mackenzie rifled Santhonax's pockets and then turned back the way they had come. 'Leave him. To hell with the chaise. I smell trouble. For all I know he's already discovered Walmsley . . . there is not a moment to lose.'

Drinkwater ran back, following Mackenzie into the stable. In a lather of inexpert haste Drinkwater tried to get a horse saddled in imitation of Mackenzie. The other came over and finished the job for him. They drew the horses out of the stable and mounted them. Drinkwater hoisted himself gingerly into the saddle.

'Are you all right?' hissed Mackenzie.

'I think so . . .' Drinkwater replied uncertainly as the horse moved beneath him, sensing his nervousness.

'Listen! If we are pursued, get to Memel and your ship! Go direct to London. Ostroff and I will take care of Walmsley . . . Come, let's go!'

They rode across the yard and through the archway.

Behind them General Santhonax stirred and groaned.

Santhonax got slowly to his feet, clawing himself upright by the wall. His head throbbed painfully and his jaw was severely contused. He staggered forward and the courtyard swam into his vision. He looked dazedly about him. A young man was staring at him and then seemed to vanish. Santhonax frowned: the young man had been wearing something very like a seaman's coat.

His head cleared and then it came back to him. The two men, the sudden guilty hesitation and the deceptive confrontation by one of them while the other struck him with a clubbed pistol. The apparition of the youth and the smell of a stable full of horses spurred him to sudden activity. He crossed the yard and met Walmsley at the stable door.

'What's happening?' asked Walmsley in English, mistaking his man in the gloom. Santhonax smiled savagely.

'Nothing,' he replied reassuringly, his own command of English accent-free.

'Is that you, Ostroff?'

'Yes,' lied Santhonax, silhouetted against the last of the daylight.

'Have they gone then?' Santhonax heard alarm awaken in the

question. 'Are they getting the chaise?' Guilt had robbed Walmsley of his wits.

'Yes . . .' Santhonax pushed Walmsley backwards and followed him into the stable.

'Why, you're not Ostroff! That's a French uniform!'

'*Oui m'sieur*, and who are you?' Walmsley felt the cold touch of a pistol muzzle at his chin. 'Come, quickly, or I'll kill you!'

Walmsley was trembling with fear. 'M . . . midshipman, British navy!'

With this information Santhonax realised the extent of his own failure to keep the Emperor's secret.

'You are not wearing the uniform of a British midshipman, boy! Where are your white collar-patches? What the hell are you doing here?'

'I was acting under orders . . . attending my captain . . .'

'What captain? Where is your ship?'

Walmsley swallowed. 'I surrender my person . . . as a prisoner of war . . .'

'Answer, boy!' The pistol muzzle poked up harder under Walmsley's trembling chin.

'My frigate is off Memel.'

'And the captain?' asked Santhonax, lowering his pistol and casting an eye for a suitable horse. Walmsley sensed reprieve.

'Captain Drinkwater, of the *Antigone*, sir,' he said in a relieved tone.

Santhonax swung his face back to his prisoner and let out a low oath. 'You are a spy, boy . . .'

Walmsley tried to twist away as Santhonax brought up the pistol and squeezed the trigger. The ball shattered the midshipman's skull and he fell amid the straw and horse dung.

Among the rearing and frightened animals Santhonax grabbed Walmsley's saddled horse and led it through the doorway, then mounted and dug his spurs into the animal's sides. The terrified horse lunged forward and Santhonax tugged its head in the direction of the road to Memel.

PART THREE

The Post-chaise

"It is their intention to employ the navies of Denmark and Portugal against this country."

George Canning, Foreign Secretary,
to the House of Commons, July 1807

Accord

The two Emperors sat at the head of an array of tables that glittered with silver and crystal. The assembled company was peacock-gaudy with the military of three nations. The sober Prussians, humiliated by the indifference of Napoleon and the implied slight to their beautiful queen, were dour and miserable, while Russians and French sought to outdo one another in the lavishness of their uniforms and the extravagance of their toasts.

General Bennigsen, still smarting from the Tsar's rebuke, sat next to the King of Prussia whose exclusion from the secret talks had stung him to the quick. His lovely Queen displayed a forced vivacity to the two Emperors, who sat like demi-gods.

'She is', Napoleon confided slyly to the Tsar, 'the finest man in the whole of Prussia, is she not?'

Alexander, beguiled and charmed by his former enemy, delighted at the outcome of the discussions which gave him a free hand in Finland and Turkey, agreed. The man he had until today regarded as a parvenu now fascinated him. Napoleon had shown Alexander a breadth of vision equalling his own, a mind capable of embracing the most liberal and enlightened principles, yet knowing the value of compulsion in forcing those measures upon the dark, half-witted intelligence of the mass of common folk.

'I hope', Napoleon's voice said at his side, 'that you are pleased with today's proceedings?'

Alexander turned to Napoleon and smiled his fixed, courtly and slightly vacant smile. 'the friendship between France and Russia', he said to his neighbour, 'has long been my most cherished dream.'

Napoleon smiled in return. 'Your Majesty shows a profound wisdom in these matters,' he said and Alexander inclined his head graciously at this arrant flattery.

Napoleon regarded the banquet and the numerous guests, his quick mind noting a face here and there. Suddenly his benign expression clouded over. He leaned back and beckoned an aide. Nodding to a vacant place on a lower table he asked the young officer, 'Where is General Santhonax?'

The Return of Ulysses

Drinkwater clung to his mount with increasing desperation. He was no horseman and the animal's jerking trot jolted him from side to side so that he gasped for breath and at every moment felt that he would fall. It was years since he had ridden, and want of practice now told heavily against him. The thought of the long journey back to Memel filled him with horror.

Equally anxious, Mackenzie looked back every few yards, partly to see if Drinkwater was still in the saddle, partly to see if they were pursued.

As they left the town and found themselves surrounded by the bivouacs of the Russian army they passed camp-fire after camp-fire round which groups of men played cards, drank and smoked their foul tobacco tubes. There were other travellers on the road, officers making their way to the celebrations at Tilsit; but the news of peace had removed all necessity for caution and the horsemen continued unopposed along the Memel road.

At last they drew away from the encampments. It was dark but the sky had cleared, and a silver crescent of moon gave a little light, showing the dusty highway as a pale stripe across the rolling country-side. As Drinkwater jogged uncomfortably in his saddle it occurred to him that as he became accustomed to the horse, he became less able to capitalise on his improvement, for his buttocks and inner thighs became increasingly sore.

Drinkwater grunted with pain as they rode on, passing through a village. The road was deserted but the noise of shouting, clapping and a guitar came from its inn. A few miles beyond the village Mackenzie looked back at his lagging companion. What he saw made him rein in his horse. They were in open countryside now. The Nieman gleamed a pistol shot away, reflecting the stars, and the road lay deserted before them.

Drinkwater looked up as he saw Mackenzie stop and heard him swear.

'I'm doing my damndest . . .'

'It's not that . . . Look!'

Drinkwater pulled his horse up and turned. A man was pursuing them, his horse kicking up a pale cloud of dust, just discernible in the gloom.

'Santhonax!'

'Can you remember the content of Edward's report?' Mackenzie asked sharply.

'Of course . . .'

'Then ride on . . . go . . . get back to your ship. I'll do what I can to stop him, but do not under any circumstances stop!'

'But you? What will you do?'

'I'll manage . . . get to London overland, Captain, bringing your midshipman with me, but you go *now*!' And Mackenzie brought an impatient hand down on the rump of Drinkwater's horse.

'God's bones!' Drinkwater lost the reins and grabbed the animal's mane, his sore knees pressed desperately inwards against the saddle. He dared not look back but he heard the pistol shots, and the image of Santhonax still in hot pursuit kept him riding through the night as if all the devils in hell were on his tail.

Lieutenant James Quilhampton lay rigid and awake in the darkness. The scratching sound came again, accompanied by a sibilant hiss. He swung his legs over the edge of the cot and, crouching, pressed his ear against the cabin door.

'Who is it?'

'Frey, sir.'

Quilhampton opened the cabin door and drew the boy inside. He was in shirt and breeches, a pale ghost in the darkness.

'What the devil d'you want?'

'Sergeant Blixoe sent me, sir. Roused me out and sent me to wake you and the other lieutenant. He says there's a combination of two score of men in the cable tier. They're murmuring, sir . . . after the day's events . . .'

Quilhampton began tearing off his nightshirt. 'Get Mr Fraser and Mr Mount, quickly now, while I dress, no noise . . . then double below and tell Blixoe to call out all his men!'

He began to dress, cursing Rogers. The first lieutenant had flogged two men the previous day with the thieves' cat. Their offences were common and had not warranted such severity. One had neglected his duty, the other was judged guilty of insolence towards an officer. What made the event significant was that the man who had not jumped to his allotted task with sufficient alacrity to satisfy Rogers had not done so because he had been flogged for drunkenness only the previous day. This circumstance had sown a seed of genuine grievance among men whose usual tolerance of the navy's rough and summary justice had been overstretched during Rogers's brief tenure of command. The surgeon's claim that the man was not fit to receive punishment had encouraged a seaman to speak up in support of the protest and he had been judged guilty of insolence by an infuriated Rogers.

Before nightfall one of the men was dead and the news spread quickly through the ship. Shortly after midnight, word had gone round the berth deck of a meeting of delegates from each mess in the cable tier. It was this disturbance that had prompted Sergeant Blixoe to action.

Quilhampton checked the priming of his pistol and belted on his sword. His anxiety at Drinkwater's absence had increased with every abuse and loss of temper that had marked Rogers's behaviour. For the last few days every motion of the ship's company had been accompanied by ferocious criticism and vitriolic scorn as Rogers continued to exercise the crew remorselessly.

Drinkwater's regime had been too lax, their performances too slow. The bosun's mates were too gentle with their starters and Rogers, in a paroxysm of rage, had grabbed the rope's end from the hand of one man and laid about him in a fury, sending the topmen scampering aloft. When he was satisfied with their performance he had brought them down again, then started the bosun's mate for 'lenience' and disrated him. Quilhampton knew Rogers was exercising considerable will-power over his craving for drink. But his ungovernable rages and transports of savage injustice had become intolerable.

He emerged from his cabin and turned forward, ducking under the men still in their hammocks. There was no sentry at the midships companionway and he stood and looked down into the cable tier. The space was capacious, but filled with the great coils of ten-inch hemp, so that the huge ropes formed miniature amphitheatres, lit by lanterns, their sides lined with thirty or forty men in vehement but whispered debate.

'But the captain ain't 'ere, for Chris' sakes . . . and that black-hearted bastard'll kill more men before 'e gets back . . .'

183

'*If* 'e gets back . . .'

'If we rise, do we take 'em all?'

'Yes,' a man hissed, 'kill all the buggers, for they'll all flog you!'

'Aye, an' we're men, not fucking animals!'

'Let's act like men then!'

'Aye!'

'Aye!'

They began to stir, resolution hardening in their faces, an impression heightened by the lamplight. Quilhampton realised he had to move fast. He cocked the pistol and descended the ladder.

The silence that greeted his appearance was murderous. He stared about him, noting faces. 'This is mutinous behaviour,' he said and judging a further second's delay would lose him the initiative added, 'the Captain's due back imminently.'

'That may be too late for some of us,' a voice said from the rear. It found an echo of agreement among the men.

'Go back to your hammocks. No good can come of this.'

'Don't trust the bastard!'

Quilhampton uncocked the pistol and stuck it in his belt. 'The marines are already alerted. Mr Mount and Mr Fraser are awake. For all I know they've called Mr Rogers . . .'

'We are betrayed!'

Quilhampton watched the effect of this news. Fear was clear on every man's face, for they knew that once Rogers identified them, each man present would likely die. They had only two choices now, and Quilhampton had already robbed them of their weapon of surprise.

'Get to your hammocks, and let me find this place deserted.'

They remained stock still for a second, then by common consent they moved as one, slipping away in the darkness. Quilhampton waited until the last man had vanished, stepped forward into the encirclement of the cable and picked up the lantern. Reascending the companionway he walked aft. A few of the hammocks swung violently and he caught sight of a retracting leg. He ascended to the gundeck and met Lieutenant Mount. He was coming forward with his hanger drawn, his marines behind him in shirtsleeves but with their bayonets fixed. Fraser was there with the midshipmen and the master.

'James! Where the hell have you been, we've been looking for you?' Fraser asked anxiously.

'I went to check the cable tier.'

'You *what?*'

'Have you informed Lieutenant Rogers?'

Fraser and Mount looked at each other. It was clear they had been debating the point and had decided not to.

'Because if you have, you had better tell him it's a false alarm. The cable tier's quite empty . . . except for the cables of course . . .'

'This is no time to be flippant!' snapped an irritated Mount, lowering his hanger.

'This is no time to be wandering around,' said Quilhampton, with affected nonchalance. 'Good night, gentlemen!'

General Santhonax recovered consciousness aware of a great weight pressing upon his leg. His skull, sore from the pistol blow on the left-hand side of his head, now bore a second lump on his forehead where he had struck it as his horse fell. The animal was dead and it took him several minutes to assemble his thoughts. In the east the first signs of daylight streaked the sky and he recalled the urgent need for pursuit. Then, triggered off by this thought, the events of the previous night came back to him. He swore and pulled his leg painfully out from beneath the horse.

He needed another mount, and would have to go back to the horse lines of the nearest Russian cavalry regiment for one. He began unbuckling his saddle. Should he then ride on to Memel? Or was he already too late?

He paused, forcing his aching head to think. Drinkwater would be within ten miles of Memel by daylight. Pursuit was pointless, but return to Tilsit risked disgrace or worse.

Dawn showed the road ahead of him, a thin ribbon beside the grey shimmer of the Nieman, with only an early peasant and an ox-cart upon it. The devil alone knew how he could face the Emperor again, for it was certain his absence would have been noticed. A furious anger began to boil within him – he had been outwitted and by his old antagonist Drinkwater, of all people!

He had forgotten how many times their paths had crossed. He only recalled in his bitterness that he had twice passed up the opportunity to kill the man. How he regretted that leniency now! Napoleon's secret would be in London as fast as Drinkwater's frigate could carry it and she was, as Santhonax had cause to know, a fast ship. He smote his saddle in his frustration and then calmed himself and resolved on the only course now open to him. His anger was replaced by the desperate courage of absolute necessity. Dragging himself to his feet, Santhonax turned his footsteps back towards Tilsit.

It was mid-morning when Drinkwater reached Memel. His horse was blown and he slid to the cobbles of the quay, his legs buckling beneath him. The flesh of his thighs was raw and his whole body was racked with an unbelievable agony. He had covered fifty-odd miles in twelve hours and almost certainly outrun pursuit. He had no idea what had become of Mackenzie beyond knowing that he had thwarted Santhonax by some means. Pain made him light-headed and he sat for a moment in the sunshine of early morning, mastering himself and trying to think clearly. Whatever had happened to Mackenzie or Walmsley his own task was clear enough. Standing unsteadily he walked along the quay, looking down at the boats tied alongside. An occasional fisherman mended nets. None looked in condition to sail imminently. Only one man stared up at him, a broad-faced man with a stubby pipe who smiled and nodded.

Drinkwater felt in his pocket and his fist closed on some coins. He drew them out and pantomimed his wishes. The man frowned, repeating the gestures of pointing, first at Drinkwater, then at himself and then a quick double gesture at the deck of his boat and then the horizon. He seemed to ask a question and Drinkwater thought he heard the word 'English': he nodded furiously, pointing again at himself and then directly at the horizon.

Comprehension linked them and Drinkwater held out the gold for the man to see. There was a pause in the negotiation, then the man agreed and beckoned Drinkwater down onto the deck. Sliding back a small hatch, he called below, and a moment later a younger version of the fisherman appeared. Drinkwater made himself useful casting off and tallied on a halliard, within minutes they had hoisted sail and were moving seawards.

As Memel dropped astern and the Nieman opened into the Kurische Haff and then the Baltic Sea, his anxiety waned. He had avoided pursuit and for a while he enjoyed the sensation of the brisk sail as the fishing boat scudded along before a moderate breeze. It was good to feel the sea-wind on his face and see a horizon hard-edged and familiar. He relaxed and smiled at the pipe-smoking Kurlander at the tiller.

'A good boat,' Drinkwater said, patting the low rail.

The man nodded. '*Gut. Ja, ja . . .*'

Soon Drinkwater could see the masts and yards of the *Antigone*. His last fear, a childish one that the ship would not be on station, vanished. His problems were almost over. He could shave and bath and soak his raw flesh, and then sleep . . .

'All hands! All hands! All hands to witness punishment!'

Quilhampton looked up from the gunroom table where he had the midshipmen's journals spread out before him. He met the look of incredulity on Mount's face.

'Christ, not again . . .'

The two officers hurried into their coats, and left the gunroom buckling on their swords. As they emerged onto the upper deck they were aware of the ground-swell of discontent among the people milling in the waist. Rogers, in full dress, was already standing on the quarterdeck, Drinkwater's copy of the Articles of War in his hands.

'I should think he knows the Thirty-Sixth by heart,' Quilhampton heard someone mutter but he ignored the remark. Quilhampton took his now familiar place and cast a quick look over the marines. There might be a need for them shortly, but even among their stolid files there seemed to be a wavering and unsteadiness. He caught Blixoe's eye. The man's look was one of anger. Blixoe had acted to forestall mutiny in the night and Quilhampton had made a fool of him. Now the advantage of warning no longer lay with the officers and marines. With the whole ship's company assembled and every man except Rogers aware of what had transpired in the middle watch, a sudden explosion of spontaneous mutiny might result in the officers and marines being butchered on the spot.

'Silence there!' bawled Rogers, opening the book and calling for the prisoner.

It was Tregembo, his shoulder still bandaged, and pale from the effects of his wound. Quilhampton could only guess at Tregembo's crime and as Rogers read the charge it seemed to confirm his supposition. It was insolence to a superior officer. Tregembo had clearly spoken his mind to Rogers. The first lieutenant did not even ask if any officer would speak for the man. Once again he was lost to reason, consumed by whatever fires were eating him, possessed only of an insane hatred that had no meaning beyond expressing his own agony.

'Strip!'

Quilhampton was surprised to see the faint scars of previous floggings crossing Tregembo's back. Then Lallo stepped forward and declared the man unfit to undergo punishment. It was an act of considerable courage and so riveting was its effect on Rogers that no

187

one saw the fishing boat swoop under the stern, nor paid the slightest attention to a fluttering of sails as it dropped briefly alongside.

'Stand aside!' roared Rogers, stepping forward.

Lallo fell back a pace and Rogers rounded on the bosun's mates standing by the prisoner. 'Secure him!'

They crucified Tregembo across the capstan, lashing his spread-eagled arms along two of the bars. A thin trickle of blood started down his back from beneath the bandage of his wound. Flogging against a capstan was a barbarism that refined an already barbaric custom; to flog a wounded man was a measure of Rogers's depravity. What he did next he must have conceived as an act of humanity. As a murmur of horror ran through the ship's company at the sight of Tregembo's reopened wound, Rogers nodded to the bosun's mate holding the cat.

'Strike low! And do your duty!'

By avoiding the shoulder, the cat would not do further damage to the wound. But it would lacerate the lower back and could damage the organs unprotected by the rib-cage. The bosun's mate hesitated.

'Do your duty!' Rogers shrieked.

'Mr Rogers!'

The attention of every man swung to the rail. Teetering uncertainly at its top, a hand on each stanchion, an unshaven and dirty figure clung. The hatless apparition repeated itself.

'Mr Rogers!'

'It's the cap'n,' said Quilhampton and ran across the deck.

'Get the ship under way at once!' Drinkwater ordered, before falling forward into Quilhampton's arms.

The Vanguard of Affairs

Drinkwater stood immobile by the starboard hance, leaning against the hammock netting and with one foot resting on the slide of a small brass carronade. It seemed to the watches, as they changed every eight bells, that the captain's brooding presence had been continuous since they had broken the anchor out of the mud of Memel road four days earlier.

In fact the truth was otherwise, for it was Rogers who got the ship under weigh and Hill who laid off the first of the courses that would take them home. The captain had vanished below, exhausted and, rumour had it, wounded as well. It was a measure of Drinkwater's popularity that when the nature of his indisposition was properly known it did not become the subject for ribald comment. Nevertheless, as soon as he was rested and the surgeon had dressed his raw thighs, Drinkwater was on deck and had remained so ever since. He moved as little as possible, his legs too sore and his gait too undignified, atoning in his own mind for the sin of absence from his ship and the troubles it had caused.

The reassuring sight of Drinkwater's figure calmed the incipient spirit of revolt among the people. The fact that they were carrying sail like a Yankee packet and were bound for England raised their hopes and fed their dreams like magic. The dismal recollections of their period off Memel faded, and only the unusual sight of a marine sentry outside the first lieutenant's cabin served to remind the majority. But there were men who had longer memories, men who bore the scars of the cat, and, while the news of Lord Walmsley's disappearance seemed to establish an equilibrium of sacrifice in the collective consciousness of the frigate's population, there were those who planned to desert at the first opportunity.

For Drinkwater there was a great feeling of failure, despite the importance of the news he carried. It was compounded from many sources: the high excitement of his recent sortie; the intense, brief and

189

curiously unsatisfactory reunion with his brother; the death (for such he privately believed it to be) of Lord Walmsley; his uncertainty as to the fates of either Mackenzie or Santhonax; and finally, the tyrannical behaviour of Rogers and the maltreatment of Tregembo. All these had cast a great shadow over him and it took some time for this black mood to pass. It was in part a reaction after such exertion and in part a brooding worry over what was to be done about Samuel Rogers. There was a grim irony in contemplating the future of the first lieutenant; Rogers had failed worst where he had succeeded best. The effort of will and the strength of his addiction had combined to produce a monster. He had been placed under arrest and confined to his cabin where, so the surgeon reported, he had fallen into a profound catalepsy.

The only bright spots in Drinkwater's unhappy preoccupation were the continuing recovery of Tregembo and the value of the news from Tilsit. As the days passed these grew in strength, gradually eclipsing his misery. At last his spirits lifted, and he began to share something of the excitement of the ship's company at the prospect of returning home. He thought increasingly of his wife and children, of Susan Tregembo and the others in his household at Petersfield, but the heavy gold watch he carried in his waistcoat pocket reminded him that, despite the lofty press of sail *Antigone* bore and the air of expectancy that filled the chatter of her messes, it was the realities of war that drove her onwards.

The fair breeze that allowed them to stand to the westward under studding sails failed them during the forenoon of the last day of June. Chopping slowly round to the west, *Antigone* was forced to be close-hauled and stretch down into the shallow bight east of Rügen, leaving the island of Bornholm astern. By noon of the following day she was five leagues to the east of Cape Arkona and able to fetch a course towards Kioge Bay as the wind backed again into the south-west quarter. They passed Copenhagen through the Holland Deep on the afternoon of 2 July, but their hasty progress was halted the following day as the wind veered and came foul for the passage of The Sound. They anchored under the lee of the island of Hven for two days but, on the morning of the 5th, it fell light and favourable.

Next morning a freshening north-westerly forced them to tack out through the Kattegat, but the sun shone from a blue and cloudless sky and the sea sparkled and shone as the ship drove easily to windward, reeling off the knots. Ahead of them lay the low, rolling, green-wooded countryside of the Djursland peninsula spread out from Fornaess in the east away towards the Aalborg Bight to the west. Astern of them lay the flat sand-cay of Anholt, and the encircling sea was dotted with the sails of Danish fishing boats and coasters – the sails of potential enemies, Drinkwater thought as he came on deck. He leaned back against the cant of the deck, his thighs still sore but much easier now. Aloft, *Antigone*'s spars bent and she drove her lee rail under so that water spurted in at the gunports.

'Morning, sir,' said Quilhampton crossing the deck, his hand on his hat and his eyes cast aloft. 'D'you think she'll stand it?'

'Yes, she'll stand it, she goes well, Mr Q, though I could wish the wind fairer.'

'Indeed, sir.' Quilhampton watched the captain keenly as Drinkwater looked about them and drew the fresh air into his lungs.

'The countryside looks fine to the south'ard, don't you think?' He pointed on the larboard bow. 'You know, James,' he said intimately, looking at the lieutenant, 'old Tregembo advised me to retire, to buy an estate and give up the Service. I dismissed the idea at the time; I rather regret it now. I cannot say that I had ever considered the matter before. What d'you think?'

Quilhampton hesitated. Such a notion would deprive him of further employment.

'I see you don't approve,' Drinkwater said drily. 'Well, the matter is decided for Tregembo . . .'

'How is he, sir?' Quilhampton asked anxiously, eager to divert Drinkwater's mind from the thought of premature retirement.

'He'll make a fine recovery from his wound. But he'll not leave his fireside again, and I can't say I'm sorry.'

There was, however, another question Quilhampton wanted answered, as did the whole ship's company, and he felt he might take advantage of the captain's mood and ask it without impropriety.

'May one ask the reason for your anxiety for a fast passage, sir?' The greater question was implicit and Drinkwater turned to face his interrogator.

'I can tell you little now, James, beyond the fact that I, and others, have been employed upon a special service . . . but rest assured that this ship sails now in the very vanguard of affairs.'

In the event it was all the explanation Quilhampton ever received upon the matter, but the phrase lodged in his memory and he learned to be satisfied with it.

*   *   *

Drinkwater was deprived of his fast passage: in the North Sea the winds were infuriatingly light and variable and *Antigone* drifted rather than sailed south-west, beneath blue skies on a sea that was as smooth as a mirror. For over a week after she passed the Skaw she made slow progress, but towards the end of the second week in July a light breeze picked up from the eastward and the next afternoon Drinkwater was called on deck to see the twin towers of the lighthouses on Orfordness.

'We've the last of the tide with us, sir,' said Hill suggestively.

Drinkwater grinned. 'Very well, stand inshore and carry the flood round the Ness and inside the Whiting Bank and we'll be off Harwich by nightfall.'

'We'll flush any Dunkirkers out of Ho'sley Bay on our way past,' remarked Hill after he had adjusted their course, referring to the big lugger-privateers that often lay under the remote shingle headland and preyed on the north-country trade bound for London.

'No need,' said Quilhampton staring through the watch-glass, 'there's a big frigate in there already . . . blue ensign . . .'

They could see the masts and spars of a man-of-war lifting above the horizon, then her hull, rising oddly as refraction distorted it suddenly upwards.

'She's no frigate, Mr Q,' said Hill, 'she's an old sixty-four or I'm a Dutchman.'

Drinkwater took a look through his own glass. The distant ship had set her topsails and was standing out towards them. He could see the blue ensign at her peak and then the relative positions of the two ships closed and the refractive quality of the air disappeared. The strange ship was suddenly much closer and he could see men on her fo'c's'le, fishing for the anchor with the cat tackle.

'She'll be the Harwich guardship, I expect, come out to exercise before grounding on her own chicken bones.' The knot of officers laughed dutifully at the captain's joke. 'Make the private signal, Mr Hill,' he added, then turned to Quilhampton. 'I shall want my barge hoisted out as soon as we've fetched an anchor on the Harwich Shelf. I shall be posting to London directly . . . you had better let Fraser know.'

'Aye, aye, sir.'

Their eyes met. The coast of England was under their lee and it would not be long before Lieutenant Rogers was taken ashore. Fraser would inherit temporary command of the ship, but with Rogers still on board, the situation would be delicate for a day or two in the captain's absence. Quilhampton wondered what Drinkwater intended to do about Rogers and the question lay unasked between them. In a low voice meant for Quilhampton's ears alone Drinkwater said, 'Under last year's regulations, James, a commanding officer is, as you know "forbidden from suffering the inferior officers or men from being treated with oppression". The first lieutenant's conduct . . .'

He got no further. The ship trembled and for a split-second Drinkwater thought they had run aground, then the air was alive with exploding splinters and men were shouting in alarm, outrage and agony. His eyes lifted to the strange ship standing out from the anchorage. The blue ensign was descending, and rising to the peak of the gaff were the horizontal bands of the tricolour of the Dutch Republic.

'Christ alive!' Drinkwater swore, seized by agonizing panic. 'All hands to quarters! Beat to quarters! Rouse out all hands!' He ground his teeth, furious with himself for being so easily deceived, as he waited impotently for his men to rush to their stations, aware that the enemy would get in a further broadside before he was ready to reply. It was too late to clear for action and Hill was altering course to enable *Antigone* to bring her starboard broadside to bear, but it first exposed her to the enemy's fire.

The innocent-looking puffs of grey smoke blossomed from the Dutchman's side before the Antigones had cast off the breechings of their own guns. The enemy cannon were well pointed and the shot slammed into the side of the British frigate. Shot flew overhead with a rending noise like the tearing of canvas. Hammocks burst, spinning, from the nettings, splinters lanced across the deck and the starboard side of the launch amidships was shattered. Chips flew from the mainmast and holes appeared in the sails. Aloft, severed ropes whipped through their sheaves and landed on deck with a whir and slap so that unbraced yards flew round and men fell like jerking puppets as langridge and canister swept the deck in a horizontal hail of iron.

'Hold your course, damn you!' Drinkwater screamed above the din, leaping for the wheel. 'She'll luff, else!'

'She won't answer, sir!'

'Bloody hell!'

He looked desperately at the enemy and then, at last, there came from the fo'c'sle an answering gun and Drinkwater saw Quilhampton leaping along the starboard battery. Close to Drinkwater at the hance, little Frey fired one of the brass carronades with an ear-splitting roar and Mount's marines were lining the hammock netting, returning fire with their muskets.

From the waist now came the steady roar of the main guns, the black-barrelled 18-pounders rumbled back on their carriages, snapping the breechings bar-taut as their crews leapt round to sponge, load and ram, before tailing onto the tackles and sending them out through the ports again. Aiming was crude; the instant a gun-captain saw the slightest suggestion of the enemy through the smoke he jerked his lanyard, the flint snapped on the gun-lock and the gun leapt inboard again, belching fire, smoke and iron.

Overhead there was a loud and distinct crack and the maintopmast sagged forward, to come crashing down, tearing at the rigging and bringing with it the foretopmast, enveloping the deck in a heap of spars, mounds of rope and blanketing sheets of grey canvas that were hacked and torn away by the fire-fighting parties in an attempt to keep the guns in action. Smoke rolled over everything and the heat and gasses from the guns began to kill the wind. Drinkwater had not lost his sense of impotence: his inattention had denied him the opportunity to manoeuvre, he had made no study of his enemy and all at once found himself pitched into this battle from which there could be no escape. As he stood helpless upon his quarterdeck, it was no comfort to realise the curious refraction in the air had deceived him as to the true range of the Dutch ship; neither did it console him to know that he had failed in this most important mission on the very doorstep of London's river. In a mood of desperation he tried to force his mind to think, to gauge the advantages of striking in the hope that he might contrive to escape with the news from Tilsit. Lieutenant Fraser loomed through the smoke. He was wounded and his expression showed a helpless desire to surrender.

Drinkwater shook his head. 'No! No, I cannot strike. We must fight on!' It was a stupid, senseless order with no chance of success, but Fraser nodded and turned forward again. Behind him the unscathed masts and yards of their persecutor rose up, closing them with a paralysing menace. Drinkwater recalled the large group of men milling on her fo'c's'le, catting her anchor. Realisation of their true purpose struck him like a blow; at any moment *Antigone* would be boarded.

'Fight, you bastards!' he roared as his officers flinched, the shot storming round them. Hill reeled and fell and Drinkwater saw a midshipman carried past him, his face and chest a bloody pulp.

Drinkwater drew his sword and an instant later saw the hull of the Dutch vessel loom athwart their hawse.

'Boarders!' he roared. 'Repel boarders!' He began to move forward, pulling men from the after-guns which had no target now.

'Come on, men! 'Tis them or us!'

Drinkwater felt the jarring crash as the two ships smashed together and to the concussion of the guns was added the howling of boarders pouring into his ship.

'Mr Mount!'

The marine sergeant appeared out of the smoke. 'Mr Mount's wounded, sir.'

'Damn! Get a few of your men, Blixoe. You must guard my person.'

'Guard your person, sir?'

'You heard me!'

'Sir.'

It was not the time for explanations, for he alone knew the value of the news he carried.

A midshipman appeared.

'Mr Wickham, what's happening forrard?'

'We're giving ground, sir.'

'Mr Quilhampton?'

'Down, sir . . . the first wave of boarders . . .'

Drinkwater swung the flat of his sword across the breast of a retreating seaman. That was a rot he must stop. He raised his voice: 'Wickham! Blixoe! Forward!' Drinkwater led the after-guard in a counter-attack that looked like a forlorn hope as it lost itself in the mêlée amidships, where the fighting heaved over the broken ribs of the boats on the booms. Steel flashed in the sunshine and the pale yellow stabs of small arms fire spurted among the desperately writhing bodies that struggled for supremacy on the deck.

On the fo'c's'le, Quilhampton had been knocked down in the first rush of the enemy boarders. He was not seriously hurt, but his exertions at the guns had left him breathless. By the time he scrambled to his feet the enemy had moved aft and the sight of their backs caused him to pause an instant before charging impetuously upon them. It was clear that things were going badly and he had no idea of the vigour of resistance amidships to the ferocious onslaught of the Dutchmen. He was surrounded by the wreckage of the foremast and the groans of the seriously wounded. He had only to lift his head to see the enemy ship rising above the rail of the *Antigone*.

With a ponderous slowness the two vessels swung together and a second wave of boarders prepared to pour over the Dutch ship's larboard waist, to take the British defenders aft in flank. A few guns continued to fire from both ships somewhere amidships but generally the action had become the desperate slithering, hacking and cursing of hand-to-hand fighting.

It took Quilhampton only a moment to take in these events. Suddenly there appeared above him the muzzle of an enemy gun. He waited for the blast to tear out his lungs, but nothing happened and in a moment of sheer ecstasy at finding himself alive he swung upwards, one foot on *Antigone*'s rail, and leaned towards the Dutch ship. The gun barrel was hot to the touch, but no boarding pike or ramming worm was jabbed in his face; the gun was deserted!

In an instant he had heaved himself aboard the enemy ship and the sudden gloom of the gundeck engulfed him. Dense powder smoke hung in the air. Further aft a gun discharged, leaping back, its barrel hot, the water from the sponge hissing into steam, adding to the confusion and obscurity. A group of men and an officer ran past and it was clear that everyone's attention was focused outboard and down into *Antigone*'s waist where the issue was being decided. From the shouts it was clear that the Dutch were having their own way.

A battle-lantern glowed through the smoke and Quilhampton made for it. He found himself above a companionway and face to face with a boy. The child had a thick paper cartridge under each arm and looked up in astonishment at the unfamiliar uniform. Quilhampton held out his right hand and the boy docilely handed the cartridges over, his eyes alighting on the iron hook Quilhampton held up. A moment later Quilhampton was stumbling down the ladder. At the foot a sentry stood with musket and bayonet. Before the man realised anything was wrong, Quilhampton had swung his hook, slashing the astonished soldier's face. The man screamed, dropping his musket, and fell to his knees, hands clutching his hideously torn face. Quilhampton pulled the felt curtain aside and clattered down a second ladder.

The wood-lined lobby in which he found himself was lit by glims set behind glass in the deal lining. Another wet felt curtain hung in front of him. Quilhampton had found what he was looking for: the enemy's powder magazine.

Drinkwater's counter-attack was outflanked as the two vessels ground together, yardarm to yardarm. As he stabbed and hacked he felt the increased pressure of the additional Dutch seamen and marines pouring down from the dominating height of the battleship.

'Blixoe! Here! Disengage!' He caught the marine sergeant's eye and the man jerked his bayonet to the right and stepped back. As the two pulled out of the throng Drinkwater looked round. The waist was a shambles and he knew his men could not hold on for many more minutes against such odds. His glance raked the enemy rail and then he knew that providence had abandoned him. In the mizen chains of the enemy ship, in the very act of jumping across the gap, was a tall French officer. Their eyes met in recognition at the same instant.

General Santhonax jumped down onto the deck of the *Antigone*, leaping onto the breech of a carronade and sweeping his sword-blade among its wounded crew. Drinkwater brought up his hanger and advanced to meet him.

'Keep your men back, Blixoe!'

'But sir . . .'

'*Back*! This man's mine!'

Then Santhonax was on him, his blade high. Drinkwater parried and missed, but ducked clear. Santhonax cut to the right as they both turned and their swords met, the jarring clash carrying up Drinkwater's arm as their bodies collided. They pushed against each other.

'I have come a long way . . .' Santhonax hissed between clenched teeth.

They jumped back and Drinkwater cut swiftly left. Santhonax quickly turned and spun round. They had fought before; Santhonax had given Drinkwater the first of his two shoulder wounds, a wound that even now reduced his stamina. Had he had a pistol he would not have hesitated to use it but, unprepared as he was, he had only his hanger, while Santhonax fought with a heavier sabre.

Santhonax cut down with a *molinello* which Drinkwater parried clumsily, feeling his enemy's blade chop downwards through the bullion wire of his epaulette. He shortened his own sword and jabbed savagely. Santhonax's cut had lost its power, but Drinkwater felt his blade bite bone and, with a sudden fierce joy, he drove upwards, feeling the hanger's blade bend as the tall Frenchman's head jerked backwards. Drinkwater retracted his arm, fearful that his weapon might snap, and as the blade withdrew from Santhonax's throat the blood poured from the gaping wound and he sank to his knees. Santhonax's eyes blazed as he tried to give vent to his anguish. With lowered guard Drinkwater stood over his enemy, his own breath coming in great panting sobs. Santhonax raised his left hand. It held a pistol, drawn from his belt. Transfixed, Drinkwater watched the hammer cock and snap forward on the pan. The noise of the shot was lost in the tumult that raged about them, but the ball went wide with the trembling of Santhonax's hand. He began to sway, the front of his shirt and uniform dark with blood; his head came up and he arched his back and Drinkwater sensed his refusal to die.

Blixoe's marines closed in round the captain, while all about them men fought, slithering in the blood that flowed from the Frenchman. Suddenly the sabre dropped from his flaccid fingers and he slumped full length. Drinkwater bent beside the dying man; he felt a quite extraordinary remorse, as though their long animosity had engendered a mutual respect. Santhonax's mouth moved, then he fell back dead.

Drinkwater rose and turned, catching Blixoe's eye. The fighting round them was as desperate as ever and the Antigones had given ground as far as the quarterdeck.

'Clear the quarterdeck, Blixoe!'

The sergeant swung his bloody bayonet and stabbed forward, bawling at his marines to keep their courage up.

Dropping his hanger, Drinkwater picked up the sabre Santhonax had used and hurled himself into the fight, roaring encouragement to his men. They began to force the Dutchmen backwards, then suddenly Drinkwater was aware of Quilhampton above him, scrambling over the battleship's rail into the mizen chains.

'Get down, sir! Turn your face away!'

'What the hell . . .?'

Quilhampton jumped down among the shambles of struggling men and Drinkwater saw him push little Frey to the deck, then the one-handed lieutenant seemed to leap towards him, thrusting his shoulder, spinning him round and forcing him down.

The next moment Drinkwater felt the scorching heat of the blast and the air was filled by the roar of the explosion.

News from the Baltic

Lord Dungarth rose from the green baize-covered table in the Admiralty Boardroom. He was tired of the endless deliberations, of the arguments veering from one side to another. He stopped and stared at the chart extended from one of the rollers above the fireplace. It was of the Baltic Sea.

Behind him he heard the drone of Admiral Gambier's unenthusiastic voice, raising yet another imagined obstacle to the proposed destination of the so-called 'Secret Expedition' that had been assembled at Yarmouth to carry an expeditionary force across the North Sea to land at Rügen. Dungarth concluded that 'Dismal Jimmy' had so much in common with the evangelical preachers that he professed to admire that he would be better employed in a pulpit than commanding the reinforcements to Lord Cathcart's small force of the King's German Legion already in the Baltic.

'But my dear Admiral,' interrupted Canning, the Foreign Secretary, with marked impatience, 'the Prime Minister has already given instructions to Their Lordships and Their Lordships have doubtless already instructed Mr Barrow to prepare your orders. I don't doubt you will experience difficulties, but for God's sake don't prevaricate like Hyde Parker when he commanded the last such expedition to the area.'

Dungarth turned from the map and regarded the group of men sat around the boardroom table. The 'Committee for the Secret Expedition' was in disarray despite the brilliant arrangements that had assembled in secret a fleet, an army corps and its transports that waited only the order to proceed from the commander-in-chief to weigh their anchors. Dungarth caught Barrow's eye and saw reproach there, aware that his department had failed to produce the definitive intelligence report on the Baltic situation that would have enabled the committee to settle on the point of attack with some confidence. Dungarth knew, as Barrow and Canning knew, that Rügen was a compromise destination, designed to bolster the alliance, a political decision more than a military one. Dungarth sighed, he had hoped . . .

His eyes lifted to the wind-vane tell-tale set in the pediment over the bookcases at the far end of the room. The wind had been in the east for a week now, and still there was nothing . . .

A discreet tapping was heard at the door. Exasperated, Canning looked up.

'I thought we were not to be disturbed.'

'I'll attend to it,' said Dungarth, already crossing the carpet. He opened the door and took the chit the messenger handed him.

'It's addressed to me, gentlemen, I beg your indulgence.' He shut the door and opened the note. Casting his eyes over it the colour drained from his face.

'What the devil is it?' snapped Canning.

'An answer to your prayers, gentlemen, if I'm not mistaken.'

'Well read it, man!'

'Very well . . .

> *H.M. Frigate* Antigone
> *Harwich*
> *14th July 1807*

My Lord,

It is my Duty to Inform His Majesty's Government with the Utmost Despatch that it is the Intention of the Russian Emperor to Abandon His Alliance with His Majesty, and to Combine with Napoleon Bonaparte. Particular Designs are Entered into by the Combined Sovereigns Aimed at the Security of the British Nation which are of sufficiently Secret a Nature as not to be committed to Paper. They are, however, known to,

> *Your Obed.ᵗˡ Serv.ᵗ*
> *Nath.ⁿˡ Drinkwater,*
> *Captain, Royal Navy*

. . . that is all, gentlemen.'

The crinkle of the folding paper could be heard as the astonished committee digested this intelligence.

'It isn't possible.'

'Where is this officer?' asked Canning, the first to recover from the shock. 'Who is he? D'ye trust him, damn it?'

They were looking at Dungarth and Dungarth was staring back.

He was no less stunned at the content of the letter than the others, but he at least had been willing such an arrival for weeks past. 'A most trustworthy officer, Mr Canning, and one whose services have long merited greater recognition by their Lordships.' Dungarth fixed Barrow with his hazel eyes but the point was lost in Canning's impatience.

'If he's kicking his damned heels in the hall below, get him up here at once!'

'At once, gentlemen,' acknowledged Dungarth turning a second time to the door, with the ghost of a smile upon his face.

The sun was setting in a blaze of colour beyond the trees of St James's Park as the travel-stained naval captain and the earl crossed Horse Guards' Parade in the direction of Westminster. As they walked Drinkwater recounted those details of the strange cruise of the *Antigone* in the Baltic that he had not already mentioned in his verbal report to the Committee for the Secret Expedition.

'And you say this Dutch ship was commandeered by our old friend Edouard Santhonax?'

'Aye, my Lord, and forced out of the Texel in the teeth of the blockading squadron. I was only thankful that she had not taken on board her full quantity of powder, for if she had, I should not have lived to tell the tale.'

'And your fellow, Quilhampton, boarded her.'

'He is reticent upon the matter, but a determined cove nonetheless. I cannot speak too highly of him.'

'Nor I of you, Nathaniel. So you consider *Antigone* no longer seaworthy?'

'I think not, unless she be doubled all over and she will likely lose her fine sailing qualities. She suffered severely from the blowing up of the *Zaandam*; much of her starboard side was damaged and the first lieutenant was among the victims.'

'I see.'

They walked on in silence. Drinkwater had fought hard to keep *Antigone* afloat as they worked her into Harwich, and she lay now beached on the mud off the old Navy Yard there. Of Rogers he said nothing more, since nothing more need be said. In his own way Rogers had died in the service of his country; it was epitaph enough for him.

'And how is old Tregembo?'

'Like the *Antigone*, not fit for further sea-service.'

They dined at Dungarth's house in Lord North Street, the conversation muted until Dungarth's single manservant had withdrawn and left them with their port.

'Canning is well pleased with you, Nathaniel,' Dungarth smiled, lighting a cigar and leaning back to blow a pale blue cloud over the yellow glare of the candles.

'I suppose I should be flattered.'

'He has had an expedition fitting out for the Baltic for several weeks now. It was destined to support operations in Rügen until your news arrived. I've been warning Canning that something was afoot but until we knew for certain the outcome of events between the Russians and the French we should not show our hand.'

'I thought you must have expected something. When I got your note, I thought . . .'

'What? That I was a necromancer?' Dungarth smiled and shrugged. 'No, but the unusual nature of my duties reveals odd things, and I am not necessarily referring to secrets. For some reason war draws the very best from men who are idle and dissolute creatures else, intent on pleasure, petty squabbling and money grubbing. Give a man a guinea and he will buy a bottle or a whore; give a people freedom and they will turn to riot and revenge . . .' Dungarth poured himself a second glass and passed the decanter. 'And this war . . .' he sighed and watched Drinkwater fill his own glass. 'It is said history imitates itself and men's motives are not always derived, as they would have you think, from their own reason. Some are, I conceive, instinctive, like Santhonax's persistence or your own quixotic abetting of Ostroff. It isn't circumstantial, you know, Nathaniel, and I have always felt that these events are conjoined, like tiny links in a great chain that unwinds down the ages.' He took the proffered decanter and paused as he refilled his glass again. 'Or like some gravitational pull, which orders our affairs in spite of ourselves and wants only a second Newton to codify it.' Dungarth smiled. 'An odd, illogical fancy perhaps, but then we are all subject to them. Your own fascination with that witch Hortense Santhonax, for instance. No, don't protest your unimpeachable fidelity to Elizabeth. You are as prone to profane thoughts as the next man.'

Drinkwater reached into his waistcoat pocket. 'I did not know you read me so well,' he observed wryly and leaned across the table. His thumb flicked open the back of a gold hunter and Dungarth looked down at the timepiece.

Grey eyes stared up from the pale oval face of the miniature.

'Good heavens! Santhonax's watch?'

Drinkwater nodded, closed it and slipped it back into his pocket.

'It's very curious, is it not?' Dungarth shook his head ruminatively.

'And you, my Lord, were you then moved by the gravity of history to send word, by Horne of the *Pegasus?*'

Dungarth barked a short laugh. 'You turn my metaphor against me. Yes, and no. Perhaps I was and perhaps not . . . I cannot truly tell you.'

'What then will be the destination of this Secret Expeditionary Force – not Rügen, surely?'

'Oh, Lord, no! Not now we know what Napoleon intends. Our most immediate worry is the Danish navy. The French are on the point of occupying the country and the Danish fleet is in an advanced state of readiness.'

'I thought that we had finished that business before, at Copenhagen.'

'Would that we had, but time does not stand still. If the Danes cannot be coerced into surrendering their fleet in return for a subsidy, we shall have to execute a *coup de main* and take it into our safe-keeping.'

Drinkwater frowned. 'You mean to cut out the entire Danish fleet?'

'Yes.'

'God's bones! What a savage master this war is become.'

'Like fire, Nathaniel,' Dungarth replied with a nod, 'and like fire, it must be fought with fire.'

'Lord Dungarth has made me privy to the circumstances in which you were compelled to leave your command, Captain Drinkwater.'

Mr Barrow, the Admiralty's Second Secretary, smiled, his pedantic mouth precise in the exact allowance of condescension he permitted an officer of Drinkwater's seniority. He placed his hand palm downwards on the little pile of documents that Drinkwater had submitted. 'I would have thought it your first duty to report to their Lordships but, in view of the importance of the information you have brought, these matters will be overlooked.'

Drinkwater's mouth was dry. After the congratulations of Canning and Dungarth, Barrow's attitude was rather hard to accept. He counselled himself to silence.

'It is also important, I might almost say of *paramount* importance, that the sources of this information are not divulged. I think *you* understand this, Captain. War with Russia is now certain and our agents in that country are in great peril. The matter is therefore a secret of state. You do understand, do you not?'

'I do.'

'Your absence from your ship therefore did not take place,' said Barrow, proceeding like a Domine leading a class through a Euclidean theorem. 'You will surrender your log books and destroy any personal journals. The death of your first lieutenant is really most convenient.' The thin smile appeared again on Mr Barrow's face. 'I leave an explanation of Lord Walmsley's death for the benefit of his father entirely in your hands, Captain Drinkwater. Lord Dungarth says you have a ready wit in these matters.'

Drinkwater felt a rising tide of anger within him at Barrow's condescension and his self-control slipped further at Barrow's next remark.

'The over-riding importance of secrecy does not permit you much licence. Your people . . .'

'Will gossip, Mr Barrow,' Drinkwater put in sharply, exasperated by Barrow's bland assumption that a man-of-war might be sealed off like some packet of secret orders.

'It is unlikely that your men will have much opportunity to gossip.' Barrow paused to make his effect more telling. 'As for your officers, they are to remain under your command . . .'

'Until death discharges them?' Drinkwater snapped, the sinister and inhuman implication of Barrow's intentions striking him fully.

'Or peace, Captain, or peace. Do not let us be too pessimistic,' Barrow continued smoothly. 'In the meantime I shall see what's to be done about a new lieutenant.' Barrow began to gather up the papers and tie a pink tape around them.

'And the shattered state of my ship, sir, have you considered that?'

'Of course! There are orders for you being prepared in the copyroom. You will turn your ship's company over directly into the *Patrician*, a razeed sixty-four and a particularly fine sailer. She is at Chatham and wants only men . . . your men.'

'And myself, sir?' he asked, numbed by this news but thinking of his wife and Tregembo and the simple desire of a man to go home. 'Am I also affected by this *proscription?*'

Barrow looked up. 'I think it best that you are on shore as little as possible, Captain Drinkwater. The increasing desertions of men are most often noticeable where the commanding officer sleeps out of his ship. You know the regulations.'

Drinkwater stood and gripped the back of his chair in an effort at self-control. 'I had believed that I and my ship's company had earned a measure of respite, having rendered the State a signal service, Mr Barrow. Some of my men have not stepped ashore since the last Peace, God damn it!'

Barrow stared at him and Drinkwater saw with a certain degree of satisfaction that he had at last provoked the man. 'There is no doubt that your service has been most satisfactory, Captain Drinkwater. I thought I had been at some pains to make that clear to you,' Barrow said frigidly, 'but there is no respite for any of us. Every effort will continue to be made . . .'

'I do not think I need to be taught my business, Mr Barrow!'

The two men glared at each other. Barrow's ruthless ability was an admired fact; he was an accomplished administrator with a task of great complexity, but he had little appreciation of a captain's predicament. Duty was obvious, while Drinkwater's sense of obligation to his crew was a tiresome liberality. Nothing of this conflict seemed clear to Barrow.

'No, I am sure I do not, Captain,' Barrow conceded. Then he added, 'But do not forget to forward your logs – privately, you understand.'

Drinkwater stared for a moment at the little heap of Admiralty papers that were now being neatly bundled up in pink tape. How fatuous his conversation with Lord Dungarth now seemed. As Barrow's fingers formed a bow in the pink tape the act was symbolic of dismissal. Tired, angry and disgusted, Drinkwater made for the door.

'One thing more, Captain Drinkwater.'

Drinkwater turned on the threshold.

'The matter of the eighty thousand sterling you conveyed to the Baltic. Unfortunately His Majesty King Gustavus saw fit to impound it for his own use. It never reached the Tsar. Unhappily you will be deprived of your customary percentage . . .' Drinkwater recalled his promise to his men, but Barrow had not yet finished with him.

'One wonders, if it had reached Alexander as intended, whether he might not have remained faithful to the alliance. Good day, Captain.'

Half choking with anger Drinkwater stepped out into the corridor.

Copenhagen

Admiral Gambier's fleet of over three hundred men-of-war and transports lay at anchor off the village of Vedboek. To the west of the anchored ships, amid the low wooded hills and red-roofed villages of the island of Zealand, an expeditionary force of the British Army and King's German Legion advanced on the Danish capital of Copenhagen. Field howitzers were already bombarding the city's defences and the thunder of the cannonade, the whistling of the arcing shells and the violent concussions of the exploding carcasses could be heard miles away.

In accordance with his instructions the army commander, Lord Cathcart, had demanded the surrender of the Danish fleet in exchange for an annual payment to be made for as long as was necessary. The Danes had refused the terms, voluntarily submitting their capital to bombardment rather than their honour with their ships.

When darkness fell the night was bright with the traces of shell-fire, and over Copenhagen the dense pall of smoke rose into the sky, its billowing under-belly orange with reflected flame.

A few days later the rape of the Danish fleet was completed, and Admiral Gambier sailed homewards with his prizes.

Author's Note

The means by which the British Government learned of the secret articles of the Treaty of Tilsit remains a mystery to this day. Whilst historians may speculate upon probabilities, the novelist enjoys the greater freedom of exploring possibilities. Nevertheless I have tried not to abuse this privilege and have spun my yarn with the few known facts.

The most likely contender for the role of the spy beneath the raft is Colin Alexander Mackenzie, a known British agent who had seen service in the Russian army and was a good linguist. A century after the event his family revealed his close connection with the incident (*English Historical Review*, Vol. XVII, p.110, 1902). Although this is inconclusive, Canning's steadfast refusal to name his source does suggest a vulnerable individual who remained at large in a suddenly hostile Russia. But Mackenzie was known to the Tsar, and dined with Alexander when he entertained Talleyrand. He may, therefore, have been too conspicuous to have been the actual eavesdropper, though he knew all about it. Circumstantial evidence of his possible arrival in London is not confirmed, but is put *after* 16 July, when Canning wrote his instructions to Gambier and Cathcart for the attack on Copenhagen. Talleyrand himself may have supplied some information, for his betrayal of Napoleon dates from Tilsit, and he occupied the Foreign Ministry of France throughout the transition from Napoleonic to Bourbon rule in 1815, when the French copy of the treaty is alleged to have disappeared. However, he was not under the raft, nor were any of the other Britons known to have been in Russia at the time, such as Lords Leveson-Gower and Hutchinson, Robert Wilson or Dr Wylie, who were kept at a discreet distance.

The intrigues of the Russian court will never be known, but there are several contenders for the role of, at least, accomplice. The Vorontzoff family have been closely connected with the secret, even cited as providing the spy. Leaked information may also have come from Bennigsen, and the British Foreign Office is said to have papers alleging his part in a plot to kill Alexander.

The most intriguingly 'useful' fact is the existence of a letter quoted by Dr Holland Rose, dated 26 June from Memel, from an anonymous officer in the Russian service.

The speed with which the intelligence arrived in London could have been achieved by land or sea. It was a hot summer, 'the labourers fainting in the fields', with little wind and an anti-cyclone over the North Sea. My preference for the frigate *Antigone* is obvious, but lent credence by Richard Deacon's remark in his *History of the British Secret Service* that much information was gathered by cruisers of the Royal Navy. Government secrecy, of course, ensured that *Antigone*'s log book cannot now be found in the Public Record Office!

Much of the credibility of the story rests on the exact nature of the 'raft'. Lariboissière's engineers certainly had a hand in its adaptation and there are hints of the employment of local labourers. The anonymous Russian officer, quoted by Holland Rose, calls the thing a *pont volant*, suggesting the use of an existing 'flying bridge' such as are believed to have been used for moving cattle across the lower reaches of the river. It is this supposition I have favoured in view of the period of concealment and the details claimed by the Mackenzie family.

The free movement of strangers among the military is affirmed by Savary, Duke of Rovigo: 'this meeting attracted visitors to Tilsit from a hundred leagues round.' The opening exchange between Napoleon and Alexander is too widely quoted to tamper with. For, as Napoleon's secretary Bourienne points out, the meeting at Tilsit was 'one of the culminating points of modern history . . . the waters of the Nieman reflected the image of Napoleon at the height of his glory'. Who that reflected image concealed in the water below is here revealed as the mysterious 'Ostroff'.

Wilson's presence at Eylau, the seizure by Gustavus of the Tsar's subsidy and the loss of the arms shipment are all verifiable and the Danes have not yet forgiven us the seizure of their fleet in 1807. Morality has never been a conspicuous feature of war, and, as Fortescue says, 'it was Denmark's misfortune to lie between the hammer and the anvil' while, on Britain's part, 'the law of self-preservation [was] cogent'. Even as the British struck, Marshal Bernadotte received Napoleon's orders to invade Denmark. Finally, Fouché, Napoleon's Chief of Police, says in his memoirs, 'The success of the attack on Copenhagen was the first thing that deranged the secret article of the Treaty of Tilsit, by virtue of which the fleet of

Denmark was to be put at the disposal of France . . . I had never seen Napoleon in such a transport of rage.'

The circumstances under which Edward Drinkwater found himself in Russia are more fully explained in *The Bomb Vessel*.